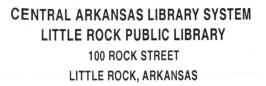

Also by Terrill Lee Lankford

EARTHQUAKE WEATHER

ANGRY MOON

SHOOTERS

Blonde Lightning

*B*londe *L*ightning

A Novel

Terrill Lee Lankford

Ballantine Books　New York

Copyright © 2005 by Terrill Lee Lankford

All rights reserved.

Published in the United States by The Random House Publishing Group, a division of Random House, Inc., New York.

BALLANTINE and colophon are registered trademarks of Random House, Inc.

ISBN 0-345-46779-5

Printed in the United States of America on acid-free paper

www.ballantinebooks.com

2 4 6 8 9 7 5 3 1

First Edition

Text design by Laurie Jewell

For Fred Olen Ray,

who knows where the bodies are buried,

and for the two Jills:

one was a muse, the other just amusing

Hell is—other people!

—JEAN-PAUL SARTRE

That which does not kill you . . .

can truly fuck you up.

—CLYDE MCCOY

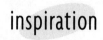

inspiration

chapter one

When you first get to Los Angeles, it does not take long to realize that the ground you walk on is untrustworthy, even when it is not moving underfoot. On June 17, 1994, precisely six months to the day after the Northridge earthquake rocked the city off its foundation, a very different kind of shock wave ripped through the land. This event would not attack the city's tectonic plates but split the people of L.A. along racial and economic lines instead. It started far more subtly than the 6.7 asskicker of a temblor we had survived, but the effects of this event would be even more long lasting and psychologically destructive than the physical scars left on the city back in January on Martin Luther King's birthday.

I was sitting on my favorite barstool at my favorite bar, Viande, having my favorite meal (Cajun blackened steak), and enjoying my favorite beverage (Tanqueray and tonic), watching the Rockets battle it out with the Knicks in game five of the NBA finals on the big-screen TV when the Juice made a run for the border. We found out the hard way. The network suddenly put the game in a little box in the corner of the TV screen and made O. J. Simpson's slow-speed chase the main attraction. This did not sit well with the hoops fans gathered at Viande.

We were five days into the Simpson saga, and already we had seen enough. O.J.—or *someone*—had killed his ex-wife, Nicole Brown Simpson, and a waiter friend of hers named Ronald Goldman who had stopped by her condo to drop off a pair of glasses that Nicole's mother had left at the restaurant where he worked in Brentwood. It looked like Goldman had caught the killer in the act and had gotten himself killed for his troubles. Talk about bad timing. O.J. was on a Chicago-bound plane ninety minutes later, as if that would make a good alibi. I guess he thought the cops had never seen his Hertz commercials. Now, five days later, he was interrupting a championship basketball game with this silly-assed attempt to flee justice. As Charles Barkley would say, it was *outrageous.*

The motley bunch gathered around the bar cursed and screamed and shouted—like that was all it would take to get the network executives to pull their heads out of their asses and put things into proper perspective. The Game was news; O.J. running for the hills was inevitable. If we *had* to track his progress, *that* was the picture that should be down in the corner of the screen. Not the Game. Bob Costas was on the tube calling the whole thing "surreal," but it would take more than that to alter the network's priorities.

I finished my steak just as Orenthal James Simpson crossed back over the city limits into Los Angeles. Realizing the jig was up, he had changed his plans to visit Mexico and was crawling back to his plush Brentwood crib. He was being driven in a white Ford Bronco by fellow ex–football player Al Cowlings who had gotten on the cell phone with the police to let them know that the Juice had a gun and would use it on himself if they tried to pull them over. O.J. had taken himself hostage, just as Cleavon Little did in *Blazing Saddles*—with similarly impressive results.

The cops took Simpson very seriously. They were giving him plenty of space. They did not want him to hurt his prisoner. Crowds of Angelenos were gathering on freeway overpasses—cheering him on. Bozos! I just wanted him to drive faster so the cops could arrest him and we could watch the end of the game. Would that start another round of riots? Possibly. But let's settle this NBA dispute first, please.

I saw my neighbor Clyde McCoy enter through the front door of Viande. I hadn't spoken to him since the night of the Simpson murders—not because he had anything to do with the crimes, but because he had shown a chilling insensitivity to the fact that a friend of mine had died the night before (of completely unrelated causes, of course).

Charity James had been my roommate—after a fashion—for a few months and my friend for even longer, and she had died under sordid circumstances. But when the police came to inform me of the details of her passing, all Clyde could think about was a stack of his screenplays he had asked me to read, hoping I might option one. I was pissed at him—for that and a number of other reasons too complicated to think about—and I had no intention of rekindling our friendship over drinks. I was hoping he wouldn't pull up a stool next to mine, but, as so often happens in life, my hopes were dashed.

"Hey, man," he said as he scooched up to the bar, "can you believe this shit?"

I grunted and pulled thirty dollars out of my pocket and paid my tab. I started to stand up, and Clyde grabbed my arm.

"Where you going?"

"Home."

"What's the hurry?"

"I just want to go."

"Wait a minute. Sit down and have a drink with me."

"I've had enough."

"To drink or of me?"

"Both."

"C'mon, don't be like that. Give me a chance to explain."

"There's nothing to explain."

"You think you know me? You think you know why I do the things I do or say the things I say?"

"Why should I care?"

"We're neighbors. And I thought we were friends."

"I thought so, too. But friendship with you seems to be a one-way street."

"That hurts."

"Sorry. But that's been my observation."

"Listen, if this is about your friend, I'm sorry. I didn't mean to seem callous, but I don't do well around death. I've kind of developed automatic blinders."

"Some kind of allergy?"

"You could say that. I've lost a lot of people in my day. And now, when people I know lose loved ones, I'm not a good shoulder to cry on. I shut down. I'm sorry. Stay and have a drink with me. I'll buy."

I looked at his face, searching for any hint of disingenuousness or trace of ulterior motive. He appeared to be sincere, but with Clyde McCoy, anything was possible. He was an onion with layers upon layers of façade.

"One drink. But then I'm leaving."

"Whatever you say."

He motioned for the bartender and said, "Two more of whatever he's having."

The bartender, a hot French Canadian brunette name Maryse, nodded and went to work. Clyde was a binge drinker who seemed to have the ability to turn his addiction on and off at will. He was known to be trouble when it was *on*.

"I'm drinking gin," I warned.

"Gin's fine with me. Hope it's good gin."

"Tanqueray."

"Good enough."

Maryse set the two drinks in front of us. Clyde sipped his hesitantly at first, trying to get the taste for gin back on his tongue. He was a bourbon, whiskey, and rum man by trade.

"Just like lemonade," he said.

"Yeah. With a kick."

The awkward conversation I was expecting didn't materialize. Clyde seemed content to sit silently, sipping his drink and watching the idiots on the TV cheer for O.J. The Bronco had pulled off the freeway now, and it was winding through the streets of Brentwood, followed by more cops than were on Goldie Hawn's ass in *The Sugarland Express.*

Emily Woolrich, Clyde's girlfriend, a third-degree black belt turned martial arts movie star, entered the restaurant and squeezed in next to Clyde. "Let's go, Clyde. The movie starts in ten minutes."

"We can't go to the movies. They're about to shoot O.J. Simpson."

"They're not going to shoot O.J. They just want to question him."

"Yeah. With Tasers."

"He lives in Brentwood. They don't use Tasers on the citizens of Brentwood."

"They might make an exception in his case. He *did* kill two people, you know?"

"No, I don't know that. And neither do you."

"Please. Don't get crazy."

"I'm going to the movies. With or without you."

"I'm staying. This is news. Besides, Mark and I are having a drink and making peace. Aren't you going to say hello to Mark?"

She looked over at me and said, "Hello, Mark." She didn't sound like she meant it.

"Hi, Emily. Nice to see you."

She went back to ignoring me and pulled on Clyde's sleeve. "Let's go. You promised."

"Damn, woman, can't you see I'm having a drink?"

"Clyde, you get your ass off that barstool right now or the last you'll see of *my* ass will be when it walks out that door."

"Well, if you're going to get selfish . . ." He gulped down the last of his drink, stood up, and pulled out his keys. "I'll go get the car."

She took the keys from his hand. "I'll drive."

"You're pushy tonight. I'm going to hit the head before we go."

He tossed some money on the bar, walked down the hallway toward the back door, and disappeared into the men's room.

Emily looked over at me with disdain on her pretty features. "He's been drinking for three days straight. I wish you wouldn't encourage him."

"I was just sitting here, minding my own business, trying to watch the game."

"Just don't enable his bad behavior."

She walked down the hallway to wait for Clyde by the bathroom door. Up on the TV, O.J. Simpson was pulling into the driveway of his Brentwood mansion. His grown son ran out of the house to try to convince him not to kill himself. I couldn't see the score of the basketball game, and at the rate things were progressing, I had a feeling that it wasn't going to matter anyway. We were now living in Juiceland.

chapter two

It was a bright sunny day at Forest Lawn. Not the gloomy, overcast, or rain-soaked atmosphere that was standard for a funeral scene in the movies. There were only a handful of people present for the ceremony. Charity James didn't have a lot of friends around her at the end. Only dealers and users. The few people who made the funeral dated back to the time before Charity hooked up with my late boss, Dexter Morton. There were two or three guys, all ex-boyfriends, and a number of starlet-in-training types who looked like they might have gotten off the Greyhound bus the same day Charity did. They were attractive in that plastic way that young women often think works in Hollywood, but usually gets them only as far as the casting futon. The ex-boyfriends and the starlets-in-training were all sizing one another up for the after-party.

And then there was Alex Richards and the cops. They had arrived together, and I assumed they would be leaving together as well. Alex had also worked for Dexter Morton. We were both creative executives at Dexter's production company, which had had a first-look deal—and plush offices—at Warner Bros. Dexter had been a film producer specializing in big-budget action fare, and we were the two guys hired to help him find and develop his product. Little did Dexter know that the day he hired Alex Richards was the day he signed his own death warrant. Alex had been dating Charity James, and he made the mistake of introducing her to Dexter. Dexter outbid Alex, and Charity soon moved into Dexter's house atop Mount Olympus so she could look down at the mortals shuffling about below in the flats of L.A. Unfortunately, it didn't take Charity long to fall from those hallowed heights. A combination of drugs and dirty dealings by Dexter Morton sent her spiraling out of control until she found herself here, asleep forever in this gray box before us.

Long before she actually died, Alex felt Dexter had destroyed Charity James, and he decided to do something about it. He bashed Dexter on the head and drowned the man in his own swimming pool. But it was too late to save Charity James. Her path had been chosen. And now she had reached its dark terminus. At least she would get to sleep with the stars, here in Forest Lawn.

The cops had been on to Alex early, despite the torture they put me through during their investigation. There's a sadistic streak in a lot of cops, and I think encounters with movie people bring out the worst in them. They put me through my paces as if I were a suspect, while they were certain it was Alex all along. Perhaps they wanted to see if I was in on the scheme. After all, Alex and I had been coworkers and fairly close friends—until I confronted him with my suspicions that he had killed Dexter. Then he threatened to tear my head off with a fire poker.

The eulogy was brief and miserable. A priest who had never met Charity James said words that could have applied to many people, but certainly not the deceased. It was a grim affair, and it couldn't be over soon enough. No one was glad to be there. There was a small reception planned at the Smokehouse Restaurant across from Warner Bros., courtesy of Alex, who had fronted the bill for the whole affair—including the funeral—because Charity James had no relatives willing or able to burden the expense. The knowledge that he wouldn't be needing a lot of money in Corcoran State Penitentiary probably made the expenditure an easier pill to swallow.

When it came time to pile dirt on top of Charity's casket, Alex just stood there, shovel in hand, staring down into the dark hole, thinking about his lost love. When he finally started shoveling, he found he could not stop. The six-foot hole was half filled in before he collapsed beside it, and then was led away by Detective Campbell.

After that display, I was surprised to see Alex and the detectives enter the reception area at the Smokehouse. Alex went straight to the buffet table. They were giving him a long leash, and it looked like he had regained his composure.

I noticed quite a few more people at the reception than had been at the funeral, which was typical for this town. There will always be more revelers at the party after the premiere than attended the premiere itself. A lot of people don't want to do the work of sitting through the main event, but they are more than happy to show up for the free grub and the chance to network at the after-party.

Detective Campbell spotted me in the still relatively thin crowd and walked over to enlighten me with his wisdom. Campbell had taken great pleasure in watching me squirm under the glare of their investigation. If he had been born three or four hundred years ago, he could have found solid work during the Inquisition.

"You'll be glad to know this is the last public appearance your buddy will be making for quite a while."

"You're finally arresting him?"

"Right after the reception."

"That's cold."

"*You* wanted us to pick him up a week ago."

"Yeah. He was promising to kill me."

"He was under surveillance. You weren't in any danger."

"It might have been nice if you told me that last week."

"And risk compromising an investigation? That's not how we work."

"Anyone ever complain about how you work?"

He grinned. "All the time."

I walked over to Alex. He was building a Dagwood sandwich at one of the deli platters.

He looked up at me and said, "Figured I better load up on the good eats before I go to the slammer." He no longer seemed angry at me. It was as if we had never had cross words.

"So, they finally pulled the trigger, eh?"

"I went to them. I knew it was only a matter of time. I got tired of waiting."

"Maybe that will make it go easier for you."

"I doubt it. But I figured the only way to avoid jail would be to kill you and make a run for the border. And we saw how good runs to the border work nowadays. After the O.J. spectacle, I realized running was not an option. They wouldn't have 'escorted' me home like they did for Juice. They would have beat me like a rented mule."

"At least they let you come to the funeral."

"That was the deal. I wanted to be with Charity one last time. I told them it was a condition to getting my full confession."

He was wheeling and dealing all the way into the hoosegow. "Alex, you may not want to admit this, but you're a born romantic."

"Yeah. I know. That's why I'm going to jail."

"Killing Dexter was not a good career move."

"It got me an agent."

"You're kidding?"

"Nope. Signed with Klopert and Maciejeski just yesterday."

"Bloodsuckers."

"Yeah, but they're *my* bloodsuckers."

"There're laws in this country against using the media to profit from your crimes."

He laughed. "*You're* kidding now, aren't you? These guys know all the angles. They're already talking mid–six figures for the book deal. The movie rights will set me up for life."

"I think the state is already planning to set you up for life."

"Oh, come on. I'll be sent away for six or seven years. I may not even go to jail. They might just ship me to the loony bin."

"Don't count on it."

"Whatever happens, it beats working for that asshole."

"If you say so."

"Still, the timing sucks."

"How's that?"

"This Simpson scandal is blowing my story away. That shit's going to have to die down before we go to auction on my movie rights."

"Die down? This thing's not going to die down for years. I think you missed your window of opportunity."

"God, let's hope not."

chapter three

After the depressing afternoon spent in the company of the dead—some of whom were still walking—I did not feel like returning to the gloominess of my apartment. Valley Billiards is a pool hall on Ventura Boulevard, a few blocks from my place. It's a clean, well-lit joint that services upscale hustlers and slumming yuppies. It's got a bar where you can order beer, wine, and a rather amazing selection of food, considering they have only a microwave and a small pizza oven with which to cook. I decided to drop in and kill some time—and brain cells. Maybe I'd even shoot some pool.

I went to the bar, ordered a pitcher of beer, then started going through the want ads of the newspaper I had bought from the machine out front. Not surprisingly, I could find no listings for movie executive positions. I had hired a head hunter to help me find a studio gig, but he was having no success. It looked like I might have to start considering another line of work, but I wasn't qualified for much else. I got halfway through the pitcher of beer before nature called. I put the paper aside and headed for the bathroom. As I made my way through the pool hall, a voice called out to me.

"Howdy, neighbor!"

It was Clyde McCoy. He was off in a corner shooting pool with Emily and a lanky blonde who was bent over the table provocatively, trying to line up a shot. I walked over and shook hands with Clyde and waved at Emily across the table. She didn't seem to notice.

"How you guys doing?" I asked.

"Couldn't be better," Clyde said with a smile. Emily just nodded. They were shooting rotation, and she must have been losing. She was intently watching the other girl line up her shot as if she were Minnesota Fats and a couple thou was on the line. The girl was well worth studying. She had long blond hair and almond-shaped eyes. She wore a white blouse and a medium-length skirt that hugged her body in a way that gave me a very good idea of what it would be like to see her out of it all. She had the kind of full, sensual lips that usually indicated collagen injections, but I could tell she was all natural. She wore almost no makeup yet seemed ready for a photo shoot, and she looked great bent over the pool table. I had the overwhelming urge to get behind her and help her with the shot. She seemed to have stepped out of a dream. She was female perfection—at least as I imagined it.

Then she took her shot. The cue ball crossed a field of green, missed every ball on the table, and dropped into the far corner pocket as if aimed there deliberately. The spell was broken.

"Shit," the blonde said. She straightened up to a good five-feet-eight-inch height that did nothing to diminish her femininity.

Emily smiled and attacked the table.

The blonde looked over and noticed me. She took a few steps closer and extended her hand. "Hi, I'm Tracy."

I shook her hand. "Nice to meet you. I'm Mark."

"That's perfect," Tracy said. "We've been looking for a *mark* all day."

"You guys are out hustling pool, eh?"

"Yeah, didn't you see how she slopped that shot right into the corner pocket to try to build your confidence?" Clyde said. "Oldest trick in the book. She's gonna take you for a ride."

I looked at Tracy and tried to stop a sexist comment from boiling to the surface, but it was hopeless. "That would be fine with me," I said, like some sitcom reject.

Tracy smiled and took the crude innuendo in stride with the kind of casual aplomb that indicated she had heard every line in the book and was accustomed to the advances of all creatures male—and probably quite a few of the female persuasion, as well.

Emily was working the felt and shooting like a pro. She quickly cleared the table and told Clyde to "Rack 'em, loser."

Clyde frowned and started to rack the balls.

"I'm going to the little girls' room," Emily said.

"We'll alert the media," Clyde retorted.

"Tracy?" Emily said.

"Yeah, sure," Tracy said. Then she looked at me and asked, "You gonna be here?"

"Uh, I've got to be getting back."

"Too bad," she said with a pouty face; then she smiled like a vixen and added, "For you."

The women giggled nastily and headed for the ladies' room.

"You are such a tramp," Emily said.

"I just couldn't help myself," Tracy replied. "He looks so . . . hungry."

They both laughed and disappeared around the corner. I could feel my face flush with embarrassment.

Clyde finished racking. "If I were you, I'd forget about that one. She's a major DGS sufferer."

"What do you mean?"

"You know, the old Damaged Goods Syndrome. She's sick with it. Can't you tell just by looking at her? She's so fucked up by all the shit she went through as a kid that she can't deal with life as it comes down now. She's talking to you, but she just sees this big angry dick. Probably her uncle or her stepdad. Ask her. She'll probably tell you all about it."

"I doubt it."

"No. Go for it. DGS victims love to talk about it, no matter how embarrassing it gets. You'll be surprised. Just one thing, though . . ."

"What's that?"

"If it doesn't go well between the two of you, don't blame me."

"No problem."

I went to the men's room and did my business. As I was washing up, I caught a glimpse of myself in the cracked mirror. I looked guilty. I had just buried my last "conquest," and here I was trolling for some new action, just a few hours later. It was shameless. I splashed water on my face and tried to shake off the past. It didn't work. At least my face would be clean, even if my conscience wasn't. I returned to the bar, paid my tab, tossed the newspaper in the trash, picked up the remainder of my pitcher of beer, and rejoined the group. The ladies were back, laughing and carrying on. Clyde was sitting in a tall chair, watching them kibitz.

"Back for more, eh, stranger?" Tracy said. She had a knowing look that told me she understood exactly what my wishes and desires for her were. She didn't seem overly offended by the idea.

"Want to play doubles?" Clyde asked. "You two are getting along so well, you can play against Emily and me."

"Sure," I said.

"You'll regret it," Tracy said. "I suck."

"I think that's what he's hoping for," Emily replied.

"You bitch," Tracy said with a giggle as I turned bright red.

It's tough when you're in a room full of mind readers.

We played four games, and Tracy and I got thoroughly beaten all four times. Tracy was right. She couldn't play worth a damn, but she looked great in action. If I was going to lose at something, it wasn't so bad losing with her. It was losing with *style*.

We paid the bill, then retired across the street to Viande for a night-cap. The cocktail waitress was new, second day on the job, very pretty, but a bit slow on the draw. I had a black and tan, Tracy ordered a White Russian, and Emily and Clyde had iced tea.

"You guys aren't drinking?" I asked.

"I gotta work tonight," Clyde replied

"And I'm in training," Emily said. "I'm shooting a picture in a few weeks, and I'm trying to keep the weight off."

"Thank God I don't have to go in front of the cameras anymore," Tracy said, sipping her drink. "I *do* like my White Russians."

"You were an actress?" I asked.

"Yep, but I just couldn't stand the adulation. I had to give it up for the sake of art."

"What do you mean?"

I thought I saw a moment of concern flash between Emily and Tracy, but I might have been reading into it.

Tracy said, "I work at an art gallery down at Bergamont Station. Rain. You know it?"

"No."

"I run it for a rich German guy who's never there. You should drop in sometime."

"I will."

"I bet he will," Emily said. "Soon."

"How's the movie going, Clyde?" Tracy asked, trying to get Emily off the subject of my desperate desires. I was liking Tracy more by the moment.

"It's coming along," Clyde said.

"What movie?" I asked.

"Remember that script of mine? *Blonde Lightning*?"

"Yeah."

"I've got some people interested in putting up the dough to make it."

"Really?"

"Don't sound so astonished. It's not that bad."

"It's not that. I actually liked that script. I thought it was the best of the bunch. I'm just surprised you didn't tell me you had an interest in it before you gave it to me to read."

"This just came up a few days ago. Guy I know needed a project. Gave me a call. I'm tweaking the script before we move forward. You should have jumped on it when you had the chance."

"I don't have the kind of money you'd want for an option."

"You never know until you ask."

There was an uncomfortable lull in the conversation, finally filled by Tracy asking Emily, "Hear anything new from Mace?"

"Oh yeah," Emily replied. "Mace manages to do something shitty to me every day. Every damn day."

Clyde chimed in, "Yesterday the fucker took a bad review of Emily's last movie and faxed it to producers and execs all over town. The little rat fuck probably planted the review himself. It was in some rag called *Martial Arts News Now!* I never even heard of it."

"Who's Mace?" I asked.

"I know this guy," Emily said. "He approached me a few years ago, after I had done some of the Hong Kong films. I hadn't shot anything in the States yet, but he said he could hook me up. He wanted to be my manager."

"Manager—*ha*!" Clyde said. "That fucker couldn't manage his sock drawer."

"You want to tell this, or should I?"

"Go 'head."

"Okay. So I tell the guy I don't want a manager, but if he puts together a film that I can star in, I'll give him a piece of whatever I get. We never specified the details, and he never gave me any paperwork."

"You got to have paperwork," Clyde said.

"You should know. You've been ripped off enough times."

"Are you going to tell the story or not?"

"Yeah, if you shut up and let me."

"I'm shutting."

"Anyway, this guy, Mace Thornburg, he takes me around and introduces me to some people. Nothing happens. I go off to do a film in Thailand, and when I come back, one of the guys Mace introduced me to invites me to a party. At the party, I meet a woman named Adria who says she has a good project for me. I read the script, it's pretty good, so I say I'll do it. She gives me twelve thousand dollars as a retainer so she can use my name to raise money at the Cannes Film Festival, and all of a sudden I get a call from Mace saying he wants half the money."

"For what?"

"He said that since I met Adria at a party thrown by one of his connections, he should be my full partner on the deal. He wanted half of whatever I made on the movie."

"That's ridiculous."

"No kidding," Clyde said. "Can you imagine if everyone in town had to commission anyone and everyone connected with business done at a party? And fifty percent? What kind of commission is that? He's a thief."

"We never had a formal agreement," Emily continued. "I thought he would be asking agent or manager fees if anything ever happened that he was specifically associated with, but I didn't think he was going to expect half of anything I ever made within the L.A. city limits."

"So, what happened?"

"Well, Mace raised such a stink about the whole thing that Adria suggested we pay him off, but before we could, he started slinging the word *lawsuit* around, and her investors got cold feet. The picture didn't get made, but Mace still wanted half my money. My attorney threatened him with legal action, and Mace started leaving sick messages on my phone machine. He began to stalk me, and he started interfering in my business matters, calling people I was working with and people I wanted to work with, telling them all kinds of lies. He's sort of an amateur publicist for his girlfriend, Monique Eden, so he's pretty well hooked into the information highway around here."

"Isn't she a porn star or something?"

"She did soft-core in the seventies, but then she got a boob job and tried to be a female Stallone in a bunch of lousy action movies in the eighties. Mace latched on to her, became her manager, and they've been together ever since."

"They've got a real weird thing going," Clyde said. "Very S and M."

"You don't know that."

"He's a coprophile."

"Can we keep on the topic? This subject bores me, and it's probably boring Mark, too."

"Are you kidding?" I said. "This is interesting stuff. I want to hear it all."

"There's not much more to tell. The guy keeps harassing me. The police can't do anything about it. I filed a restraining order on him and changed my phone number, but I still get weird calls late at night. I've been up for some studio jobs, and every time I get close, the producers receive anonymous packages filled with negative reviews and libelous gossip-column pieces about me. They know the situation, but it still makes hiring me look like a risky venture. My tires were even slashed once while I was having lunch with a Paramount exec at Le Dôme. That's why I have to make my living by shooting films outside the country. Who wants to hire someone who's got crap like that hanging over their head? The studios don't want that kind of intrigue complicating their shoots."

"This guy sounds dangerous. How come you never told me about him before?"

"He got real quiet after the earthquake. I thought maybe his house had caved in on him or something. Come to find out, he was overseas trying to make deals for the last six months. He took the first flight out of LAX that had an open space after the shaking stopped in January. The quake freaked him out. He cut and ran, he's such a chickenshit, and used business as his excuse. Now that the aftershocks have died down, he's back and making my life miserable."

"He's a pussy," Clyde said. "I could make him go away in ten seconds if she'd let me."

"You sic your goons on Mace, and *I'd* be the one who ended up in jail."

"They're not goons. They're . . . family."

"Yeah, which family?" Tracy asked. "Manson? Or Corleone?"

"You stay out of this."

"Clyde's got some friends," Emily said to me. "Scary types. He wanted them to straighten Mace out, but I told him that's conspiracy down at the DA's office. To say nothing of racketeering."

"You're being ridiculous," Clyde said.

"I'm not going to stoop to Mace's level."

"You wouldn't have to. You wouldn't even have to know anything about it. I'm about to start a movie myself, and I'd rather not be looking over my shoulder the whole time, wondering if that asshole is going to drop a sandbag on my head when I'm not looking."

"You're being paranoid."

"No such thing in this town."

Emily got very serious all of a sudden. "Let's drop it," she said sternly.

"Fine. Drink your tea. I've got work to do. I need to go home and work on the rewrite."

"Don't let us stop you. The world needs another volume of bile."

"You keep this up, and you're going to drive me to drink."

"If you need an excuse, I guess I'm as good as any other."

Clyde looked at her for a stony moment; then he stood up, threw some money on the table, and said, "Night, everybody. It's been fun."

"Clyde, c'mon . . . ," Tracy pleaded.

"It's no biggie. Fuck it. Let Lady Kung Fool handle her own messes. I don't give a shit. I'll see you later." He turned and walked away.

Tracy leaned into Emily and said, "Little rough on him, weren't you?"

"He had it coming," she said. "He's going to get me in trouble with all his childish gangster talk."

Tracy looked at me and tried to explain. "Clyde likes to consider himself connected."

"He's got these friends in Las Vegas who strong-arm people," Emily added. "I don't want anything to do with that nonsense. And he's pissing me off because he won't let it alone."

"Aren't you afraid he'll start drinking again if you push him like that?" Tracy asked.

"He's a big boy. He starts drinking again, that's his problem. If it gets out of hand and becomes *my* problem, I'll just stop seeing him."

"You're cold, Emmy."

"I won't go through that again."

I knew enough not to pry into this one. I had already heard more than I should have. And I had seen how Clyde got when alcohol took hold of him, so I knew what Emily was talking about.

"I kind of liked him better when he *was* drinking," Tracy said. "I mean, all the time. Not just once in a while."

"Oh yeah, he was the life of the party, till about three in the morning. Then he was a complete asshole."

"But he was funny. He hasn't been funny in a long time."

"He's getting too old for that stuff. Doctor said if he starts drinking seriously again, his blood pressure will shoot through the roof. To say nothing of the liver that is operating on borrowed time already."

Emily tried to hide it, but concern was creeping into her voice. She finished her iced tea and put a few more dollars on the table. Tracy started to gather her belongings.

"Don't get up," Emily said. "I'm sorry we spoiled the evening, but you guys should stay here, get acquainted. I'm just going to go check on the grumpy old man. Make sure he hasn't thrown himself out the ground-floor window."

Tracy looked at me, wondering what I was going to say. It was another one of those defining moments.

"I wouldn't mind another drink if you want one," I said. "I'll buy."

Tracy smiled at the tawdriness of the gesture. "Well, if *you're* buying."

"Have fun," Emily said as she made for the door.

I waved the waitress over and ordered another round. Tracy and I sipped what we had left in our glasses and contemplated our next move.

"Been friends with them long?" I asked.

"I've known Emily since high school. She introduced me to Clyde not long after she started dating him a few years ago, but I can't say I'm friends with him. I don't see him very often. He usually stays holed up in his apartment. They don't go out on the town much as a couple."

"Yeah. I know."

"How long have you been living next to Clyde?"

"A little more than a year. But I didn't meet him until the morning of the big quake. It took that much shaking to bring him out of his cave. But I have to say, he certainly seems to be getting over the recluse act in a big way. I've been running into him a lot lately."

"I think he got cabin fever working on that book of his. Emily said he's considering moving, just to look at some different walls for a while."

"Really?"

"Yeah. But he probably won't. He's been in that apartment for longer than Emily and I have known him. He's dug in."

"It's funny. I feel like they're my friends, but I really don't know much about them. How'd they first hook up?"

"On a movie. How does anyone meet anyone in this city? It's either at a shoot or a party or a bar. Or church. And you won't find Clyde in church. He wrote some narration and looping dialogue for one of Emily's Hong Kong films that they were dubbing for video release here. You know, they don't really have official scripts over in Hong Kong when they shoot those movies. They just have a rough idea of the story and they kind of move their lips and then figure it all out in post-production. They don't even shoot sound over there."

"That's weird," I said. Actually I knew how they shot the Hong Kong flicks, but I liked hearing her talk about it, and it seemed to make her feel good that she knew something arcane, that she had something unusual to offer to the conversation.

"They spent three days in a dubbing studio together, and when it was over, they started dating. They've been on again, off again for years now."

"Why so tumultuous?"

"Artistic temperament, jealousy, alcohol—same old stuff."

"How about you? Do you have a boyfriend?"

"No."

"I find that hard to believe. Why not?"

"My husband wouldn't like it."

I felt the color flush into my cheeks, then drain down my legs into my shoes.

Tracy reached over and grasped my forearm. "Hey, don't worry about it. We're separated. I'm staying with my folks right now."

"Do you mind if I ask what happened?"

"He's abusive. I don't really want to say much more."

"Okay."

Our drinks arrived, and the waitress took away the empty glasses. We drank, and I was at a complete loss for words. But Tracy was a true mind reader.

She took my hand and looked me in the eyes. "Listen, you seem like a really nice guy, and we've been having you on tonight. Not the stuff about Clyde and Emily, but the stuff where she's been kind of throwing you at me. She'd love to see me get involved with you—with just about anybody but my husband—but the truth is, it's not going to happen and she knows it. I don't want to lead you on. I love my husband, and I know I'll be going back to him eventually."

I pulled my hand away—not angrily, just coldly. Somehow I felt betrayed. By all of them. "Then why don't you go back to him tonight?" I said. "Why prolong the agony?"

She thought about it for a moment, and I could see tears welling in her eyes. She held them back. "Maybe you're right," she said. She took another sip of her drink, got up, kissed me on the cheek, and said, "You're a doll. If I wasn't married . . ."

She turned and walked out of the restaurant.

I sat there looking like a dope and feeling like a fool. If the last thirty seconds had been part of a screenplay that I had optioned, I would have ordered an immediate rewrite so the guy in the scene wouldn't say stupid things, like "Why don't you go back to him tonight?" What the hell was I thinking?

She didn't even pay her bar tab.

chapter four

I went up to my apartment, a two-bedroom affair that was the only second-floor apartment in the four-unit complex. The complex itself was conveniently located about a hundred feet from Viande's back door.

I sat in the hammock strung catty-corner between two posts on my balcony and stared at the cellular relay tower disguised as a metal palm tree on Morrison Street while I mused on recent events. Clyde, who lived in the downstairs apartment directly next to the entrance to my stairwell, was going back into production—with or without me. I had no job, but I did have savings—more than twenty thousand dollars that I had socked away over the years by not having that fourth drink every night. I was pooling my funds in the hopes of putting together seed money with which to develop movie projects. Twenty grand didn't go very far in Hollywood, but maybe I could buy a small piece of Clyde's action if his producers were selling shares to raise the budget. But could I buy enough to have a say in things—and, more important—get some kind of producer's credit on the project?

I went into the kitchen, picked up the phone, and called Clyde.

He answered gruffly. "What?"

"Clyde, it's Mark."

"What's up? I'm in the middle of a spat with the old lady."

I could hear Emily curse at him in the background.

"I'll call back later."

"Fuck that. What do you want? You want to talk about the movie, don't you?"

I hesitated for a moment, thinking he was going to bite my head off. "Yeah."

"I think I might have something for you on the picture."

"Okay."

"Meet me for dinner tonight at nine."

"Where?"

"Let's just eat at Viande since it's staggering distance to both our apartments. I feel like getting drunk."

I could hear more cursing from Emily. She was really getting mad now. Then something crashed and broke in the background. Something large and made of glass.

"Hayes, you still there?"

"Yeah. What broke?"

"She just threw a bottle of Maker's Mark through the television screen."

"Damn." I heard glass rattling on the other end of the phone as he sifted through the rubble.

"It's okay. The bottle didn't break. They really know what they're doing in Kentucky."

development

chapter five

I was on my perch at the bar when Clyde came through the door at nine sharp. The shocking thing was that Emily accompanied him. They looked happy, as if nothing violent had happened between them just a few hours earlier.

"This is a surprise," I said as they approached the bar.

"Yeah. We worked things out"—Clyde winked—"the hard way."

Emily laughed and punched him on the shoulder. "You really want an ass-kicking, don't you?"

"Ouch. You already trashed my apartment. You want to break my arm, too?"

"If that's what it takes."

"Hayes, never date a woman who can beat you up."

"Good advice."

They ordered drinks from Maryse, and then Clyde got right down to business.

"Vince Timlin called me a couple days ago. He's got a deal with some foreign investors, and they want to do *Blonde Lightning,* with Vince producing and starring, of course."

Fifteen years ago, Vince Timlin had been an up-and-coming young star. Then, in the late eighties, sensing a growing lack of interest from the studios and feeling the heat of the new wave of hot-new-things on his back, he began partnering up with lower-budget producers in exchange for partial ownership of his films. Ownership and *control.* He was a star-producer now.

"Who's going to direct?"

"I'm thinking about taking a crack at it myself."

"I thought you didn't want to do that anymore?"

"It's that or let Vince direct it, which would be like setting fire to the script. There's not enough money in the budget for a decent director. Besides, they always want to come in and 'fix' everything. Next thing you know, the picture's neither fish nor fowl. Fuck it, I'll bite. I'll give it one more shot. It will be good to get out of the house again. You want in?"

"What would my job be?"

"Watching my back. And once a day, clean the daggers out of it. We could probably swing an associate producer's credit for you."

That was the equivalent of *director's nephew* in Hollywood jargon, but I didn't want to insult Clyde with my lowly opinion of the offer. "What would it pay?" I asked.

"What were you getting at Dexter's?"

"Seven-fifty a week."

"Not that much."

"Terrific."

"Hey, it's just an offer. You don't have to take it. I just thought it might tide you over until something better came along. Believe me—it won't be a long gig. And it might look good on your résumé."

I didn't have the heart to tell him I probably wouldn't put something like that on my résumé. I wanted to keep working at the studio level. They didn't give a damn about low-budget fodder. The less of it you did, the better. You'd think they'd appreciate any experience you had, but low-budget guys get marked. It's okay to do one or two of them, but any more than that, and the studios think that's all you'll ever do. Often they are correct. And often it's just a self-fulfilling prophecy. Still, I had a feeling that I would be needing the income, and if I couldn't be the producer of *Blonde Lightning,* maybe this would be the next best thing. I could be involved in the production without assuming the same level of risk as the actual producers would. If the movie did not succeed, I wouldn't be responsible. If it was a success, it could open some doors for me.

Something across the room caught Clyde's eye. I looked where he was looking. Seven people were seated at a table by the big glass windows in the front of the restaurant. They seemed to be having a rather subdued business dinner. Clyde must have recognized someone at the table, because his face was suddenly red with anger.

"Son of a bitch," he said, getting off his barstool. "That motherfucker has the balls to come here? I'm gonna kick his ass!"

Emily put her hand on his chest to stop his forward progress, then looked to where he was looking. The color drained from her face and her hand vibrated a little, but she kept Clyde at bay. "Leave it be, honey," she said. "It's a free country. He can eat wherever he wants."

"He knows not to come in here. He's fucking with us!"

"Who is it?" I asked.

"It's that guy we told you about—Mace Thornburg—and a bunch of his scumbiz friends. They're pissing on my front porch."

"Let's just go," Emily said.

One of the men at the table—a skinny redheaded fellow wearing mirrored wraparound sunglasses (despite the fact that it was night)—looked over and nodded at Clyde. He smiled like the Cheshire cat, then got the attention of another man at the table, a big guy with pockmarks all over his face, and pointed in our direction. The two men got up from their table and announced to the others that they were going to the bar.

"If Mohammed can't go to the asshole, the asshole will come to Mohammed," Clyde said to Emily.

"Don't get into it, okay? You do, and I'm going home—and I don't mean *your* home."

"I'll be a perfect gentleman."

"Uh-huh."

The redheaded man and the crater face approached us.

"Back on the sauce, eh, McCoy?" the redhead said.

"We were just celebrating," Clyde said. "They passed a new law this afternoon banning maggots from public places. I'm afraid you're going to have to leave."

"Material like that, I'm surprised you couldn't find work writing for tee-*vee.*"

"What are you doing in here, Mace?" Emily asked. "I've got a restraining order that says you've got to stay one hundred and fifty feet away from me at all times."

"And I have the exact same order against you," Mace said. "So we're both breaking the law. And I have a reservation to eat here. Do you? Wanna call the cops and see who they arrest?"

"I want you out of my face."

"We just came over to say hi. Who's the new guy? Breaking in a new drug dealer?" He was looking at me while he spoke. I ignored the comment and finished my beer. I had the feeling we were about to leave.

"Get the fuck out of here," Clyde said. He slammed Mace in the chest with the palm of his hand. It wasn't enough to hurt him, just enough to shove him back a bit.

The big, quiet guy with the pockmarked face punched Clyde in the jaw before anyone had any idea what was happening. Clyde fell back against me, and I knocked over what was left of Emily's beer.

"Sorry, ma'am," Crater Face said to Emily. "But I can't let people go hitting Mace. You understand, don't you?"

Emily said, "Sure," and extended her hand to the pockmarked guy, like she wanted to shake and make friends. I don't know if the guy was stupid or if it was just an impulse reaction, but he stuck out his hand, and Emily wrapped her fingers around his thumb and pulled it back with a quick twist. A loud snap filled the room, and the big guy howled like a gut-shot hound dog.

"Fuck! My thumb! It's broken!" Crater Face exclaimed. He went down onto his knees and cuddled with his busted thumb, trying not to shed tears.

"If you try to stand, I'll give you a nose to match," Emily said.

The man looked at her with fear. He had no plans to challenge her. He just stayed on his knees and complained. "Fucking fuck me fucking Jesus fuck . . . it fucking hurts so much. . . . Fuck!"

"You are in *so* much trouble!" Mace said to Emily. "I'm gonna sue the shit out of you, and this time I've got a hundred witnesses." He looked around the room at all the waiters, waitresses, and diners. Every single one of them looked away as if to say *I didn't see a thing.* The people at his own table were so far away and so preoccupied with their own conversations that none of them had noticed the conflict.

"Bartender!" Mace yelled at Maryse, who was also acting as if she had better things to do. "Call nine-one-one! My friend needs an ambulance."

Maryse said, "Um, this phone isn't working. There's a pay phone in the parking lot next door."

"Don't give me that shit, bitch," Mace snarled. "I been watching you talk to your boyfriend on it all night long!"

Maryse looked startled. "What did you call me?"

"Bitch?"

"I'm going to go get the manager." Maryse lifted the panel on the bar that allowed her to exit, and she walked back into the kitchen.

Emily looked at Clyde, who was rubbing his jaw. He did not look pleased by the fact that he had been defended by his girlfriend.

"You okay?" Emily asked.

"Yeah, is mama's boy okay?" Mace taunted.

Clyde moved toward Mace, and Mace jumped back, not as brave as he had been when his muscle had two hands.

Emily stopped Clyde before he could reach Mace. "Don't, Clyde! Can't you see that's what he wants? He wants you to screw up. You want to go to jail?"

Clyde looked around the room. People were staring at us again. I could see the humiliation on his face. "You're in charge, Mama." Clyde turned and went down the long hallway and out the back door.

"Now, there goes a man who knows who wears the pants in his family," Mace said.

"Fuck you," Emily said; then she went down the hallway after Clyde.

I brushed past Mace to follow Emily and bumped him in the process. He shoved me in the back. I stopped, turned, and went back to confront him face-to-face. He didn't flinch this time. I guess I wasn't as intimidating as Clyde or Emily.

"Listen, ass wipe," I said in my best Clint Eastwood (which probably came out more like Woody Allen). "You don't know me. Don't ever touch me again. Don't fucking do it. Got that?"

He just stared at me, but it was like I was having a stare-off with myself, because all I could see was my own reflection in those damned mirrored sunglasses. I could tell he wasn't going to respond. Some of the guys who were sitting at his table by the front door were coming over to see what was going on. I backed away a few feet, then turned and went down the hall.

"See you in court," Mace called after me.

By the time I got to the alley, Clyde was pulling out of the parking lot in a battered black Maserati Bi Turbo that had seen far better days. Emily was standing on the back steps of the restaurant, and we watched Clyde burn rubber down the alley.

"He's pissed," she said. "I shouldn't have done that."

"You had no choice."

"Sure I did. I could have let Clyde hit the guy."

"That guy was twice his size."

"Yeah, but he's only got half the heart. When Clyde McCoy breaks loose, you just have to duck and cover."

It was true. I had seen Clyde wipe the ground with a much larger opponent just a few months earlier. He had picked up quite a few pointers living with a third-degree black belt. "But you were right. If he'd gotten into it big-time, he might have gone to jail. I think you minimized the risk."

"Maybe. But now I embarrassed him. Clyde doesn't handle humiliation well. He's kind of a macho jerk when it comes to this sort of thing."

"What are you going to do?"

"Find him. I'm sure he's going to the Dresden Room. We were supposed to meet some people there later on, after dinner."

"You want me to drive you there?"

"Yeah. That would be nice. Maybe you can help calm him down."

I doubted it, but we went to my car, a silver '88 Camaro with a leaky T-top, and got in.

"Do you know where the Dresden is?" she asked.

"Hollywood, right?"

"Yeah. Hollywood."

I turned the ignition, the car groaned and fired, and we were off. I jumped on the 101 Freeway and headed south, toward Hollywood and the unknown.

"Who was the guy with Mace?" I asked. "The guy with the fucked-up thumb."

"Wilson. Mace says he's his *assistant*. I think he just keeps him around for protection."

"That didn't work out so well."

"The guy isn't too bright, but I wouldn't want to take him on in a straight bar fight."

"You handled him pretty easily."

"I went for his weak spot: his brain."

I laughed. "What's Mace need a bodyguard for, anyway? That seems extreme."

"Mace has a lot of enemies. He rubs people the wrong way. Last year he got mugged. Someone beat him up pretty bad."

"Who?"

"No one knows. It seemed random—you know, just another robbery in Hollywood—but Mace accused everyone he knew of being behind it. Including Clyde and me."

"Didn't he see who did it?"

"Oh yeah. He said it was a big black guy. Where have we heard that one? Guy took his Porsche, took his jewelry, even took his clothes. Mace said the man just walked up behind him after he got out of his car and told him to give up everything he had. After he complied, the guy still slapped him around. I guess Mace didn't move fast enough."

"Did the guy have a gun?"

"That's the funny thing. Mace usually brags about being a badass, but he admitted the guy didn't show him a weapon. Not even a knife. He said the guy was so big and dangerous looking that he didn't want to argue with him. It was so pussy, everyone believed him."

"If he saw his attacker, how could he accuse you of being involved?"

"Mace said the guy knew where he lived and had targeted him. He told the police he was certain one of his enemies set him up for the robbery. He gave them a nice long list of suspects, and they actually questioned us, among others. Can you believe it? It was worth it, though, just to hear the story."

"Do you think it happened the way he said?"

"I don't know. Mace is such a liar. He may have been ripping off his own insurance company, for all I know, and then hassling his enemies as a bonus. But he did seem genuinely shaken after the incident. He hired Wilson a few weeks later. How many agents or managers do you know who have their own bodyguards?"

"I know a bunch who ought to."

We got lucky and found a parking space on the crowded Hollywood streets in less than ten minutes and had to walk only three blocks back to the Dresden Room.

The Dresden is a schizophrenic joint. Half the place is a divey piano bar, the other half a restaurant with plush white leather booths that look like they were designed for a David Lynch movie. Very retro. A wall separates the two halves of the room, but there are two large entryways at either end of the bar to make it all flow as smoothly as possible.

Two lounge music legends, Marty and Elayne, perform their variations on jazz standards in the piano bar six nights a week. Despite their age, they draw a young, loyal crowd of hipsters.

Clyde was sitting in the restaurant side of the Dresden when we entered. He was sipping a drink and staring at the menu. He didn't look surprised or upset to see us as we approached him.

"This may work out after all," he said. "I like the prime rib here. Maybe Mace's visit was a sign."

"A sign we should eat at the Dresden Room?" Emily said as she crowded in next to him.

"The Lord works in mysterious ways."

I slid into the booth on the opposite side from them. Clyde's troubles seemed to be forgotten. A waitress arrived and took our drink order, then brought two more menus.

"Did you kill everybody in the room?" Clyde asked Emily.

"Yep. They're all dead. Even the evil Mace Thornburg."

Clyde snorted. "I wish." He looked at me. "You know, that's not even his real name. His real name's Harold Jenkins, but he thought

Mace Thornburg sounded cooler, so he had it legally changed. I'm sure Mace Neufeld is none too happy about it, having that jerk running around town using his first name."

I nodded and laughed. "Yeah. Neufeld's a pretty good guy, but he doesn't suffer fools lightly."

"Hey, how'd you do with your pool partner after we left this afternoon?" Clyde asked.

"I struck out," I said. "I think I sent her scurrying back to her husband."

"That won't last long."

Emily scowled at him from over her menu but said nothing.

"When the girl we're meeting later shows up, don't go crazy on her," Clyde continued. "She makes Tracy look like a boy, but we may have to work with her, so I don't want any additional complications."

"I doubt anyone could make Tracy look like a boy."

"You haven't met Michelle yet."

"Michelle?"

"Michelle Kern. She's going to be the hot new thing. I saw her in a failed pilot last year, and she blew me away. I'm thinking of offering her the lead in *Blonde Lightning*."

Emily put down her menu. "Maybe *you're* the one who's in danger of going crazy."

"My interest in her is strictly professional."

"We'll see."

The waiter arrived and we ordered. I took Clyde's advice and had the prime rib. He was right. It was great. So great that I overate and was feeling pretty bloated when Michelle Kern and her manager, Judy, arrived tableside.

Clyde had not been exaggerating. Michelle was gorgeous: tall, slender, buxom, and beautiful. She had a face the camera would love. I doubted you could take a bad picture of her if you tried. She was perfect from any angle. But she was no blonde. And the lead actress in

Blonde Lightning not only had to be blond, she had to be an über-blonde. Michelle had long, flaming red hair. I assumed Clyde had a plan in mind for that.

Introductions were made all around, and then they crowded in with us, Michelle sliding in next to Clyde, the writer/director. She was going to go far in this town.

Michelle's manager, Judy, was a hard-boiled broad who had been in the business for decades. At one time or another, she had repped everyone from Joan Hackett to Meg Tilly. Michelle was her latest project, and she planned on protecting her like the girl was her own private property.

"We've read your script, Clyde. It's good. But we're not sure it's the direction we want to take Michelle right now."

"You mean she's not ready for starring roles yet?"

"No, I mean we're looking for something with a studio attached. A big project. Pollack has been talking to us about a new picture with Redford."

"And he wants Michelle as the co-star?"

"No. A supporting part. But fourth billing on a Pollack–Redford picture beats top billing on a straight-to-video pic any day."

"It will only end up straight-to-video if the performances aren't up to snuff."

"I can play the hell out of that part," Michelle said.

"Clyde, Clyde, Clyde," Judy said. "You always know how to take advantage of the new girl in town."

Emily snorted in agreement.

"I'm just telling it like it is. The two leads in this thing don't deliver, and it won't get a theatrical release. I know Vince is up to the task. I think Michelle is, too. But I guess we'll never know."

"Stop it, Clyde. It's not going to be that easy."

"No. It won't. I'm not even offering the part without a test."

"You want Michelle to screen-test for a less-than-a-million picture?"

"Vince insists. He wants to make sure he has chemistry with the leading lady."

"I know all about Vince's chemistry tests," Judy said. "Michelle will not fuck for this part."

"Don't be ridiculous, Judy. There will be none of that bullshit on my film. Vince will behave. But he has a right to see how they look together on the screen. And, of course, Michelle has to go blond."

"Not for the test. This thing falls apart, and she'll be stuck as a blonde with no place to go."

"We can use a wig for the test."

"Let me talk to Pollack tomorrow. I'll see how serious he is."

"That's fine. But I need to know by end-of-business, or I have to keep looking."

Michelle looked at Judy like she was mad at her but was trying not to show it.

"End-of-business, then."

We ordered drinks, and the conversation drifted away from our specific business and more toward the general gossip about town: who was in, who was out, who the up-and-coming players were. Judy knew it all. It was her business to know. She was a fountain of information. And it was clear that whatever she learned from us would become part of her currency.

As the drinking continued, Michelle slowly oozed closer and closer to Clyde. He acted like he didn't notice, but Emily certainly did. She was getting more irritated as the night wore on. Judy, sensing that this would not be the best time for her client to seduce the director, pulled her out of the place at a little after midnight, claiming she had a callback in the morning.

I was glad I would be riding in my own car on the way home. I had the feeling that Emily would be on the warpath again once she had Clyde to herself.

chapter six

Clyde called on Monday and said he had mentioned me to Vince Timlin and I had the job on *Blonde Lightning* if I wanted it, but Vince liked to meet everybody at least once before they signed a contract so he could feel like he was giving them his approval. They wanted me to drop by their office for a face-to-face. He gave me an address in Van Nuys and said I should be there at five.

I had some time to kill, so I drove down to Santa Monica to see if I could undo the damage I had done with Tracy. Bergamont Station is a group of industrial buildings on the edge of Santa Monica that have been converted to art galleries. I found the gallery where Tracy worked very easily. It was one of the largest on the lot, and it had a big sign over the door that said RAIN in blue neon.

I parked near the gallery, went up the metal stairs, and entered through chrome doors. The space was very large. Paintings dotted the aluminum walls, and a few steel sculptures grew out of the wood floors. It was very austere. Even the lighting was minimal. Small halogens on wires spotlighted each painting and statue, leaving the rest of the room bathed in dim ambient light.

No one seemed to be in the building. I walked through the room, studying the paintings. They were grim pieces. Dark, brooding, abstract. I turned a corner and went into another room filled with more of these nightmarish images. Clearly, they were all created by the same hand, which might explain why there was so much empty wall space. The artist didn't have enough work to completely fill the large gallery. Or maybe they just couldn't keep him in stock due to the town's insatiable appetite for depressing images.

A voice suddenly spoke from above me. "I figured you'd find your way down here eventually, but I didn't think it would be so soon."

I turned and looked up. Tracy was standing at the railing of a second-floor office that overlooked the gallery.

"I was in the neighborhood."

She smiled knowingly. "I bet."

"Sort of."

"I'll be right down."

She disappeared from the rail. I went back into the main part of the gallery and walked toward the staircase in the back of the room. Tracy came down the stairs wearing a yellow flowered sundress that transformed her into the best piece of art in the entire building. She was a van Gogh in a sea of Bauhaus.

"Like what you see?" she said.

"You're beautiful."

She laughed. "I meant the art."

I looked at the painting nearest to me. It was a nightscape with stick figures lost in a swirl of gray on what looked like a rocky beach.

"It's . . . depressing."

"Every one of these paintings is by a man named Robbie Ankers. He killed himself when he was twenty. Back in 1973. Drank rat poison. His parents kept all these pieces in their house, and now that they are getting on in age, they decided to share them with the world. He was a complete unknown until this show opened last week, but he's going to be very, very famous."

"Lucky him."

"It's a major discovery for the art world."

"Have you sold any of them yet?"

"They're all sold."

"All of them?"

"Yes. The show was a complete sellout. We're just waiting for the various collectors to pick up their pieces. But there's no hurry. We don't have a new installation scheduled for another week."

"About what I said to you at Viande . . . I think I spoke out of turn."

"What do you mean?"

"I think I hurt your feelings."

"Don't be silly. You were the perfect gentleman."

"Maybe that was a mistake."

She smiled and took my hand and led me to another painting. "I want to show you my favorite piece."

More gray. But this one had fire in it, as well. Traced in the flames, I could make out the features of a man's face, screaming.

"Can you see the face in the fire?" she asked.

"Yes."

"It's a self-portrait."

"And this guy killed himself? That's surprising."

"He was a very troubled artist."

"Funny how often trouble and art go hand in hand."

"Trouble goes with everything."

"Speaking of which, I'm hoping you didn't take my advice that night."

She realized she was still holding my hand. She started to pull away from me, but I held on and pulled her to me instead. Despite the overactive air conditioner in the room, her body was very warm against mine. For a moment I thought we were going to kiss—then she said, "I'm afraid I did."

I froze. "You went back to him?"

"No. But I called him. We're going to have dinner tonight and talk about it."

"You know how much I want you?"

"I think I have a pretty good idea. But it's . . . complicated."

Light from outside flooded the gallery as two people came through the chrome doorway. Tracy stepped away from me and straightened her skirt. She looked at me sadly, and I returned an even sadder look.

"Those're the Thompsons. They're picking up their piece."

I envied them. "Okay," I said. "I've got to get back to the Valley for a meeting anyway."

"Drop by anytime."

"I will." I caressed her shoulder and walked toward the door.

As I passed the Thompsons, who were gazing in wonder at the monstrosity they had purchased, I paused and said, "That'll look great over the couch."

The production office was small and shabby. Clyde and Vince had taken over a dilapidated ex-bookstore on Magnolia Street. The previous owners had let the place really go to hell. Clyde had a small art-department crew puttying the walls in preparation for a paint job.

Partitions had been set up to create rooms for the various production departments. Vince was bouncing from room to room, talking to the different department heads as if he were directing the picture himself. Clyde was much more stoic. He seemed perfectly calm, almost uninterested in the minutiae of the production. He told me that it was a good sign. The panic was contained on the inside.

They had begun to crew up, despite the fact that they had not raised their complete budget yet. Vince had another project looming after the targeted completion date of *Blonde Lightning,* and he wanted to do the pictures back to back and have them ready for the American Film Market in February. They would be deep into preproduction before all the money was secure in the bank. A risky venture, but it was not that much riskier than making a movie in the first place.

When Vince finally gave me the honor of his presence, the meeting was mercifully brief. Vince is a short man, like most actors of stature, and a complete Southern California pretty boy. His father had been a fairly good actor in his day, but Vince had already outperformed him in the industry, financially at least. Dad worked for Son nowadays, when Son would toss him a bone. Marcus Timlin was scheduled for a three-day gig on *Blonde Lightning*. Just enough to keep his health insurance paid up with SAG.

Vince introduced me to Gloria, his fiancée. She was a cute blonde with enhanced breasts and a nice smile. They had met on a movie Vince produced and starred in for Showtime. A sand-and-silliness picture shot at Zuma Beach. Gloria was Vince's discovery. He plucked her from a stack of headshots and thrust her into B-movie stardom. She had done three films in the last year, each one revealing more skin. Vince finally decided enough was enough. He was going to make an honest woman out of her. And since she was soon to be the next Mrs. Vince Timlin (number four, to be exact), there would be no more nude scenes in her future. At least not *on* camera. Or at least not *movie* cameras. For the viewing public. Who knew what Vince's private filmmaking hobbies included?

Vince was moving Gloria behind the scenes. She was going to be a co-producer on the film. This meant a glorified title and a paycheck, and she probably would manage to make a nuisance of herself, trying to do a job that didn't exist except in her own mind. Vince assured me that this was not so. She would actually be handling the bookkeeping chores. She would be working budgets, cost-to-date data, overages, and she would be the production liaison to the payroll company. She was handling a lot of the line producer's duties, a tall order for the uninitiated. Vince assured us that she was up to the task. I wanted to believe him, but something about the setup just didn't feel right. The faint scent of fiscal disaster was in the air. They gave me a copy of the current budget, and I was astonished to find that they planned on making the film for less than half a million dollars in cash and approximately two hundred thousand in deferments. The whole thing was to be shot in twelve days. Having read the original script, I didn't think it was possible.

"I'll make it work," Clyde said. "If we get the right people, it will be a cakewalk."

I told Clyde that I still wasn't sure I could take the position, because I had a few meetings set up for studio positions (which was a lie). He shrugged and said it was fine by him either way. No matter what happened, I wouldn't be needed for at least another two weeks. They couldn't afford to put me on the payroll this early. Deep down I hoped something better would come along before then. He let me take the budget home so I could study it if need be. I felt like stacking it on top of my old copies of *National Lampoon.* It was just as funny.

chapter seven

A few days later, as I was leaving my apartment to get a bite to eat, I ran into Clyde and Emily in the parking lot, preparing to get into Clyde's car. Emily was the first to speak. Clyde seemed to be giving me the cold shoulder.

"Hello, Mark. How have you been?"

"Busy," I lied.

"What's the hurry?"

I stopped and looked at her, feeling uncomfortable. "No hurry."

"We're meeting some people for dinner at Dan Tana's. Want to come along?"

I looked at Clyde. His expression told me nothing. "I better not. I've got some reading I have to do later."

"C'mon, Hayes," Clyde said. "You can read anytime. Come to dinner. We'll treat. I'll put it on the picture's tab."

"That's very tempting."

"Get in, then."

Emily opened her door and smiled at me. I felt awkward about the whole exchange, but I walked toward them. Emily pulled the seat forward so I could get in the backseat.

"You made me an offer I can't refuse," I said, then climbed into the back of the Maserati.

We made small talk as we drove over the hill to Dan Tana's, mostly discussing the progress of the O. J. Simpson saga. The media was pronouncing that Simpson was assembling a team of the finest legal minds in the country—or at least the finest legal minds that make a business of defending celebrity slashers. A closer inspection of the roster would have told the wags that it was actually a collection of Simpson cronies, big-name has-beens, and strutting media-manipulators. Almost none of them had successfully defended a client in a murder trial. Still, in an unprecedented PR coup, they were being called "The Dream Team" by the media, further sullying basketball history by adopting the moniker of our country's Olympic basketball team of 1992. Simpson just couldn't leave us hoops fans alone.

Emily and Clyde made no mention of the movie during the first part of the drive. I had a feeling Clyde felt rejected by my lack of enthusiasm for his job offer. I finally broke the ice. "How's the production shaping up?"

"We're having some financing problems," Clyde said. "That's one of the reasons for dinner tonight. We're wining and dining some investors."

"You sure you want me around for something like that?"

"You're the associate producer, aren't you?"

I didn't know what to say.

"At least you are tonight," Clyde added, filling in my silence. Now I got it. I was being brought along to make the production look more professional, more crewed up. I was a shill.

Dan Tana's is an Italian steak house that looks like it was lifted straight out of the heart of New York City and plopped down in the middle of West L.A. Red leather booths, checkered tablecloths, and wine bottles hanging from the ceiling. It's packed nightly with old-time Hollywood royalty, meeting and greeting, wheeling and dealing, but you can still get a table most of the time if you call ahead. It isn't one of the hip new places that requires reservations days or weeks in advance. It's a solid establishment that has survived since the 1960s, while thousands of trendy joints have come and gone. Dan Tana is such a Hollywood character that Robert Urich used his name in the hit TV show *Vega$.* (The producers added an extra *n* in *Tanna,* just to be creative.)

The bar was packed when we got there, but Clyde forced his way through and ordered drinks for us. We stood near the bar and watched the players play while we waited for our table and the potential investors.

"Listen," Clyde said to me, "these people are a little religious, so be careful what you say to them. They're born-agains. And they don't have very good senses of humor when it comes to God and whatnot."

"I don't plan on saying anything to them."

"Well, don't just sit there like a bump on a log. They'll think something's wrong."

"Okay. You want me to talk up the project?"

"Hell no. Just play it loose. We'll talk *around* the movie, not about it."

"Gotcha."

"Just follow my lead. Don't talk a lot, but don't act like you're a monk who took a vow of silence either. If you fuck this up, Vince will have your head."

"Why isn't Vince here himself?"

"Are you kidding? With his reputation, we're lucky these people are even considering a movie he's starring in. If they knew how involved he is in the production end of the project, it would blow the deal for sure."

"How you going to keep that from them?"

"They're just investors. It's business. They'll put up some money in return for points in the picture. They won't be involved with the creative end of things. I'll make sure of that."

"Here they come," Emily said.

Three smiling people made their way toward us through the crowd. A man and a woman in their late twenties and an older man who looked to be sixty-plus. I was introduced to Tremayne Harris and his twin children, Tod and Tressa. Tremayne had made a fortune by opening fast-food restaurants in the inner city. He had found religion a dozen years ago and was now trying to find new ways of spreading the Gospel. Burgers and fries just weren't doing the job anymore. Tremayne had produced a movie two years earlier that had heavy religious overtones. It hadn't made a lot of money, but he recouped enough through foreign sales that they didn't lose any either. And he'd made enough connections with foreign sales agents that he was now producing two other films and needed a third picture to satisfy contracts in three territories.

"I need Benelux, Italy, and Germany," Tremayne said while we were enjoying our appetizers.

"Germany?" Clyde was horrified. "We can't give you Germany. Germany is huge."

"I need it. Or I can't put up the money. Germany is the main reason I want to be involved with this film. I need to fulfill a contract there."

"The other investors won't give up the coin Germany brings. That's one of the most lucrative territories."

"I'm not as interested in the revenues as I am in being able to deliver Germany. It's the key to the completion funds on my two other films. They want three pictures or nothing."

"What if we let you sell Germany, but we take a piece of the action?"

"That might work, but I still want to recoup my investment before anyone starts profit sharing."

"Of course."

"We may be able to work this out."

Dinner arrived. I had the New York Steak Helen, named after Mace Neufeld's wife. No one at the table mentioned Mace's evil namesake, not wanting to alarm the born-agains with tales of Mace Thornburg's misdeeds.

As we ate, Tremayne let us know that his son and daughter were very interested in pursuing careers in the film business and wondered what they could do to help Clyde on *Blonde Lightning*. I could see my associate producer's credit drifting away on the winds of finance.

Tod and Tressa were relatively quiet during the meal, letting their old man handle the business. Although Tod did bring up one odd caveat to the deal. "Dad, what about Karen Black?"

Tremayne nodded. "Oh yes. Clyde, Tod had a very good idea about casting the part of Georgia. Karen Black."

"Karen Black?"

"Toddy's got a big crush on Karen Black," Tressa said. Tod kicked her under the table.

"It's true the boy has a bit of a fixation on Ms. Black," Tremayne said. "Ever since he saw that movie about the mean doll when he was a little boy. But when we read your script, we realized it would be the perfect part for her. Think you can get her?"

"I know Karen. I'll talk to her."

"Good."

The ideas kept coming. Clyde worked Tremayne, never giving in completely to any of his demands or suggestions, but never completely rejecting any of them either. He was completely noncommittal, yet in such a positive tone that Tremayne seemed to be under the impression he was winning on every point.

We had dessert and more drinks and more movie talk. Clyde paid the check, and we all walked out of the restaurant together. Clyde let Tremayne give his ticket to the valet first. He wanted to say the words that would cinch the deal, but Tremayne beat him to the punch and brought up something that had been mercifully absent from the dinner conversation.

"I have some script content problems, Clyde."

"Like?"

"Do you really need to use so many four-letter words in your writing?"

"Do you think the Germans will mind?"

"It's not the Germans I'm worried about. It's the members of my congregation. It's my friends and neighbors. It's having to answer their questions when they see my name on a picture that contains so much profanity."

"Perhaps you could use a pseudonym. Or we could leave your name out of the credits since you are providing a limited investment and only receiving certain territories in return."

"Credits mean a lot in this business."

"Many powerful players have left their names off controversial projects that they invested in for reasons similar to what you are suggesting."

"Really? Like who?"

"George Lucas was executive producer of *Body Heat*. His involvement helped get the picture made, and he took a check, but he left his name off the credits to avoid tarnishing his *Star Wars* family-friendly image. He wanted to support the movie, but he knew that some people wouldn't understand. George Lucas is pretty good company to be in."

"You may have something there."

Clyde seemed to have pulled off some kind of psychological checkmate. He was finding a way to get the investment and minimize the investor's involvement and potential collateral damage to the movie.

Tremayne's white Rolls-Royce pulled up at just the right moment. The twins loaded into the back. Tremayne and Clyde shook hands, and Tremayne went around to the driver's side. He reached into his pocket and feigned looking for cash. Then he looked over the roof of the car and said, "I didn't bring any folding money, Clyde. Can you take care of this fine gentleman?"

The valet looked over at Clyde, wondering if he was about to get stiffed.

"No problem, Mr. Harris."

Tremayne smiled. "Talk to you tomorrow." He slid into the driver's seat, and the Rolls took off like a rocket.

The valet came over, and Clyde gave him his own ticket. "I'll catch you when you get back," he promised. The valet looked at the ticket and headed for the parking lot in the back of the building, now fearing he was going to get tipped for one job after doing two. A reasonable fear.

"How do you think it went?" I asked.

"I think you got it," Emily said to Clyde.

"Well, I better have," Clyde said. "This was expensive."

We drove two miles down Santa Monica Boulevard and stopped in at Trader Vic's to visit with some friends of Emily's: stunt people and martial artists who were planning to shoot a movie of their own in Australia after the first of the year. Emily had already promised to do a cameo in their film in exchange for two round-trip airline tickets and an all-expenses-paid vacation to commence after her four days of shooting. She was going to take Clyde along with her—if they were still together by then. They were currently listing their relationship as "day to day."

Trader Vic's is stylistically about as far from Dan Tana's as you can get. It's an air-conditioned Polynesian hothouse plopped down on the edge of Beverly Hills. Vic's bartenders specialize in lethal rum concoctions that look deceptively like innocent froufrou drinks. Vic *invented* the mai tai! After I was introduced to the group, I ordered the notorious scorpion bowl from a sexy waitress in a grass skirt. Clyde ordered a hurricane, and Emily went for a fog cutter. That's the trick with froufrou drinks. They look so innocent that even casual drinkers dive in where it would be best to wade slowly.

The one thing Vic's shares with Dan Tana's is a celebrity clientele, and tonight was no exception. Warren Zevon was having a quiet dinner with a lovely lady at the table next to us. Shannen Doherty was having a not-so-quiet dinner with a table of friends at the other end of the room. Gary Busey and Mel Gibson were yukking it up at the bar. And the entire room grew quiet as Hugh Hefner entered the place with four gorgeous blondes in tow. Even Gary and Mel gave them a moment of silence as they passed through the bar area on their way to a more private room in the back. There's royalty, then there's *royalty.*

Our table was consumed with talk of Australia and plans for improving the movie before they got there. Emily had some good ideas for the director, a stunt coordinator who had shot a lot of second-unit but never helmed a feature before. As tough as he was on the outside, I could tell the prospect of finally making his dream project was beginning to unnerve him. *Everyone* at the table had ideas for him. Not all of them good. Emily gave the soundest advice, probably because she was one of the few people at the table who had no interest in ever directing anything.

There was a break in the conversation as Tracy, looking casually stunning, and a tall blond guy who looked like he just stepped off the cover of *Surf Rider Monthly* joined us at the table. I was startled by Tracy's sudden, unexpected arrival. I felt my heart race, and at the same time I felt great disappointment in seeing her with another man.

"I heard there was a party going on back here," Tracy said.

More intros were haphazardly thrown about, and I learned that the big handsome guy accompanying Tracy was her husband, Adam. I immediately hated him. During the intros, Tracy and I made brief eye contact and we shared a microsecond of discomfort. Emily had told her earlier that they would be hitting Trader Vic's, but I don't think she had anticipated my presence at the party, and Emily had also neglected to mention to me that Tracy might show up. I guess the matchmaking hadn't gone well enough to warrant warnings for each of us. I must not have registered very highly on Tracy's Richter scale.

The conversations around the table grew loud and boisterous. Emily and Tracy were having a good time, laughing and carrying on. Tracy's husband seemed out of place. He didn't engage in any conversations that lasted longer than a few sentences. He looked stiff and uncomfortable in the middle of this bunch. I considered moving to his side of the table and making conversation with him; then I remembered I hated him for having that which I could not have, and I let him sit there. At one point he got up and went to the men's room.

Tracy took the opportunity to come over and speak to me. "How are you?" she asked with a big smile.

"Terrific. How you doing?"

"I'm . . . okay."

"I see you've worked things out with hubby."

"I wouldn't say that."

"He's here, isn't he?"

"Only to keep an eye on me."

"Oh, it's like that, is it?"

"He'd never admit it, but, yeah. It's like that."

"Maybe he'll do the world a favor and give up on you."

"It's quite possible."

"If that happened, could I call you?"

"Sure."

Adam returned from the bathroom and came over to see what was up. His wife wasn't talking to Emily anymore—she was talking to some *guy.*

Tracy stood up to introduce us. "Hey, Adam, this is Clyde's neighbor, Mark. Remember I told you about him? The guy who worked for Dexter Morton?"

"Uh, yeah," Adam said, shaking my hand a little too firmly, trying to prove something. "We did some work for Dexter last year."

"Oh, what is it you do?" I asked.

"I've got a landscaping company. Sometimes we do work on locations for films. We did some greenery for the mansion shoot-out in *Bel Air PD.*"

"That was a good scene." Yeah, in a godawful movie.

"Hey, aren't you the guy they thought killed Dexter?"

"One of the guys. There were a lot of suspects. I'm surprised they never called you in."

"Me? Why would I kill Dexter?"

"It didn't take much for Dexter to get on someone's wrong side."

"I liked the dude. He paid well and on time."

"He had that going for him."

Adam couldn't tell if I was having him on or not, but he had heard enough. "Well, nice meeting you," he said, and then he guided Tracy back to their side of the table. I noticed Emily was watching it all, and she looked at me sympathetically before looking away.

Clyde leaned into me and whispered, "Don't worry, pal. Around here, all things come to those who wait."

After a few more uncomfortable minutes, Tracy and Adam said their good-byes to Emily and waved to the group, who were busy discussing business among themselves and didn't really seem to notice.

Emily came over to my side of the table. "I guess I should have warned you that they might drop in."

"It would have been less of a shock."

"I'm sorry. I didn't realize you liked her that much."

"What's not to like?"

"You've got good taste. Hang in there. Maybe things will work out."

"That's what I told him," Clyde interjected.

"I bet you did."

We stuck around for last call. The froufrou drinks were getting to me. I was feeling downright surly. If we were in New York, I probably would have started a fight with one of the cocky stuntmen after a few more rounds of drinks. Luckily for me, L.A. rolls its sidewalks up early. I just sulked in the backseat of the Maserati as Clyde drove us back to the Valley.

chapter eight

I didn't hear from Clyde for a few days. In the meantime, my job search crawled along without success. I checked my development fund and found that I had dropped below the twenty-thousand-dollar mark. It was now a war of attrition. I needed work. Any work.

I called Clyde and asked him how the film financing was going.

"Pretty good. Looks like the born-agains are in for fifty K. We're giving them the right to sell Germany, but we're taking fifty percent of the revenue. We only need another thirty grand and we're good to go."

I thought about my twenty, and then quickly talked myself out of it. I was looking to make money, not blow the last of my savings.

"Let me know if there's anything you need me to do to help. I'll shill for you again if need be."

"Cool. You did pretty good with the fish. I told Vince all about it. He's happy to have you aboard."

It was as if we had never had the conversation about me possibly not working on the film. I guess I had a job coming up after all. Low pay is better than no pay.

"That's great," I said.

"I'll show you the revised script as soon as it's finished."

"Terrific."

He hung up without saying good-bye. So, I had a job without asking for it—if they could raise that last thirty thousand dollars. I wasn't going to start counting on my mediocre paycheck yet. I'd seen many projects that looked much more secure than this one crash and burn at the last moment for any number of bizarre reasons.

Tracy came into Viande that night while I was eating dinner. She looked frazzled, but I didn't comment on her appearance. I kissed her on the cheek and told her how happy I was to see her.

"I had to get out of the house," she said. "It was driving me crazy. I just wanted to talk to someone. I thought Emily might be here."

"Will I do?"

She blushed, then said, "I'm such a liar. You were really the one I wanted to see."

My heart swelled with optimism. At least I think it was my heart. "You want to talk in private?"

"Yes."

"We can go to my place."

She gave me a "you've got to be kidding" look, then surprised me by saying, "Okay."

I paid my tab, and we went up to my apartment. I opened two beers, and we stood out on the balcony as she laid out the news for me.

"I'm leaving him," she said.

"What happened?"

"That's not important. The only thing you need to know is that I'm leaving him. It's over. I can't stay there anymore."

"What are you going to do?"

"I don't know. I packed some clothes. I don't want to go back to my parents' house again. I'm getting a little old for that. I guess I'll stay in a hotel for a few days, until I can find an apartment."

"You can stay here." I made the offer far too quickly. I sounded desperate.

"I couldn't do that."

"Why not?"

"Look, I came here to tell you I left Adam. It's obvious what I meant by that, but I'm not going to just move in with you."

"I just thought . . . until you got on your feet . . ."

"Sure you did. I *know* what you're thinking."

"Then I don't really have to say anything else, do I?" I leaned forward and kissed her.

She didn't resist, but didn't go wild either. "I'm not going to sleep with you," she said. "I can't."

I pulled back and looked at her seriously. "Why not?"

"I don't know you well enough. And there's a lot you don't know about me."

"I know enough."

"You don't. There are things about me that would repulse you. Physical things. And I don't feel like going through any more rejection right now."

"I don't know what you think is wrong with you, but I think you are one of the most beautiful women I have ever seen."

"You haven't seen me with my clothes off. I'm hideous."

I laughed. I immediately knew it was a moronic thing to do, but I couldn't help myself. It seemed so ludicrous. She obviously had a body to die for.

She pulled farther away from me, and I could see that she was shivering. "Please don't do that," she said.

"I'm sorry. It just seems crazy to me. You are gorgeous. And I can tell that you would be even more gorgeous without your clothes, so I don't know what you're talking about."

"No, you *don't* know."

"Clyde warned me about you."

"He did? What did he say?"

"He said you suffered from DGS."

"Him and his damaged-goods bullshit. I've heard it all before. What does he know about me? Nothing! I'm telling you there's a problem, and it's not psychosomatic. It's physical."

"Okay. What is it? Tell me. Please."

"I had cancer. Breast cancer."

I just sat there, numb in the dim glow of the alley streetlight. She didn't say anything else. It was as if she did not want to go on. As if she had already said too much.

"Are you okay?" I finally asked.

"They think so. But you never know. It could come back."

"What happened?"

"They found a lump, then two more. They tried to treat it with chemo, but finally they had to cut. One of my breasts is totally mangled. I'm a freak."

"I can't believe you're saying this. Do you think I give a damn if you've been cut? Do you really think I'm that shallow?"

"Probably. But I'm here anyway."

I moved closer to her and kissed her again.

She was even more tentative this time. "I don't want you to prove anything. You don't have to play 'give the freak a treat' with me."

"Damn, lady, can't you tell how I feel about you? There's nothing you could be hiding that can change that."

"Really? So if I didn't look the way I look, you'd feel the same way about me?"

"Of course."

"It's my sparkling wit that has you entranced, right?"

"Right."

"Good. Then the sex thing doesn't have to enter into it. We can just be brain buddies."

"Sure. If that's how you want it."

I kissed her again, and this time she responded. We moved into the hammock and one thing led to another and suddenly we were both sixteen again and the balcony was really the backseat of a '69 Mustang. We made out for half an hour. I tried to stay away from her breasts, not wanting to upset her. She was probably just as upset that I avoided them. It was a catch-22. I didn't know what the hell I was expected to do. Things got hot in spite of my reluctance to round second base, and I suddenly found her straddling me and giving me the dry hump of my life. I tried to pull at her clothes, but she resisted.

A whoop came from the parking lot. Late-night revelers leaving Viande had spotted us in the shadows. We giggled like kids, and I suggested we go inside. We went to my bedroom and continued necking for a while. I tried to get her out of her clothes again, and she resisted again. She spotted my blue bathrobe hanging on the door. She got up, excused herself, and took the robe into the bathroom.

I lay there waiting for her. After almost ten minutes, she came into the bedroom wearing my robe. She turned off the lights, and the room became pitch-black. I reached up and opened the blinds to let light from the alley spill into the room.

She sat on the edge of the bed and touched my hand softly. "Close it, please," she said.

"Why?"

"I don't want you to see me."

"But I want to."

She gathered the robe around herself and stood up. "Maybe I should go."

"Okay, okay, I'm sorry. I'll close them." I shut the venetian blinds, and we were plunged into darkness again. She did not climb back into the bed. I stood up and moved to her, gathering her close. She pulled away—but not very forcefully.

"Please stay," I said. "I won't rush anything."

She didn't answer, but she let me hold her. I traced the line of her face and neck with my fingers and kissed her gently on the lips.

"You'll regret this," she said. "It's ugly."

"There's no way anything about you is ugly. Why don't you have a little faith?"

I kissed her again and felt along the side of the robe. I came to where her right breast should be, but it wasn't there. Or at least most of it wasn't. What *was* there was small and mangled and scarred. I caressed the area, and she pulled away from me violently.

"Don't touch me there! I'm not a freak show for you!"

"I just want to make love to you. I don't care what you think is wrong with you. I think you're the most beautiful woman I have ever known, and I just want to be with you."

I stepped closer to her. She was trembling. I picked her up and put her down on the bed.

"Just don't touch me there," she said nervously.

"Okay. I won't."

She let me open the robe on the left side and feel the other breast, the one that the doctors hadn't mangled.

Another guy might give you all the juicy details about what happened from that point on, tell you all about the way we made love, describe the contours of her tragically beautiful body and lovely face, wax poetic about the passion we felt for each other that had been denied, and how she finally let me open those blinds and see all there was to see and love all there was to love, but I'm not that kind of guy.

Let me just say this—it was worth the wait.

Afterwards, we lay in the hammock on the porch with the overhead lights off and watched the clouds move across the night sky. Light from the city to the north of us made the low clouds glow as if they were on fire.

Tracy sighed so deeply that she actually shuddered. I could feel the sadness creeping through her body like a fast-moving cancer come back to enact its revenge.

"What's wrong?" I asked.

"It's hard for me to be still like this. My mind goes to places I don't want it to go. That's why I like to stay busy."

"Are you thinking about Adam?"

"I wasn't, but thanks for bringing him up."

"I'm sorry."

"It's okay. I'm being snippy. No, I was thinking about what we did in there."

"You didn't like it?"

"I liked it fine. But what is it? What is it we do with one another, men and women?"

"Try to make one another feel good?"

"That's the physical part. Animals do it all the time. Not as often as civilized people, of course, but when the time is right, they carry on just like we did. Except they don't have the soft music or the romantic lighting or scented candles burning to hide what they are. They just fuck."

"I don't have scented candles."

"You know what I mean. There's no pretense to what they do. And no entanglements. They mate to procreate. But we fuck just to fuck. And what for? I can't even have children. The chemo fixed that. Don't you see? I'm just going through the motions. I'm a ghost, and I don't even know it."

"You feel pretty damn real to me."

"One day I'll be dead. And you'll be dead. And everyone we know will be dead. Then what was the purpose of it all? Why do we struggle and claw and fight our way along, trying to achieve something, when we all end up as dust?"

"That's been the big debate, hasn't it?"

"Sometimes I feel my chest, where my breast used to be, and it feels like it's still there. Phantom pain is what they call it. But then I realize that not only is my breast gone, but I should be gone, as well. Forty years ago, what I had would have been one hundred percent fatal. I would not have survived. And then I think of my friend Carla and how it took her so fast, and realize that I got lucky, even for today. But for what? I can play out my time, but let's face it—life won't get any better than it's been. We're getting older. It's not as much fun as it used to be. I'm not as fast or strong as I used to be. And neither are you."

"No, but I'm craftier now."

"It's different for you. You know what you want to do with your life."

"I would not say things are looking good on my career front."

"But you still have the fire. I don't anymore. Work means nothing to me. When I was growing up, I wanted to be an actress. I thought if I could be a movie star, it would be like living forever. But when I started getting parts and seeing myself on the screen, I realized how foolish I had been. Being in a movie doesn't change anything. As a matter of fact, it made me feel like I was already a ghost."

"How's that?"

"When those movies I made come on TV and I watch myself, it's so clear that it's not me anymore. It's just a transparent image of something I was a long time ago. Movies don't make you immortal—they just make you into a ghost. All movies are ghost stories. Eventually."

"That's funny. I always thought that all movies were really love stories. It takes some kind of love to get a movie made. Love of filmmaking, love of money, love of something."

"I think I've lost the ability to love."

"I don't believe that."

I touched her hand. A fireball suddenly filled the sky in the far northwest of the Valley.

"Oh my god, what's that?" Tracy asked.

"It's a rocket going up from Vandenberg," I said. "It happens all the time."

The light disappeared into the atmosphere, but a vapor trail was left behind, squiggling like a slow-moving snake in the gentle breeze, illuminated by the full moon.

Tracy said, "It's beautiful."

"Aren't you glad you were around to see it?"

"That's just my point. One day I *won't* be around. And I won't have a consciousness to remember that I even saw it tonight. It might as well not have happened."

"But it *did* happen. Can't you live for the moment? Can't you just enjoy what we have today and not think about tomorrow?"

"I always thought I'd find someone I could share nights like this with and that it would make it all make some kind of sense. Adam's not much of a ruminator, so I always feel alone when I'm with him. I thought if I shared a moment or a thought or a sight with someone I cared about, someone who understood, life would seem more permanent. But now that I'm here, in this place with you, a person who 'gets it,' a person maybe I could love, I realize it still doesn't make a difference."

"It does to me."

"Yes, but so what? I mean, not to make it small, but what we have won't last."

"How do you know that?"

"Because *nothing* does. Look at my grandparents. They were together for fifty years. Then he died. Now she's alone and miserable."

"Fifty years is a long time."

"It will pass in a blink. Then we'll be gone. All of us. Everyone we know."

I had my arm around her, and now I pulled her closer. I caressed her side. I could feel the disfigurement through the cloth of the robe and did not try to avoid it. I traced my fingers on and around the area as if she had the most beautiful breast in the world hiding under the robe. Our level of intimacy had grown enough so that she did not pull away this time.

"You're obsessed with it, aren't you?" she said.

"What?"

"My breast. Or more specifically—what *isn't* my breast anymore."

"I'm not obsessed with it. I'm obsessed with you, and it's part of you. Should I avoid touching you there? Does it still bother you?"

She climbed out of the hammock, pulled the robe around her, and stood at the rail. A light drizzle of rain was beginning to fall. "You think I'm going to get used to this just because we had sex? You think your cock is a psychological miracle cure?"

"That's not what I meant."

"I think you're trying to prove something."

"What?"

"That it's not disgusting to you. And maybe that it doesn't scare you."

I got out of the hammock and went to the rail, but I didn't crowd her. "It doesn't disgust me," I said. "But yeah, you're right. It scares me a little. It scares me to think it could come back."

I brushed hair from her eyes, and I could see she was crying. I pulled her close to me. I could feel her quivering in the cold, and she began to sob. I kissed her softly on the lips and tasted the salt of her tears. I parted the robe and kissed the scarred and mutilated flesh where her breast used to be. I cupped her close to me and squeezed her tight, trying to hold on to her precious life force and not let it slip from her body. I was crazed with a sense of all-consuming love. I kissed and sucked her unmarred breast, and the beauty of it took my breath away. She pulled me back up into a standing position, and we made love again, gently this time, leaning against the stucco wall and the wood railing, the warm night rain sprinkling our faces.

When the fever broke, I wondered how much of my emotion stemmed from the loss of Charity James. Was I just using Tracy to try to make up for my failure to help Charity? Was I trying to infuse myself with passion so I would not make the same mistakes of apathy that marked my relationship with my dead friend? I didn't know. But whatever the reasons, I felt a sense of madness. A sense that my actions were not my own. I'd never been very good with soap-opera moments with girlfriends, but Tracy was inspiring them by the bushel. Yet I sensed that the ghost of Charity James hovered over the proceedings as if she were now my constant companion.

Tracy told me she could not spend the night. She dressed, then said, "Please don't tell Clyde or Emily about this. Not yet, at least."

"I'm not like that. This isn't about them."

She smiled and opened the front door. "Good answer. I'll probably run into them in the parking lot anyway."

"You can say I abducted you, and you struggled to free yourself."

"That's not far from the truth."

"Can I call you?"

"I better call you. The next few days are going to be difficult."

"Okay."

She winked and closed the door.

Life was good.

chapter nine

After Tracy left, I was full of energy and did not want to stay in the apartment. I showered and went over to Viande for a nightcap. I found Clyde sitting at the bar, having a drink and rolling one of his cigarettes. (He preferred rolling his own, which he said slowed his intake.) When he spoke, I detected a slur. That wasn't a good sign. I wanted to work on his movie, but not if he was going to turn into some kind of Peckinpah-like drunken maniac. I'd seen him on a bender before, and I did not want to deal with it on a professional level. I'd work as a temp again before I'd put up with that. Not wanting to antagonize him, I decided not to mention anything about the drinking at this time.

We sat and talked about *Blonde Lightning.* He recapped the story for me in a nutshell. It sounded like a fairly standard detective thriller. He said it was an homage to Hammett and a virtual remake of a film he had directed a few years earlier for two producers who had "ripped him off," but with all the names and locations changed. I assumed he meant the movie I found on his résumé when I looked up his credits a few months earlier, the one on which he had used the pseudonym Colin Noble for the director's credit. When I asked him if he would get in trouble for ripping *himself* off like that, he asked me whose side I was on: his or *theirs*. The specific duties he had in mind for me as his associate producer seemed vague at best. He said he wanted somebody to watch his back and to chronicle everything that happened on the set just in case some mysterious coup was launched or some bizarre bit of treachery was perpetrated against him by the producers. His previous experiences had savaged him to the point of paranoia. Considering the people Clyde associated with, I had a feeling that a good dose of paranoia on his part wasn't such a bad idea.

Emily came looking for Clyde, and when she saw him drinking at the bar, she was not happy. "I figured I'd find you over here," she said humorlessly. "What the hell are you doing?"

"We're having a preproduction meeting," Clyde said, trying not to slur.

"Like the good old days, huh?"

"Not really."

"Bullshit." She then turned her wrath on me. "I thought you had better sense than this, Mark."

"Hey, I'm just sitting here. I'm not his keeper."

She looked at me like I was a total jerk, and I had to admit I was doing a pretty good imitation of one.

"Clyde," she said, "if you don't get up and come home right now, I'm leaving you. This time for good."

"I'll be there in a bit. I just have to wrap things up with young Hayes here."

Emily was fuming. Her face turned bright red, and she stormed down the hallway and out the back door.

"Maybe you should go after her," I said to Clyde.

"Nah, this will be good for her."

I had a feeling Emily was back at his apartment, packing her stuff, and I felt somewhat responsible. "I'll be right back," I said, standing up.

"Where you going?"

"I want to get my wallet. I left it in my apartment."

He nodded and went back to his drink. I went out the back way, crossed the alley, and knocked on the door to apartment 3.

Emily opened the door. I could see a large suitcase open on the couch, half-filled with neatly folded clothes.

"You're not really going to leave him, are you?"

"Yes, indeed. I've had it. I told him I wouldn't go through it again, and I meant it."

"This is all my fault. I shouldn't be drinking with him."

"If it wasn't you, it would be one of his other cronies. He doesn't need an excuse to drink, but he likes to have one handy anyway." She went back to packing things in the suitcase.

"Where will you go?"

"What? I don't live here. I own a house in Pacific Palisades. I just have stuff here so that I don't have to drive home all the time."

"Oh. Well, is there anything I can do to help you?"

She stopped for a moment and looked at me very seriously. I thought for a moment she was going to cry, but of course she didn't.

"Keep an eye on him. Don't let him get too wasted. And for God's sake, don't let him drive drunk."

"I'll do my best."

I left her to finish packing.

By the time I got back to the bar, Clyde was halfway to nirvana. His eyes were no longer synchronized, and his slur was more pronounced.

There was a small stack of freshly rolled cigarettes sitting next to his drink. Due to numerous complaints from diners about the cloud of toxins that usually hovered over the bar and drifted into their airspace, owner Dale Jaffe had recently instituted a controversial no-smoking policy at Viande, so Clyde couldn't smoke in the restaurant, but he'd be ready when he hit the street. So much for the "roll 'em to slow 'em" technique.

"C'mon, man," I said. "Let's go home. Maybe you can catch Emily before she takes off."

"Fuck her," he snapped.

I was taken aback. He had never spoken about her that way before. At least not in front of me.

"Let me tell you about Emily," he continued. Then he motioned with his empty rocks glass, and the bartender hit it with a shot of Jack. "She just hangs with me to stay away from her own place. She's afraid Mace or one of his goons will try to kill her."

"But I thought . . ."

"She doesn't own me. I don't own her. I wanna drink, I fucking drink."

I ordered a beer and pondered Clyde's words. "Emily's a third-degree black belt. She knows how to handle herself. Why is she afraid of Mace?"

"There's a big difference between being a tough guy and being a tough *gal.* Sure, she could kick a lot of guys' asses, but a guy who knows what he's doing? There's no contest. That stuff you see in her movies, where she kicking all this martial-arts booty? It's make-believe. Angles, cuts, planning. It's choreographed. You know, blocked out. I thought you had some idea how it all worked."

"Of course I do. But you have to be a hell of an athlete even to fake those stunts."

"Doesn't matter. Anybody can be killed. The only reason any of us are still here is that no one or no thing has really tried hard enough to kill us."

"I guess that's true."

"The great thing about being with Emily is that she's gone half the time. A relationship can be a real drain. A lot of maintenance is needed. And then when it breaks up, you're left regretting all that time and effort you put into what ultimately amounts to nothing."

"But there are good times, too, right?"

"Sure. But in some ways, that's even worse. You don't get anything done when it's cruising along smooth like that. You turn around, and a year's lost. I spent a decade catering to the needs of women. I completely wasted the eighties."

"You made a lot of movies in the eighties."

"Nothing worth bragging about. I was too busy getting drunk and chasing pussy to concentrate on the work. And when push came to shove with the producers, when they tampered with the material, half the time I walked away quietly and let them do what they wanted to do. It never made one movie better, the tinkering those bastards did. It invariably weakened the films, sometimes ruined them. But I let them get away with it, practically without a fight."

"You sure didn't get a rep as a guy who walked away from trouble."

"Let me tell you something about that. Most of the stories you hear about me are total bullshit. These guys *want* to brand you as a troublemaker if they can. That way it makes it harder for you to get work and easier for them to put the squeeze on you. You don't like the way things are going? They'll replace you. You put up an artistic argument that they don't like or refuse to write the extra scene for their girlfriend or call them on it when they pay you late or their check bounces, and they brand you a troublemaker. Then the work dries up. They always win in the end, one way or the other."

"That's true. I've seen it happen, even at the studio level."

"Of course it happens at the studios. It happens everywhere. I got burned just as bad by the studios as by the low-budget guys. Sometimes worse."

"Well, if you wanted to control the way things got done, you should have kept directing. Why didn't you?"

"You really want to hear the story?"

"Yeah."

He took a long drink and seemed to be considering whether he should go down this path or not. He was steeling himself, preparing for something painful.

"I knew these two people—they were friends of mine. I had actually introduced them to each other on a film I was shooting pickup scenes for, a movie called *The Vigilantes.* Ever see it?"

"No."

"You and everyone else. It was lame. No matter how hard you polish a turd, you still just have a shiny turd. But that's beside the point. These two people were both working on it, Elsie and Stavros; she was an actress, he was a grip, neither one of them the smartest people you ever met. But we all became friends, and soon old Stavros was racking Elsie. I didn't want any part of her action, so I was the perfect third wheel. I had no interest in Elsie whatsoever. This is twelve years ago, and my sex drive was a lot higher in those days, but for one reason or another, this girl just didn't turn me on. She was a very manipulative piece of work, and I just don't dig that, no matter how good it looks. But Stavros bought into it. He was low-class, a working boy who didn't really want to work.

"They started dating—then they moved in together. They bought a house, got a dog, and dreamed of making movies. She quit acting and ended up working for a distribution company as a sales rep. A perfect gig for someone with her personality flaws. He kept up the blue-collar shit, but he couldn't keep up with her earning power. You know the drill. Woman starts making more dough than her man; man starts feeling his balls shrink. Thing is, old Elsie had balls enough for both of 'em."

I laughed and he looked at me sharply, like there was nothing humorous in what he was saying.

"Okay," he continued. "We cruise along, and I'm goin' pretty good. I got ten, twelve films to my credit as a writer, and once in a while I produce one, but I never direct again. Every time I get the chance, I back away, thinking I'm not up to the gig or sniffing some treachery laced into the deal. So I kind of accept my life as a writer and just drink and fuck the eighties away, not a care in the world. Stavros and Elsie are more serious. They decide to get married. They even ask me to be their best man. Why not? I had introduced them. I wrote a fucking congratulation speech for their reception that had people laughing one minute, crying the next. It was beautiful. Best thing I ever wrote and it was for *free.*

"So they get married. They've got it all now—the house, the dog, the license, his and her fucking BMWs, the works. They're missing only two things: a kid and a career for Stavros. He couldn't keep being a grip the rest of his life. So Elsie decides he could be a writer, a producer, and one day, a director. He tries his hand at writing, and it's abominable shit. Not only can't he tell a story, he's dyslexic to boot. Which never stopped Cannell, but Cannell has talent.

"They ask me to help him out on the script, so naturally I give it a shot, but Jesus Christ, there's only so much a man can do. It was rancid stuff. So that's that for Stavros's writing. Next up, they want to produce a movie. They can't do it based on his stuff, so they ask me if I want to direct one of my unproduced pieces. At first I say no way. I had seen them in business situations enough times to be wary of stepping into that lion's den. But they kept twisting my arm and making promises until it started to sound good. They were going to put up the money and work the physical production end, but leave the creative process totally up to me. I had complete control and final cut. I thought, How many offers you going to get like that? It was too good to be true."

"Didn't go well, huh?" I interjected.

His eyes flared at my interruption. I had broken his flow. "Shit. You're not ready for this, are you?"

"Yeah," I said. "I want to hear it all."

"Then stop interrupting me. Okay?"

"Okay."

He took another sip and burped one of those burps that starts as deep in your body as it can and physically transforms you as it rises to escape.

"Okay. So we decide to make this movie, and it's right before the SAG strike is about to hit, so we've got to rush, and the piece they want to do is this thing I wrote called *Crimson Night* that I had sold to this Israeli production company. One of the mucky-mucks in the company sent a memo down saying erotic thrillers were out that year and pulled the plug on the project. So I make an offer to buy back the script for the balance of what they owe me on my contract. Cost me fourteen grand. But I get the piece back, and we launch into superfast preproduction.

"I go without sleep for two weeks straight, doing everything a director should do . . . and a casting director . . . and a producer. Because everyone they have hired to do those jobs are friends of theirs looking for their big break, and I'm suddenly surrounded by a bunch of talentless wannabes and I have to pull the whole thing together my own fucking self. And Stavros, he's the worst of them all. This poor bastard couldn't find his ass with both hands and a magnifying glass, but he's going to try to produce a movie for a hundred and fifty grand. It was ridiculous. Have I ever explained to you the Inverse Law of Film Production?"

"No."

"Well, you should know this if you want to be a producer. The Inverse Law of Film Production goes like this: The more money you have, the less talent you need. The less money you have, the more talent you need. The bigger the budget, the less hard you will have to work. The smaller the budget, the harder you will have to work. The more money they give you to make your movie, the less you really need to know about the craft of moviemaking, and vice versa. It goes on like that for about an hour, but you probably don't need to hear the rest."

"I get the gist."

"Right. It's the ironic key to why everything is so fucked up in this town. And we got to see the law in action on our little production. See, we had very little dough, and Stavros is basically a moron. He'd be qualified to run a studio or produce a Steven Seagal movie, but he couldn't hack getting the job done on a picture of this scale for that small amount of money. You really need to know what you're doing when you have no budget. His wife was constantly on his back because he wasn't doing his job, and then she was taking her frustration out on the rest of us because she was so pissed at him.

"They hire Stavros's brother, Raiford, as the caterer, and this fucking guy is so busy trying to lay any set skank he can get his hands on that lunch was late every day. You ever see a crew when they don't get lunch on time? It's not pretty. Then Stavros and Elsie did something unforgivable—they lied about having enough money in the bank to shoot the picture. So we've got an incompetent producer, his bitchy wife busting everyone's balls, and his lazy, good-for-nothing brother working as our caterer. It was a recipe for disaster."

"Why didn't you just pull the plug?"

"I tried to quit two or three times during preproduction. Stavros and Elsie were at each other's throats, and I thought one of them was going to kill the other, so I said we should just shitcan the thing, but they wouldn't have it. Every time I tried to cancel the shoot, Elsie would turn on the waterworks and beg me to stay with the project. That's how she controlled situations. She'd start crying and make you feel like a heel until you did what she wanted. A complete manipulator. I made them promise not to hold me responsible if it all blew up in their faces, but they did anyway."

"What happened?"

"We start shooting the movie, and right away I know we're in trouble. The first day of principal photography, I'm on the soundstage and I'm all ready to shoot, but we've got no *film*. Stavros forgot to buy the film stock! So we all stand around with our thumbs you-know-where until the stock arrives, two hours later. We've got a dolly, but no dolly track. He's too cheap to spend the three hundred bucks for track, so we're supposed to push the camera around on this big-ass old dolly and its rubber wheels. No way you're gonna get a smooth shot that way.

"Then we're supposed to break for lunch at noon, but where's Raiford? Who the fuck knows? The crew sits it out for an hour while we wait for this big, fat, lazy asshole to show up with the food, and when he does, it's crap. Now the crew is furious. I had fourteen pages to shoot the first day, including two love scenes and a complicated murder scene with makeup effects, but even with all the bad producing going on, we make the day—and the stuff is pretty good.

"Then Stavros has the nerve to tap his watch while we're wrapping and look at me and say, 'We're an hour over, Chief. What are we gonna do about this?' like he's David O. fucking Selznick or something. I mean, Christ, *he's* the one who wasted our time, him and his asshole brother. And after I've busted my ass for almost three weeks straight with no sleep, this putz is in my face, telling me how to do my job. I was angry, but I didn't say anything. I knew he was in over his head, so I just promised to do better.

"But as we went on, it proved impossible. He had no qualified production people helping us whatsoever. They had hired all their cronies in the slots that real production personnel should have occupied. These rotten fucks sat on their asses, playing cards, eating the craft service food, and talking about what Junior Spielbergs they all were while my crew busted their humps on the stage and made the movie for them. By the third day, members of the crew were wearing *Death to Production* on their hardhats.

"For some reason, Stavros and Elsie thought I had put them up to it, but that was bullshit. That crew hated them all on their own. They were working them like mules and not paying any overtime. Raiford was late with lunch every single day, and when it got there, it was garbage, so a

lot of my guys took to eating at Mickey D's across the street from the
stage. At one point I asked Raiford to get some Cokes for the crew, and
he said 'Those fuckers don't deserve it.' Can you believe it? Right in
front of them. I'm lucky the crew didn't walk out on us, but they were
a great bunch. We all just put our heads down and made the fucking
movie without the 'producers' and their staff."

"It sounds like a nightmare."

"That's just the tip of the iceberg. We get into three or four skir-
mishes about schedules and money, and they say I'm shooting too
much film, doing too many takes and such, so I start shooting the
movie the way they want me to instead of the way I know it should be
done, just to save them dough. A lot more dependence on master shots,
a lot less coverage. I wasn't happy about it, but I just wanted to be finished with the thing. Then one morning I step onto the set, and Stavros
says to me, 'You get the extras for today?' and I say, 'That's not my job,'
and he pulls my Rolodex out of my bag and says, 'Better get on the
phone, Chief.' I thought I was going to puke. I'm there trying to shoot
fifteen pages a day, and this guy wants me to sit on the phone and call
my friends to be free extras. They had hired one of Elsie's pals to wran-
gle extras, but of course he had dropped the ball like all their other
friends, and now they were making it my problem. Then I said the
words that would eventually bring the whole house down."

"What?"

"I looked at Stavros and said, 'I'm getting tired of doing your job for
you.' "

"Uh-oh."

"Right! So the shit hit the fan. Stavros asked me to step offstage with
him. Mind you, only three or four people had arrived by this time, but
he took it as a major insult. So we walk off, and we stumble right into
the middle of a fight between Raiford and my gaffer over what was
scheduled for lunch that day, and Raiford's calling my gaffer a fuckwad,
and I tell Raiford I can make the movie without *him,* but I need the

gaffer, so for a minute it looks like we're gonna have a four-way donny-brook.

"But the situation levels out, and finally I settle in to talk to Stavros and I tell him I can't make this movie without his help, and I beg him to work *with* me and not against me. He asks what the problem is, like he's been doing his job and shit, and I run down his list of crimes, and then I run down Raiford's list of crimes, and he finally, after, like, forty-five minutes, agrees to get his shit together, and we shake hands like men, dust off, and get back to work. The rest of the day went smooth as silk, and I'm starting to think, Hey, the worst is over, right?"

"The wife," I said, knowing where this was going.

"You got it. I'm getting ready to go to the set the next morning, thinking everything's cool, and I get a call from Elsie. She says Stavros told her what happened the day before and that it's 'highly unaccept-able' behavior on my part. I say I thought we had it all worked out, and she just keeps on hammering at me. Finally I ask her what she wants me to do about it, and she has no answer, but I knew right then and there that I was fucked.

"She had it in for me. See, for them it wasn't about making a good movie. It was about *making* a *movie*. Any movie. They just wanted to be photographed standing next to the camera so they could self-promote their yuppie asses all over town. They knew the flick wasn't going to win any awards, and they knew the crew hated them for being assholes, so they decided to make me their fall guy. They decided to sacrifice their best friend so that they would come out of it looking like victims, like they were 'good producers'—as they always used to call themselves—and I would be labeled the maniac who fucked everything up. I already had a rep around town as a hothead, so they played it up. It was real easy for everyone to believe the problems were all my fault. I was the perfect goat.

"But the coup de grâce was yet to come. When it came time to cut the picture, they locked me out of the editing room! They didn't even let me make a first cut. It was crazy. If you don't get to cut your own movie, you might as well not have made it. They fired my editor and hired some TV cutter who Elsie knew, and this woman didn't have the faintest idea what that movie was supposed to be. They wasted thousands of dollars trying to figure out problems I could have solved in moments for free. They even went out and shot new scenes—*three days* of pickups. You know what I could have done with three extra days? And all they got was two minutes of new footage that didn't even match the rest of the film. It actually *destroyed* the narrative.

"Then, after all this is said and done, they blame me for going over budget! They blow all this money on faux postproduction, and it's *my* fault? Give me a break. I went *one* day over schedule. They blew all the extra dough shooting scenes we didn't need and doing an incredibly lame and overpriced music score and sound mix. They didn't know who to go to, and they got ripped off. The movie didn't even make sense when it was finished, and they went around town blaming *me*. I'm not allowed to cut my own film, and then it's all my fault when it fails? They had me fucked good, no matter which way I turned."

"What happened to the movie?"

"Straight to video. What else? You know what the funniest part of the whole thing was?"

"What?"

"The main reason they went ahead and made the film when they clearly weren't ready was that they had told their *friends* that they were going to make a movie. It was their so-called *summer project,* if you can get the humor in that. Like they were Paramount or something. Have you ever heard a dumber reason to make a movie? It was insanity. After that experience, I swore I'd never direct again. I mean, if that's what your *friends* can do to you, why should I expect a fair shake from strangers?"

"You shouldn't judge the industry by that one experience. These creeps sound like real amateurs."

"Yeah, but I've dealt with the pros, too. Everyone gets fucked in this town. You've got to be a real narcissistic piece of work to survive as a director. You've got to believe your shit is gold-plated to run that gauntlet."

"So why are you directing this one?"

He shrugged and waved at the bartender for a refill. "I don't know. Restless, I guess. I'm done with my book. I don't know what else to do with myself. And I've got a lousy memory, so I had forgotten most of that stuff even happened until now."

"Sorry for stirring it all up."

"No. It's okay. It's good. I *should* remember it all. So I don't make the same mistakes again."

"Do you think things will go smoothly this time?"

"You never know until it's over. But that's why I've got *you* around. You're going to be my canary in the coal mine. I look over and see you passed out on the floor, I'll know it's time to get the fuck out of Dodge."

"That's reassuring."

Clyde kicked back his drink, then looked around the bar with the boredom of one who had sat on barstools for far too many nights. "Let's get out of here," he said. "This place is a morgue."

"Yeah. I should be going home. I'm tired."

"Fuck home. Let's go down to Boardner's."

"I don't want to go all the way to Hollywood."

"It's late. There's no traffic. We'll be there in fifteen minutes."

"Nah. I'm beat. I'm gonna call it a night."

"Suit yourself. I'm going." He finished his drink and stood up on wobbly legs.

I said, "You're in no condition to drive."

"Don't get like Emily on me. I don't need *two* nags in my life."

I thought about Emily and what I had promised her. I wasn't about to become Clyde McCoy's guardian, but if he totaled his car tonight and killed himself or, God forbid, someone else, then I would feel personally responsible.

"All right, let's go," I said. "But I'm driving."

"Good man," Clyde said. Then he paid the tab, and we were off like a dirty shirt.

preproduction

chapter ten

As was usual when trolling the bars of Hollywood with Clyde, we ran into friends of his at Boardner's. When two A.M. hit, the owner locked the doors with a dozen of us still inside, and it became our own private club. We drank until near the break of day, and I slept late into the afternoon, waking only to drain the lizard and down some aspirin.

Clyde called around four and told me to get ready—we were going out on the town with Vince Timlin. Clyde had the updated version of the *Blonde Lightning* screenplay, and we were going to rendezvous with Vince, make copies, then head back down to Hollywood to see his fiancée's mother sing at the Roosevelt Hotel. It was meant to be some kind of bonding session with "the team." And it would put Vince in good with the future in-laws.

I showered and dressed, then did a fetus imitation in the hammock until I heard the beep of Vince's Bronco in the alley below. I stumbled down the stairs and met Clyde as he was coming out of his apartment. He waved a manila folder filled with pages in the air and said, "Pure magic."

We got into Vince's white Bronco and headed for Kinko's to make copies of the script. I rode shotgun; Clyde stretched out in the backseat. Vince looked just as haggard as we did. His SoCal pretty-boy features were drawn and rough. A dark stubble marred his face.

"What the fuck happened to you?" Clyde asked.

"Went to Billy Maitland's bachelor party last night," Vince replied. "I still haven't slept."

"It's five in the afternoon."

"There were strippers. It got ugly."

Clyde laughed. "Let's hear it," he said, as if he knew we were going to get the story whether we wanted it or not.

"Four girls, two of them new to the business—one of the two, it was her first night, so she was nervous as hell—but they put on a great show."

"How'd the new girl do?" Clyde asked.

"That's the best part. At a certain point in the act, they were simulating sex with one another and they got down on the floor and the new girl got all nervous, so I had to get down there with her and talk her through it."

"Good thing you were there."

"You got that right. I put her head on my lap and stroked her hair and talked all soothing to her. Next thing I know, the girl who was kissing on her starts actually going down on her. Fuck, it was great. She's whining and acting nervous, but I can tell she's starting to like it, so I talk her through it, and the next thing you know she's coming like crazy and begging for more. I thought I was going to bust my chinos."

"You are the definition of a true humanitarian."

"You can say that again."

I laughed, and Vince looked over at me and smiled.

"I'm notorious when it comes to strippers," he said. "I'll get right up their assholes with a flashlight and a Polaroid camera if they'll let me."

"What are you looking for?" I asked.

"His destiny," Clyde said.

We laughed so hard, tears began to roll.

"Isn't it about time you had a bachelor party yourself?" I asked Vince.

"Every day's a bachelor party for me."

"Tell the truth," Clyde said.

"What are you talking about?"

"Gloria won't let you have a bachelor party. She's too smart."

"Now, that's just not true."

"What? That she won't let you have the party or that she's too smart?"

"Don't talk about my woman, mofo."

Vince's concentration faltered, and he let the Bronco drift a little into the oncoming traffic. He was met with blaring horns. Clyde kicked the back of his seat.

"Just keep your eye on the road, lothario. I don't want to be killed with your sorry hungover ass."

"Ow," Vince cried. "C'mon! My fucking head hurts!"

While we were getting the script copied at Kinko's, I got a firsthand glimpse of what it's like to be a movie star, no matter how minor a star one might be. A group of schoolgirls spotted Vince from across the room and began a titter party that should have been more embarrassing to him than complimentary. They had obviously seen a few of his Shannon Tweed lovefests on Showtime while doing their homework. Vince acted like he didn't notice, but I could see his ego glowing involuntarily from across the room. A recognizable leading man in this town has the power to render all men around him invisible to women.

Gloria's mother's show wasn't until eight o'clock, so we had an early dinner at Musso & Frank Grill, the oldest restaurant in Hollywood. Time had stopped at Musso's. The place looked no different today than it had in 1950. High-sided mahogany booths, a classic bar on one side of the room, a breakfast counter on the other, and career waiters dressed up in bright red jackets, serving the people in style. Only the prices reflected the times.

I had the pork chops, Clyde had a filet mignon, and Vince, the health nut, had a Caesar salad and a double vodka.

Brian Benben and his amazing wife, Madeleine Stowe, were having dinner at the booth next to us. I haven't the faintest idea what they were eating. I spent most of the meal trying not to stare at Ms. Stowe, all the while wondering to myself who negotiated Benben's pact with the devil, what it read like, and how I could get a similar deal. Where do I sign?

I was suddenly relating to those bimbos in the print shop who had been gawking at Vince. I guess leading ladies can have the same kind of mind-numbing effect on guys that the leading men have on women. Only I think I would have been drooling even if I wasn't familiar with Ms. Stowe's *oeuvre. Hot* is *hot.*

After dinner we walked down to the Hollywood Roosevelt Hotel, one of the older, weirder establishments on Hollywood Boulevard. The place reeked of early Hollywood. It is rumored to be haunted by the likes of Marilyn Monroe, Montgomery Clift, and even a little girl named Caroline who wanders the halls looking for her mother.

Pictures of the greats lined the walls. W. C. Fields, Mae West, Jimmy Cagney, Bette Davis, Katharine Hepburn, Cary Grant, Bogie and Bacall, Jimmy Stewart—they were all there, reminding us of the glory days. A statue of Charlie Chaplin pointed the way to the Cinegrill Starlight Room, where the event would take place.

Gloria met us at the door of the Cinegrill. She was dressed in a beautiful green satin dress that hinted of the Orient. She was working the door the whole night, aiding her mother in the pursuit of her latest comeback. Her mom had been quite the rage in the early 1960s. A talented singer and actress, she had hung out with Elvis and Sinatra, done the Vegas thing, appeared in some Beach Blanket movies, then married a producer who put an end to it all and made her stay home where she would be "safe." Colon cancer finally brought Sol Rubinstein down, and now Mama Rubinstein was gonna *sing*!

The show was entertaining, in a mothball kind of way. The lady was a torch singer. Her voice was good, the staging adequate, but I just didn't see how this was going to lead to a comeback. The room was packed with industry types—agents, managers, producers, and all other manner of suckfish. Each of them gladhanded Gloria's mother after the show and promised to call in the morning. I hoped she would get some of those calls, but somehow I doubted this event would lead to anything meaningful.

After the show, we had drinks. Then Vince announced that it was going to be a short night and suggested that Clyde and I take a cab back to the Valley so he could accompany Gloria and her mom back to their house in Beverly Hills. We took our cue and walked down to Boardner's for a nightcap. Everyone was glad to see us. It was as if we had never left.

Halfway through my first drink, I got up the nerve to ask Clyde about Emily.

"She's leaving for San Diego soon," Clyde said. "She got a few weeks on a chop socky."

"Are you guys okay?"

"Sure. We worked it out over the phone this morning. She said she didn't want to go away mad. Just go away. She'll be over it by the time she gets back."

He spoke nonchalantly, as if it didn't matter to him, but I sensed that was a façade. I didn't press it. Clyde surprised me and summoned a cab long before last call. "Got to get straight before we start shooting" was all he offered as an explanation. I wondered if Emily's absence in his life wasn't scaring him a bit. Maybe he knew that without her as an anchor, he could drift so far from shore that there would be no coming back. Whatever his motivation, it was good to be getting home at a decent hour. I was still worn out from the night before and couldn't take another all-night drinking session.

chapter eleven

Clyde gave me a copy of the new script and asked if I could read it overnight. I said yes, but when I got home, I found two messages from Tracy on my answering machine. The first one gave me her new telephone number, and the second one told me to call her whenever I got in, no matter how late.

Screw the script.

I dialed Tracy's number, and she answered on the second ring. "Mark?"

"How did you know it was me?"

"You're the only one who has this number. It's my new cell phone, and I haven't given it out to anyone else yet."

"Where are you?"

"I'm staying at the Marmont for a few days, until Adam moves out."

"He's moving out?"

"That's what I said. I gave him a week to find a place to stay—then I want back in my house."

I wasn't sure what to say next. I didn't want to sound too anxious. She made it easy for me. "Mark?"

"Yes?"

"Do you want to come see me?"

"Yes."

"Room forty-four." She hung up.

I drove back over the hill and parked in the Chateau Marmont's overpriced garage, then found my way to the fourth floor. John Belushi had blown out his heart with a speedball in one of the bungalows by the pool, but Tracy had taken a less expensive one-bedroom suite in the hotel proper to play out her own form of heartbreak.

The door opened the moment I knocked, as if she had been waiting on the other side in a panic. She kissed me passionately. I had a feeling the loneliness had set in and she really needed me there more to chase the ghosts away than to provide actual companionship.

"Where have you been?" she asked. "I called your apartment about a hundred times yesterday, and no one answered."

"There were no messages on the machine."

"I didn't leave any until tonight. I wasn't sure what to say. But where were you?"

"I was out with Clyde."

"All day and all night?"

"Most of it."

"Out carousing, eh? Did you guys get lucky?"

"I wouldn't use that phrase. What's with the third degree? Are you jealous or something?"

"If I'm going to be involved with you, I have to be sure you're not sleeping with anyone else."

"I'm not."

"Take a look at this."

She led me over to one of the windows overlooking Sunset Boulevard. The seven-story-tall Marlboro Man loomed large on a billboard just outside her room.

"Can you believe it? Here I am, a cancer survivor, and I've got that guy blowing smoke into my room all night long. Funny, huh?"

"Why don't you ask for a room on the other side of the building, overlooking the pool?"

"And have Belushi's ghost haunting me? Uh-uh. I'll stick with Joe Cancer here."

She turned the lights off, and the room was illuminated only by the glow of Sunset Boulevard and the Marlboro billboard. We sat together in an oversize chair by the window and watched the traffic stream along Sunset. It was late, but Saturday night on the strip is prime cruising time. Traffic was thick and slow-moving, punctuated by drunken confrontations as revelers took out their frustrations on other revelers whenever their vehicles sat too long in one spot and nothing exciting happened.

We watched the human comedy play out for an hour or so, not saying much, just enjoying being close to each other and, at the same time, a safe distance from the mob outside. Finally she got up and closed the window and pulled the drapes, plunging the room into complete darkness. This time I didn't fight the darkness. We got into bed and made love until the traffic sounds out on Sunset faded to nothing and the night just melted away.

I read Clyde's new draft of *Blonde Lightning* in the morning while Tracy slept. He hadn't changed it that much since the last time I read it. Cut a few scenes, condensed some others, smoothed out the dialogue. It was still a modern-day riff on classic film noir. The plot was familiar. Chandler territory, even though Clyde denied the influence. A private detective (to be played by Vince Timlin) is hired by a gangster to find a femme fatale. When he does, they fall in love and end up on the run. But does she really love him, or is she just using him? Those questions (and many more) are answered in a blaze of sex and violence.

Even the title, *Blonde Lightning,* sounded like something out of the past. The nudity level would separate it from the classics of old, but Clyde wasn't breaking any new ground here. On the plus side, the writing was crisp and the dialogue often funny. I could see why Clyde had worked so often as a script doctor. His strengths lay more in characterization than in plotting.

I called Clyde and started to make some general suggestions about things I thought he could improve. His reception was cold. I thought he wanted me to read it so I could give him my opinions. I was wrong.

Clyde said, "If I wanted fixers tampering with my material, I'd be working at the studios."

"I'm sorry. I thought you wanted me to give you notes."

"You're not a D-boy now, Hayes. You're an associate producer. I just wanted you to familiarize yourself with the script so that you could understand production problems as they arose. This isn't going to be a movie-by-committee. If you don't like the material, don't come to the screening and don't rent the videotape when it's released."

"I'm sorry."

"Don't worry about it." He hung up the phone.

I looked over at Tracy and discovered she was awake and watching me. I put the phone in its cradle and said, "Good morning."

"Morning. Who was that on the phone?"

"Clyde."

She frowned. "I thought so."

"You don't like him much, do you?"

"I just think he's a bad influence."

"On *me*? Or Emily?"

"On the world in general."

I laughed. She'd get no argument from me on that one.

chapter twelve

I spent every night of the following week with Tracy. We spent much of the time in bed. She said she had not been able to have sex with such abandon since her last operation. It wasn't that I was such a great lover. Or that Adam was particularly bad in the sack. I think it was just that I meant so little to her that she could drop her inhibitions. She wasn't embarrassed about what I would think of her, because she didn't *care* what I thought. I was a temporary player in her life. She made that clear early on and reinforced the concept whenever I started taking things for granted. I gave her a key to my apartment, but she didn't put it on her key ring. She kept it loose in her purse as if she wanted to be able to return it with great ease should the instinct to flee overcome her suddenly. We spent most of the time in her room at the Chateau Marmont, partially to avoid running into Clyde at my place. Tracy still hadn't told Emily about our involvement, and she didn't want Clyde to find out either. I felt like I was her dirty little secret.

Our postcoital conversations usually spiraled toward the existential. As someone who had contemplated the abyss as a possible next-day destination for more than a year straight, Tracy had a morbid fascination with time and its lack thereof. The inevitability of the great beyond rendered whatever we did here practically meaningless in her book. She just wanted to have fun. Or so she said. For a wannabe Cyndi Lauper, she spent an inordinate amount of time in a complete funk.

All attempts at bringing her out of this near-psychotic state of depression were met with hostility. As if *I* were the problem. When the cloud would lift, she was the perfect Valley girl. Bubbly, perky, ready to party. But I could see it hiding just under her brow. A Hyde-like apparition that wanted to take her from me. Or just take her from this world completely. A beast that would not be happy until she stopped going through the motions. She was a phantom walking the earth. And after some of the "deeper" conversations we had, I began to believe that we were all phantoms, drifting about, pretending we were going to live forever, never truly acknowledging that which Tracy carried with her at all times: the grim knowledge that it could be over at any moment and that one day, no matter how lucky you were or how healthy your lifestyle may be, you would face the reaper and be rendered unconscious forever. And after a few years, after those who knew you were gone, it would be as if you never lived at all. Ever. As if life was just a complete waste of time. A plot by an ominous society of landlords to keep their mortgages paid.

Tracy told me she had had some of these dark thoughts even before she developed the cancer. That was why she tried her hand at acting when she was younger. She hoped to leave a little piece of herself to be immortalized on celluloid. Now that her few brief appearances in movies were turning up on the *Late Late Show,* she realized that the plan had been deeply flawed from the beginning. Selling cars at three in the morning for Cal Worthington was not exactly taking an honored place in Valhalla.

Sometimes she worried that her negative ruminations had been the root of her cancer in the first place, as if she had brought the evil upon herself through the power of negative thinking. She had spent time at an ashram, and every Sunday she made a pilgrimage to the Meditation Center in Malibu for the services there (often presided over by celebrity ministers like Dennis Weaver) to purify her thoughts and drive the negativity from her mind, body, and soul, but it had not worked. The thoughts had become reality, and she had confirmed her own greatest fears. Even though she had beaten the cancer back, she knew the fight was not over. And the price already paid had been her disfigurement and a complete lack of confidence in the future. Her career as an actress had evaporated upon the arrival of her crisis of faith.

I had trouble arguing the other side of the coin with her. Who was I to preach religion? I was just another godless heathen in the city of Sodom. Besides that, I had lost three close friends of mine fairly recently, and the suddenness and stupidity with which it had happened had torn away what little faith I had brought with me into the nineties.

Of course there was the recent tragedy of Charity James, but what happened to her seemed logical and inevitable compared to the fate of my two other friends, a married couple named Kathy and Bruce. He was a sound editor, and she was an executive whom I had met during my brief stay at Paramount. They each developed health problems in their late thirties. Bruce had a bad liver, picked up a transplant, and seemed to be on the road to recovery when out of the blue Kathy discovered she had pancreatic cancer. She fought it bravely for an amazing and painful year and a half, defying all her doctors' expectations, but eventually wasted away to nothing and died. Bruce's new liver began acting up a few months later. They found a replacement organ for him, and he flew to the Mayo Clinic for the operation. Sometime during the procedure, he got screwed. They left an incision open for too long, and he developed an infection. The infection went to his brain, and within three days he was a vegetable. He never woke up. They harvested his eyes and other vital organs as he quickly went from recipient to donor.

Suddenly they were both gone. After years of struggle with the medical community, they were both dead within months of each other. They had no children. No one to carry on in their wake. I remember thinking how completely *gone* they really were. They weren't even vapor. It was as if they had never been. The total absence of them in my life was shattering, yet I couldn't hold a tangible image of them in my mind for more than a moment or two. A flash of memory, and they would fade away. And I realized it was just as Tracy said. Once all who knew them were dead, it would be as if they had never existed. The simple brutality of it was overwhelming to me in a way I could not have imagined. The cold finality of what amounted to an entire family just vanishing before my very eyes chilled me to the core. They were both single children and had no children of their own, so two bloodlines were effectively rendered extinct. They were good friends of mine, but, frankly, not the closest friends I ever had. Yet the strange one-two punch of their deaths struck me deeper and harder than any other event in my life up to that time. The abruptness of it all was nerve shattering, but it would not be until the loss of Charity James that I would understand the full impact their deaths had on me. The shock of their absences on the earth unnerved me, made me feel unsteady on my feet in a way the earthquake in January couldn't match. When Charity James joined them in oblivion, I felt like the earth was made of quicksand and I was sinking slowly away myself. My denial of death was being stripped away, and it was taking my false sense of comfort with it. I felt the need to make a stand and accomplish something while there was still time, but it just seemed impossible. Each time I took a step forward, I some-how managed to take two steps back. But in the end, what would it matter anyway?

Kathy and Bruce had remodeled their house the year before they died and spent more than a hundred grand on new hardwood floors and multitiered landscaping. The house stands atop a beautiful hill off Beverly Glen, the only monument, albeit unmarked, to their existence.

I occasionally wonder if the people who bought that house from their estate ever think of Kathy and Bruce.

chapter thirteen

On the fourth of July, Clyde called and told me he had finally sold his book, an evil rant about Raymond Chandler that he had been working on for years. He didn't get as large an advance as he had hoped for, but I was shocked he managed to sell it at all. I had read it, and not only was it wrong-headed, but I thought it was downright bad. I guess there's a market for dirt out there, even if it is inaccurate and mean-spirited. Clyde wouldn't be the first guy to cash in by knocking his betters. And he sure as hell wouldn't be the last.

He was taking his fifteen-thousand-dollar advance and putting it into the movie in exchange for the right to sell Mexico and a few Central American countries. He already had profit participation. Now he wanted to own some territories, like the born-agains. The money wouldn't arrive until we were well into postproduction, but he had amassed considerable savings by writing a ton of movies and living like a pauper, so he could afford to say no when he got too sick of it all, so he made the deal with the production now and went into his savings to bring them that much closer to having completion funds. Some of the promised investments were in escrow and would not activate until the complete budget was accounted for. They were still fifteen thousand dollars short.

Once again I considered buying into the pot, but the way things were going, by the time this movie started shooting, there would be no rights left to sell. How could I recoup my investment?

I got out the budget and studied it. I still wasn't sure Clyde could pull it off in the time alloted—and for a budget that was less than the lunches cost on a studio film. But if he succeeded, and if the movie was watchable, it looked like it could still make a tidy profit from the territories that still remained available. If it was really good, we could hit the jackpot.

I watched *Jeopardy!* and then went downstairs and knocked on Clyde's door. Clyde jerked the door open and said, "Come in, come in," without looking at me. His attention was elsewhere.

I entered the living room, and Clyde backed into viewing angle of his television. Mace Thornburg was on the tube, chattering away in front of a cheap backdrop depicting Hollywood at night. The words FINE WHINE FROM HOLLYWOOD AND VINE were emblazoned on a faux hillside using the Hollywood sign as the centerpiece of the title.

"What's this?" I asked.

"Shhh, it's Mace's cable-access show. It's on every other Wednesday. He hasn't gotten around to trashing Emily yet, but he will. Watch."

"I thought Emily broke your TV?"

"Who only has one TV? Sit down and watch or I'll kick you out of here."

Who only has one TV? Me. And it was a fucked-up one, at that. The color didn't work, so everything I watched looked like it would have looked in the fifties. My good TV had been stolen by Charity James and her drug dealer so she could afford a fix. When Clyde and I confronted the dealer, he refused to return my TV, but he gave me the piece of shit it was replacing, a nineteen-inch Sony that had fallen to the floor during the Northridge quake, knocking the color right out of it.

I sat on the couch and watched Mace's show. Clyde stayed on his feet, crouched down as if he wanted to be able to start a running tackle at the TV when the time was right.

Mace was dishing dirt on all the denizens of Hollywood, except, of course, for his own clients. He was a snippy little ratfuck, and my immediate dislike for him in the restaurant grew with every putrid word out of his foul mouth. He had absolutely nothing good to say about anyone. Finally he came to what he called his Woolrich Watch, during which a very bad picture of Emily Woolrich was lowered next to him on wires in a cheap attempt at newsroom simulation. It was the most unflattering shot of Emily I had ever seen. Possibly it had been doctored to look even worse than the original photo.

"And now for the weekly Woolrich Watch," Mace spewed. "As you know, dear friends, your humble reporter has filed a number of lawsuits against the so-called Diva of the Dojo—more like Diva of the Cookie Dough if recent photos of her widening girth are any indication of what her current training regimen is like—and in a recent scuffle with a Mace Thornburg aide, Woolrich and a number of hired thugs broke said aide's thumb in a restaurant full of horrified spectators. This cowardly attack came out of nowhere as the staff of this humble program was dining at a restaurant in the San Fernando Valley called Viande. The police were called, but Woolrich and her gang fled the scene before the gendarmes could arrive. A bench warrant has been issued for Woolrich, and she has left the country in response. Yes, dear friends, she is on the lam!"

Clyde turned the TV off with his fist. "Motherfucking hogwash!" he bellowed.

"Don't you want to see the rest of it?"

"I can't stand it. I'll shoot the fucking television. Besides, I'm taping it for Emily's lawyer. He'll have a field day with this one."

I looked at the tape machine in the console under the TV and saw the red light burning. "Where is Emily?" I asked.

"Still in San Diego. She'll be back next week."

"How can he get away with saying there's a warrant out for her arrest?"

"He can do anything he wants until someone drags him into court and forces him to stop. Then all he has to do is offer a retraction, but by then the damage is done. Once you spread bad news in this town, it becomes fact. No one's interested in retractions. They don't even believe them most of the time. Mud sticks. He knows it, and he plays it to the hilt."

"At least it's only on the cable-access channel. How many people watch that?"

"You'd be surprised what kind of damage he does to her with this show. We hear about it, believe me."

"He's a creep."

"That's putting it mildly."

"Listen, I've been thinking. The production is still short fifteen grand, right?"

Clyde smiled widely and slapped me on the shoulder. "I knew you'd come around."

chapter fourteen

I cut a deal for 1 percent of the profits in exchange for my fifteen thousand dollars. Not bad, considering the budget was sizably less than $1.5 million, even with deferments. I was ponying up less than half of 1 percent of the actual cash needed to shoot the movie, and I was receiving a full percentage point in return. A great deal if the film went into the black. Investors were in second position, after the deferments, which should allow us to recoup our initial investment, even if the picture didn't go into heavy profits. Profit sharing would not begin until all deferments and investments were paid. Nobody was skimming a percentage off the gross, which is one of the classic ways investors get burned.

True, some of the foreign territories were presold, but the investors who bought those territories would not share in the profits from the rest of the world, and they would not be recouping their investment as we took in recoupment. By taking the territories they chose, they were paid in full. They would have to sell their territories to get their money back and see profit. They were no longer our problem.

My personal development fund was demolished. The nest egg I had been hatching for years was cracked and bleeding out. What I didn't give to the production would be needed to sustain me through the shoot. My salary was $450 a week. Not even a hundred dollars a day. If this movie didn't make money, I would be filing for food stamps before O.J. even went to trial.

The production was now fully funded, and I soon began my chores on *Blonde Lightning* full-time. The production office was cramped and crowded, but there was an energy there that I had not felt in a long time, a youthful zeal for the process of filmmaking that somehow had seemed lacking at the studios. The politics in the high-pressure zones of big-budget filmmaking take a lot of the fun out of the job. When every move (or movie) you make could be your last, it makes for a rather intense experience. Most of the people who surrounded me now were youthful and filled with enthusiasm. They didn't care that they were making only fifty or a hundred bucks a day. They were working on a *movie.* For many of them, it was their *first* movie and it was a dream come true. And if it bombed, so what? They would just go out and work on another movie. It wasn't life or death for them. Yet. Save that kind of thinking for the big time.

Aside from monitoring the cash flow and the budget, my job in prep consisted mostly of answering Clyde's cell phone (provided by the production), helping him with shot lists, and keeping people off his back. I was still a flunky. But I felt useful in a way I had not in Dexter Morton's office.

Clyde seemed to be staying sober and in focus. He showed no signs of the bad behavior for which he had become notorious. All he seemed to care about was getting on with the work. He was intense and appeared to have as much energy as anyone on the crew, even people half his age.

On my second day on the job, I answered the cell phone and found someone hissing on the other end of the line.

"Revenge is a dish best served cold" is all the guy had to say; then he hung up. It was obviously Mace or one of his minions. I didn't know whether to tell Clyde or not. Finally I decided it was more risky to withhold the facts than to reveal them. What's the worst Clyde could do? Go crazy with rage? Okay. But if Mace Thornburg was actually dangerous, Clyde needed to know. A lot can happen on a film set.

Clyde took the news surprisingly well. "It was Mace. I get those calls two or three times a day," he said. Then he went back to work, but I could tell it rattled him. The rest of the day, he seemed on edge. He didn't share any of his concerns, but I knew the calls were getting to him.

The week went by fast. We had too little money and too little time to be making this movie. But that's how this kind of crew worked. They were not spoiled by the extravagances of big-budget filmmaking. What they lacked in capital, they had to make up for in ingenuity. I was quite impressed by the way the various department heads managed to stretch their minuscule budgets. They say it takes a small army to run a film set. We could afford only a platoon. But still, there were sets to construct, wardrobe to gather, schedules to create and destroy and create again, equipment to rent, expendables to purchase, meals to organize, actors to cast, effects people to hire, locations to secure, stages to rent, crew members to draft, permits to acquire. It was a lot to bite off. We were understaffed and underfinanced.

Vince's fiancée, Gloria, who was receiving co-producer credit, was nowhere to be seen. We were told she had a summer cold. I finally decided to question Vince directly about what was going on. I found him in the parking lot, rolling a joint in the back of his Bronco.

"Where's Gloria?" I asked.

"New York," he said, licking the joint and pressing the seam together.

"What's she doing there?"

"Hanging out with Don Henley."

"What do you mean?"

"She's out there visiting Henley."

"But we're starting the movie in two weeks. She should be here."

"Gloria's out. She's not co-producing anymore."

"Did you guys break up?"

"Yeah."

"What happened? I thought you were getting married?"

"These things run their course."

He seemed so nonchalant about it, I assumed he was acting. If so, it was some of his best work.

"The marriage is off?"

"Oh yeah. Very."

"But you just introduced all of us to her family. You seemed so locked in. I can't believe it."

"It happens."

"Is she sleeping with Henley?"

"I hope not."

"Why's that?"

"He's been with *everyone*."

I had to laugh at a statement like that coming from Vince Timlin, cocksman to the stars.

"What's so funny?" he asked.

"That just seems like the pot calling the kettle lucky."

"That's not funny, Hayes." I could tell I had struck a nerve. He looked angry.

"So who's going to replace her?" I asked, trying to get the conversation back on a work-related track.

"No one," Vince said. "We're just going to have to split her duties among us."

Here we go, I thought. The work piles on while the pay stays the same.

"Are we going to split her check, too?"

"Hayes, you know we're over budget already. We can't go throwing money around like that. This isn't Warner Brothers."

Like I needed a memo on that. I resigned myself to being the first guy in the door in the morning and the last guy to go home at night. I would be making less than minimum wage if you counted all my actual hours. But Vince and Clyde weren't into counting hours. I had to give Clyde credit, though. He busted his ass in the following days. Even when he wasn't in the office, he was working—taking meetings, supervising casting, working on shot lists. He was probably averaging about two hours of sleep a night. It didn't seem to bother him. I'm not sure exactly when it had happened, but he had stopped drinking completely, trying to maintain focus on the project. With the booze cleansed from his system, he was like a moviemaking Terminator.

The most important work on a film is done in prep. It's the only chance you have to prepare everything in a relatively calm environment. Mistakes can be made in preproduction, caught, and corrected far less expensively than when the shoot is on. If you don't have enough prep time, you will have major headaches when you start principal photography. Clyde assured me that he would roll film on schedule whether everyone had their shit together or not. Nothing like adding a little pressure to the workday. Despite the ridiculously small budget, I had to admit that I was kind of enjoying myself. Every now and then I had flashes of absolute pleasure.

I was introduced to an amazing array of producers, executive producers, production associates, and just plain investors without a title, all of whom had made some contribution to the funds raised for the movie and all of whom had something to say about how they wanted things to run on the production. None of them was qualified to actually help us. Clyde told me to just use my yes-man persona when dealing with them, then ignore whatever they wanted me to do, and they would eventually get bored and go away. I followed his advice, and it worked beautifully.

Clyde pushed hard to bring a real line producer onto the show, to replace Gloria, and he finally got his way. We hired a friend of his named Gary Bettman, a veteran of more shoots than all of our investors and producers put together. Once Gary was on board, things began to run much more smoothly, and I got a little breathing room in my work schedule.

Michelle Kern was hired as our femme fatale. She showed up as a blonde one day and said to Clyde, "I'm ready to work." She had even gotten a lightning-bolt tattoo on her shoulder blade like the character in the script brandished, which pissed off our makeup artist since he had made fifteen temp tattoos for the shoot that were now useless. (And Michelle's real tat was far better than what he had designed.) It was a bold move. One she would have to live with forever, but she said she liked it and would keep it even if she didn't get the part. The tat was fresh, but it would be healed by the start of filming. Vince was so taken with Michelle's brazenness, he said they could skip the screen test after all and he signed her on the spot. I guess Sydney Pollack had found another girl for Redford.

My girl, Tracy, moved back into her house as soon as her husband was out, and because of my long hours I was seeing less and less of her. We were eventually reduced to playing phone tag on our answering machines, and the tone of her messages began to sound more and more distant. I wondered if she and Adam had made up again.

The answer came in the middle of a hectic day devoted primarily to casting. Clyde and Vince were in the back area of the office running lines with the wannabes while the rest of us crunched numbers and made phone calls in our little cubicles. There wasn't enough space in my "office" to swing a cat. I had a desk, a chair, a corkboard, and a filing cabinet. I was on the phone with the permit office, my back to the "doorway" of the cubicle, when someone came in carrying one of our metal folding chairs and sat down on it across from my desk. I swiveled around and saw that it was Adam, Tracy's husband, and he did not look happy.

I covered the mouthpiece of the phone and said, "Adam, what brings you up here?"

"I don't know whether to kill you or kill myself or both."

I took my hand off the receiver and said, "I'm going to have to call you back." I hung up the phone and stared at Adam, thinking about his words. He seemed to be thinking about them, too. I finally said, "How about you don't kill anyone?"

"Tracy is my wife. I've been there for her. You're nothing. A nobody. Out of nowhere. What makes you think you can just barge in and ruin my life?"

"She didn't leave you for me. She just wanted out."

"And you just happened to be fucking her at the time?"

"No. She had nothing to do with me until she moved out of your house."

"Bullshit. You stole her from me." He leaned forward and moved his arm as if he was getting ready to pull something out of his back pocket. A gun? A knife?

I looked at my desk for a potential weapon. The most lethal item handy was the script of *Blonde Lightning*, and while it was certainly leaden in spots, I didn't think it would serve as a satisfactory bludgeon during a round of mortal combat.

Clyde's voice suddenly filled the room. "Hayes, did you get those permits I asked about?"

Adam and I looked at the doorway to the cubicle. Clyde was standing there, eating popcorn from a bag of Newman's Own.

"Uh, no," I said. "But I'm working on it."

"Well, get back to it. Adam, leave Master Hayes alone so he can get some work done. He's a real slacker, and I don't need you giving him any excuses for fucking off. Run along and catch up with him on his own time, okay?"

Adam stood up and glared at Clyde. "I never liked you, McCoy."

"That's interesting," Clyde said. "I never *noticed* you."

Adam took a menacing step toward Clyde. Clyde tilted the Newman's Own bag his way and said, "Popcorn?"

"Fuck you, McCoy." He turned and looked at me. "And fuck you, too."

"I guess we're all getting fucked, then," Clyde said.

Adam pushed past Clyde, making him spill some of the popcorn. I could see an odd-looking bulge in Adam's back pants pocket, but I couldn't tell what it was. What kind of a weapon had he brought to the office?

Clyde watched him until he exited the front door; then he looked at me. "Well, well, well, Mr. Hayes has been dipping his wick and keeping the news to himself."

"She didn't want anyone to know."

"And why is that?"

"I guess she didn't want Emily to think she's a slut."

"Christ, Hayes, this is the second half of the twentieth century. We don't have sluts anymore. That went out with the fifties."

"I don't know, then. I don't know why she wants to keep it private."

"You may want to think about that."

"Yeah."

"And remember what I told you before. Don't blame me if it goes bad on you."

Clyde walked away, fallen popcorn crunching under his tennis shoes. I thought about his words—and Adam's—then I picked up the phone to call the permit office back.

.   .   .

Tracy called me late that night to apologize for Adam's behavior and to promise he would not bother me again. She said he had called her and told her what happened, and he was very ashamed of himself. He realized that I wasn't the problem, but that he was, and he promised to be a better man whether she came back to him or not. She swore to me that she did not want to see him, but she didn't make plans to see me either. She said that our work schedules were providing us with a natural cooling-off period that would be good for our relationship. It would also allow Adam some time to reflect. I asked her how he knew about us, and she said he had been watching her room at the Chateau with high-powered binoculars from Sunset and he had seen me standing with her in the window.

I thought to myself how lucky it was that he hadn't been using a high-powered rifle instead.

chapter fifteen

A week before the production was slated to begin, I was locking the office up and Mace Thornburg walked in, accompanied by two men I had never seen before. They made Crater Face look like a puppy dog. They were big and mean. Black leather jackets and steel-toed boots. Mace looked spiffy in a long brown duster and his mirrored sunglasses. He must have thought he was America's answer to Chow Yun Fat.

Clyde and Vince were long gone, as were most of the crew. I was alone in the office except for one hapless PA who had nothing better to do than stick around until the lights went off.

"Where's your boss?" Mace snarled.

"I don't know," I said.

"I've got a message for him. Tell him he and his girlfriend better pay me what I'm owed, plus damages, or he'll never get to finish this little film of his."

"Why don't you tell him yourself? It would mean more coming from you."

Mace took two steps toward me. His goons mimicked him. I took two steps back. I think the PA crapped his pants, but other than that, he didn't move.

We heard sirens off in the distance, heading our way. Mace and his men stopped and looked at the front window.

"That's right. I called the cops the moment I saw you coming down the sidewalk."

"You pussy!" Mace reached over and tore a wardrobe drawing off the wall and ripped it to shreds.

"Let's hit it, Mace," one of the leather boys said. "I told you I wouldn't go to jail for you."

"Fuck you, Tim, no one's going to jail."

"You will if you're still here in thirty seconds," I said. "This is private property. And you're trespassing!"

The sirens were drawing near. The three men looked at one another and scrambled for the door.

"Tell Clyde what I said!" Mace yelled over his shoulder.

"Yeah. I will. I'll tell the cops, too."

They rushed out of the office. I looked at the PA and said, "Lock that damn door."

"But what about the cops? How will they get in?"

"Just do it!"

He ran over and turned the lock on the glass door just as an ambulance roared past the front of the building.

The PA turned and looked at me nervously. "I thought you called the police?"

"I was bluffing," I said as I reached for the phone. "But I'm calling them now."

The cops arrived a few minutes before Clyde, so I had to tell the story twice. Two squad cars pulled up, and four officers made their way into the office. I told them what happened, and then Clyde arrived. He had been my second phone call. I explained everything to Clyde, and he smashed his hand down on one of the desks in anger.

"Are you guys ever going to do anything about this?" he asked the cops.

One of the officers was familiar with the problems involving Mace, Clyde, and Emily. He said, "Clyde, why don't you just pay that little fellow off and get him to stop making all this trouble?"

"I'd like to," Clyde said, "But I don't think there's a number that would do it."

"You two keep messing around like this, and both of you are going to end up in jail."

"Hey, I'm just trying to make a movie here. *He's* the one who was trespassing and threatening my employees."

"Or so your employees say."

"Why would I make something like that up?" I asked.

"All kinds of reasons. The main one being that Mr. McCoy has a big grudge against Mr. Thornburg. And you happen to work for Mr. McCoy."

"I'm telling the truth. Both of us are." The PA still looked visibly shaken. He had already tendered his resignation while we waited for the police. He said he had to go back to Arizona for a few weeks to find his balls.

"It'll still just be your word against his. It's a wash."

"What the hell are we supposed to do, then—just let this guy threaten us whenever he wants?"

"You're in the film business. Get him on film. That goes a long way with a judge."

"Mace is too smart to let that happen," Clyde said.

"Can't help you, then," the cop said. "We're going to be getting back on the road now." He tipped his cap, and the four of them left the office, smiling at one another like frat boys.

Clyde watched them get into their cars and drive away. "Fucking Keystone Kops."

"What are we going to do about this?" I asked.

"Nothing. What can we do? We have a movie to make, and I'm going to make it. No pansy-ass manager is going to stop me."

"Should we tell Vince about this?"

"Hell no!"

chapter sixteen

The production office continued to receive strange calls, usually hang-ups or breathers. Occasionally we would get a bizarre COD delivery of something we had not ordered. Black roses from FTD, fifty dead chickens from a butcher in Chinatown—that kind of thing. It was a real hassle explaining to the deliverymen that we didn't order these items, and occasionally some overly eager PA would sign for something we didn't need, like the hundred pounds of horse manure that a stable delivered to the office one day when everyone with common sense was out running errands. Mace Thornburg was turning out to be a real pain in the ass.

Even more troubling, we lost Jerry, our first assistant director, a few days before commencing photography. He got the call to go off and work with De Palma. It would be a four- to six-month gig, depending on how out of control the production went, so he could not afford to turn it down. Jerry had been instrumental in the planning of the schedule. He had every timetable and company move locked in his head, and he was running off to Canada, where it would do no one any good. He replaced himself on our show with a younger, less experienced AD, but he would be able to clue the guy to the details of the production only over the phone.

The new guy had a big job on his hands. It's hard to first a show you didn't prep, especially with no lead time. Gary Bettman stepped up and took the guy under his wing. Gary had been a first long ago, and he knew what the guy was up against. Losing Jerry was a potentially deadly blow to the production.

But we were undaunted. The elements were all falling into place. We had a complete cast and crew, and everybody seemed to be on the same page about the material. Between Clyde and Vince, they had managed to assemble a far higher caliber of talent than the money would suggest possible. Almost every person on the film was a union member working for nonunion wages. Most people in the film business will take low-paying gigs to fill the gaps between better jobs, especially if they can work with people they think might eventually do bigger projects. Both Vince and Clyde had been to "the Show," and there was always the chance that they would return to form. The crew of *Blonde Lightning*—particularly the department heads—were banking on it. Their salaries would barely keep the rent paid during the shoot. But Clyde McCoy would remember who was on his side when he struck pay dirt. And he would remember who had done him wrong, as well. I definitely wanted to be on the right side of that battle.

Holy cow, we were about to go off and make a movie!

production

chapter seventeen

We began filming *Blonde Lightning* early on a Sunday morning, six A.M. sharp. We were shooting most of the movie on a cheap soundstage in Hollywood, which eliminated a lot of the risks involved in location shooting. The set couldn't have been more different from the set of *Maelstrom,* the last movie I was involved with, back when I worked for Dexter Morton. Of course, that was a studio film, but we spent more in a day on that show than Clyde would spend on this entire film. That didn't mean that the production was lacking in anything but the frills. There was food and drink and film and equipment and actors and crew, just much less of it than on a studio film. *Much* less. (But apparently more than Clyde had on the last film he directed.) And there seemed to be an urgency in the air that was missing from most of the studio-financed sets I'd been on. It was as if everyone was in on how impossible the schedule was, but they considered it a challenge, not a joke. There was little room for error. They were all going to pull together and make a miracle happen. A feature film shot in two weeks.

Clyde was the picture of professionalism: He did not drink, he did not cuss, he smoked only in designated smoking areas. He respected his fellow workers, but he did not get chummy with them. He just kept it all moving smoothly forward. He set the tone from the get-go. There was to be little or no horseplay on his set. He had a job to do, and by God, this time he was not going to screw it up.

Vince started the day cranky. He had been trying to bed Michelle for the last few days, and she was having none of it. By the time they shot their first scene together, he was ready to wring her neck—which was just the emotion called for in the script. The scene was electric. But when it was over, Vince was fuming. He took Clyde aside and tried to fire her, but Clyde convinced him it was too late in the day to find a replacement. While the crew was moving camera, Clyde had me bring Michelle to an empty dressing room, and he confronted her with his concerns that she was pissing off the star-producer. Michelle told him it was all part of her plan. She intended to cock-tease and torture Vince throughout the whole project to keep the on-screen tension high. She wanted sparks with him, but in front of the camera, not behind the scenes, where it would dissipate their energy. At first Clyde was horrified, but as he let it sink in, he was delighted. He said, if she could pull it off, not only would it be good for the film, but it would be good for Vince, too. He needed to know there was at least one woman out there who could resist his charms. It might make him appreciate the ones who couldn't a little bit more. That's Clyde for you. Always thinking about the greater good.

After Michelle left the room, Clyde turned to me and said, "She may be the best I've ever seen."

The best *what* he did not say.

chapter eighteen

On the second day of filming, we had an incident. Ted, one of the electricians, almost got fired by a 10 K, the most powerful light we were using on the stage. (It's so big that it has its own metal platform on wheels called a Crank-O-Vator, so it can be pushed around and adjusted with relative ease.) Ted moved the light to where the gaffer wanted it to go, and when he threw the switch so it would fire, he locked up on it. I was staring right at the guy, not ten feet away from him, and I knew something was wrong, but I didn't know what. He was standing on the metal fixture, one hand on the stem, and vibrating weirdly, a startled look in his eyes. But he couldn't move. He was frozen there, because 100 amps of electricity was coursing through his veins. I just stared at him, not fully comprehending his predicament.

Luckily for Ted, the gaffer knew exactly what was happening. She was a tough chick named Amy, and she took no shit from anyone. Even electricity. She crossed the stage in a flash and kicked him off the light base with her heavy workboot, not allowing herself to get locked up. Ted hit the ground and crouched there a moment, and then slowly began one of the most agonizing screams I had ever heard. It started low because he was paralyzed from the juice, but as he began to regain the ability to breathe and function, the scream leaped out of his heaving chest and built into a primal roar. The crew gathered around him, but gave him room to breathe. Amy pulled the plug on the 10 K so no one else would get shocked.

Our medic came over and checked Ted out. She suggested he go to the hospital. Ted insisted he was fine and he just needed a few minutes' rest. Vince took him into one of the dressing rooms to get him something to drink and, I'm sure, to control the playing field. He didn't want any lawsuits springing up so early in the shoot.

Clyde said to Amy, "What the fuck happened?"

Amy looked at the power cord on the 10 K. "It's exposed. It was touching the base, and the whole thing went hot." She showed us the cord. There was a short section of the rubber coating missing from one side of the power cord. Wires were exposed underneath. "This is some pretty shitty equipment you've got here, Clyde."

"Didn't you check everything during prep?"

"We gave it the once-over, but we obviously did not look close enough."

"You better. I don't want any more shit like that happening."

Her eyes flared, but she held her temper in check and said, "Neither do I."

Clyde looked around the room. The mood was gloomy. He called the first AD and asked him when lunch would be ready. Half an hour was the reply.

"Break everybody now, and give them time to check out this equipment again before we move forward, and tell the caterer to step it up so we can eat in fifteen."

"But we haven't gone six hours yet. Nowhere close."

"Just do it."

The AD frowned and began barking orders. Some of the crew headed outside to smoke, while others started looking the equipment over to make sure there would be no more surprises. Still others hit the craft service table to get a snack before lunch.

Clyde motioned for me to walk with him, away from the crew. "It feels good to be haunted, doesn't it?" he asked. "Kind of makes you feel like there's a purpose to things. Like there's life after death, or a God or something."

"What are you talking about?"

"You've been walking around in a daze ever since that girl died. And you really froze up today. I saw you. You were closer to Ted than Amy was. You just stood there and watched him fry."

"I didn't know what was happening."

"Really? Then you were the only one."

"I never saw a guy get electrocuted before."

"He just got a jolt."

"That was more than a jolt."

We stopped in the open bay door and watched a few of the crew members hanging out in the parking lot, talking about what just happened.

"I should put you in the movie, because *you* look like you've been struck by blonde lightning. That girl fried you like that 10 K fried Ted. Right now, you're about as useless to me as nipples on a tomcat. You've got to snap out of it. It's been long enough."

"There's an expiration date on grief?"

"There should be."

"Do you have no sense of compassion?"

"It's not about compassion now. It's about survival. There's too much going on around here for you to be asleep at the wheel."

"I'm not asleep at the wheel."

"Yes, you are. What is it? The dead girl or the new girl?"

"Maybe a little bit of both."

Clyde fired up one of his hand-rolled cigarettes. "Well, they've knocked you silly. You look like I looked after I was hit by lightning."

"You were hit by lightning?" Why would this surprise me?

"Yeah. Where do you think I came up with the title for the movie? I was hit by lightning back in '69. I had a job as an assistant manager at this movie theater in my hometown of Lake Worth. The Lake Theatre. I was working for a real prick, and he made me change the marquee in a thunderstorm and the marquee got hit by lightning. It was a big metal marquee on an island of ground between Lake Worth Road and the theater parking lot. Luckily for me, there was grass all around the base of the thing, or I probably would have broken my back in the fall. I got knocked off the platform and landed on the ground, flat on my back. I fell thirty feet. Knocked me right out. I woke up about an hour later, drenched from the rain, every hair on my arms burned off, staring up at some old guy in a station wagon who's looking down at me saying, 'Are you all right?' over and over again. I lay out there for an hour, and no one stopped to help me except for this old dude. There was a Winn-Dixie in the same shopping center. A thousand people must have passed me and just figured I was napping with my friends, the plastic letters."

"Where was your manager?"

"Jerking off in the theater, I guess. When I wake up, I have no idea why I'm on the ground, but I'm hurting all over, and what's left of my hair is curly and singed. There's big plastic letters all over the ground, and the marquee isn't finished. It was the title of the movie that did me in. It was *Krakatoa, East of Java.* I was on the word *Java* when the lightning hit. If they just called that flick *Krakatoa,* it would have never happened. My back wouldn't be fucked up to this day, and my whole damn life would have been different.

"So I go into the theater and the owner says to me, 'What took you so long?' I was still in shock or I would have punched his lights out. I tell him I don't know what happened out there, but I fell off the marquee. He sees I'm fucked up and immediately thinks I'm going to sue him, but I'm young, and I don't know about those things. And back then, people weren't suing at the drop of a hot coffee cup. The manager goes to turn on the marquee and it won't light up, so he calls in an electrician, and the guy says the sign's been struck by lightning, which means *I* was struck by lightning, too, but I guess the sign drained most of the juice into the ground and my tennis shoes probably kept me from being burned alive. Ever wonder why a forty-five-year-old man wears tennis shoes wherever he goes? That's the answer."

"Did you go to the hospital?"

"No. I was too broke and stupid to do that. The owner did give me five days off, though. Without pay. That asshole was too scared to go up on the marquee, so the damn sign read *Krakatoa, East of J* all week long."

"It's not even a good movie."

"You know the most fucked-up thing about it all?"

"What?"

"Krakatoa isn't even east of Java. It's fucking west!"

"Same amount of letters."

"Yeah. But why call the movie that in the first place? Especially if it isn't correct! Goddamn it!"

"Probably sounded better to the producers."

"Fuckers. Anyway, for most of the week, I was just out of it. I was walking around in a daze. I looked just like you do now, except I had a better excuse. I can't have a zombie on this set."

"Okay. I'll be more alert."

"Good. Let's go see what's for lunch."

It was chicken Kiev.

After lunch we all returned to work, even Ted, who looked ashen and unsure of himself. Amy scolded him for not wearing his work gloves (not that they would have saved him from the electricity, but he would have been easier to kick off the hot metal), and he slowly put them on. He was as zoned out as Clyde had accused me of being. Worse. But he stayed with it. And as the day progressed, he got better. Most people would have taken the day off. But that's the stubborn quality of the average low-budget-film crew member. They'll bitch and moan and complain and sometimes try to hold the production up for extra money here and there—but they won't go home if they injure themselves. It's a matter of pride. Someone else injures them, and it's a different matter altogether. But if they feel they made the mistake themselves, most of them won't go home—not unless an ambulance is called and they are wheeled away.

Clyde hadn't said anything specific about the nature of the accident to me, but I knew what he was thinking. And I knew what the subtext of our conversation had been. Maybe that 10 K power line was old and worn, or maybe someone had tampered with it. Maybe we had just witnessed our first official act of sabotage on the set. He wanted me sharp and alert, just in case Mace Thornburg had the balls to back up his threats.

By the end of the night, the incident seemed forgotten. It turned out to be a productive day after all. Clyde was right on schedule. Even with taking time out for a near-electrocution.

Michelle Kern asked me to carry her bags to the car when she was ready to go. She had been flirting with me all day long, finally realizing that flirting with Clyde wouldn't get her anywhere—except the hospital if Emily found out. She wanted a man on the inside of the production so that she could get a steady stream of intel. Despite the fact that I knew what she was up to, I let her flirt away. How often do you get the chance to be hustled by the next Sharon Stone? I just had to be careful not to actually let her know anything Clyde wouldn't want her to know. It was a fine line to walk. A line I might cross if the opportunity presented itself—and if the woman I was currently enamored with decided to return to her husband.

Michelle flirted and insinuated and gave me the sexy eyes. But she didn't tell me to get in my car and follow her home or anything like that. Still, I was walking a little bit like Festus on the way back to the stage.

Clyde was standing in the big bay door, looking down at me.

"Careful with that, buddy," he said as I approached. "You don't want to get struck again."

chapter nineteen

Working on a movie can be a very dull experience, depending on what your job entails. Most crew positions involve a fair amount of sitting around, waiting while other people perform their tasks. Then, when it comes your turn, you get to work while the others sit and watch or drift off and gab about their last project or their next project or just their dreams in general. Of course, the conversations on the set of *Blonde Lightning* usually wound up in O.J. territory before they were over. The consensus on the set was that he was guilty, but that he would eventually go free. The polls on TV were exposing a telling statistic: 75 percent of white Americans thought Simpson was guilty, while 75 percent of black Americans thought he was innocent. What amazed me most about those stats was that at least 75 percent of black America considered O.J. black. This guy was the biggest Oreo in town. He lived white until he needed to pull the race card to invent a smoke-screen defense. But murder crosses all color lines. And while most people were giving lip service to the notion that this case shouldn't be about race, it was clear that America was once again defining itself along racial lines. It was ugly, and getting uglier by the day.

The good thing about the Simpson case was that people were so consumed with it, they forgot about other things—like the murder of Dexter Morton. No one on our set seemed to realize that I had been a player in that scenario. I hoped the rest of the town would forget about my involvement, as well, so I could eventually get a studio job again.

It looked bad for Alex, though. His dreams of a big payday seemed to be evaporating. His deal with the DA made very few ripples in the media. Consequently, his other deals weren't falling into place. Dexter Morton's death didn't have the same kind of sex appeal as the murders of Ron and Nicole. Alex must have been furious. Not because he was going to jail, but because his story was generating so little press. O. J. Simpson cast a big, bad shadow over the land, and Alex was no longer the town's favorite murderer.

While everyone was talking O.J., even on our set, my job on the movie did not involve the kind of lulls that allowed long conversations about things I had no control over. I was the all-purpose cleanup man. If there was a problem that fell between the cracks of what the specialists were assigned to do, it became *my* problem.

On our third day of filming, Clyde assigned me to a unique job. Actor wrangler. Our cast consisted of an interesting mix of old-time pros whose asking prices had dropped down around SAG scale and young up-and-comers looking for their big break. One of the old-timers was a guy named Scott Hewitt, a crusty octogenarian who had been one of the next big things way back in the forties—until his bad temper and romantic attachment to whiskey, whores, and fistfights jettisoned him from the mainstream. His behavior became so volatile that the big studios wouldn't touch him, and he ended up making B pictures for Republic and the like. He was a true old Hollywood ass-kicker. He once boxed John Huston to a draw in front of the Brown Derby just for the fun of it.

Time had taken its toll on Scott's body, but his temperament remained feisty. On doctor's orders, he had traded in the booze for fruit smoothies. It had saved his life, but not made him any happier—or easier to get along with. He was scheduled for two days' work on *Blonde Lightning,* playing the leading lady's dying father. His salary? A thousand dollars a day. Quite a step down from his heyday at RKO. During those two days, my job was to babysit Scott and make sure he didn't get into too much trouble.

During preproduction, Scott had become enamored with our wardrobe supervisor, a beautiful Hawaiian girl with jet-black hair named Cambria. I guess she gave him a really exciting fitting, because afterwards he called her every day with trivial questions about his wardrobe that would lead to small talk and requests for a date. In the old days, he had been nicknamed "the Cobra" due to his sneaky and hypnotic way with women. It was said that many of his victims were flat on their backs before they even knew what hit them, as if they had been struck by a powerful paralyzing agent. Cambria was on to Scott's tricks and wanted to keep the relationship strictly professional. The fact that Scott was sixty years older than her probably had something to do with it, as well.

Scott showed up an hour early on his first day of filming and went straight to Cambria's department, where he proceeded to make a complete nuisance of himself. She quietly complained to Clyde, and he elected me as Scott Hewitt's hospitality director.

Scott wanted to spend his downtime as close to Cambria as possible, and I was a lousy substitute. I tried to make up for the fact that I wasn't a twenty-two-year-old Hawaiian hottie by helping him rehearse his lines and asking him endless questions about the old days. He was so into reminiscing that I think he managed to forget about Cambria's legs for stretches of up to thirty seconds at a pop.

The rehearsal time didn't seem to help Scott much. He had a lot of trouble remembering his lines. But, old pro that he was, he managed to blame most of his blown takes on other people: a crew member was whispering, the dolly squeaked, a car going by outside the stage distracted him, or one of his co-stars missed a cue. Everybody showed great tolerance for him. Not only because of his age, but also because they knew he could go nuts and take a walk any time he wanted. What did he have to lose? He'd probably be dead before any possible lawsuit could go to court. If he walked before completing his role, all his footage would go to waste and a new actor would have to reshoot his scenes. He had the power to hold the entire production hostage for two solid days. It was a tense situation.

My other responsibilites on the set occasionally forced me to leave Scott to his own devices. During these periods, he inevitably found himself drifting into Cambria's airspace. He showed up *six* hours early on his second day of filming just so he could visit with her. I knew I was in for trouble.

"Scott, what are you doing here?" I asked as he came through the door. "Your call time isn't until five!"

"I just like hanging out with you kids," he said. He was grinning, but his voice was like the low rumble of an avalanche heading your way.

"You have to shoot late tonight, Scott. You'll go into overtime if you clock in now."

"Keep me off the clock. I'll check in at my call time. And if they're ready for me early, I'm here."

I went to Clyde and warned him about the situation.

"He's just trying to get into Cambria's pants," Clyde said.

"I know."

"Look, I've got a big day here. Just sit on him and keep him out of everybody's way. And I don't want to hear *boo* when he goes more than eight hours tonight. No OT!"

"Got it."

I relayed Clyde's words to Scott, and he looked at me gruffly. "You kids and your overtime. That all you ever think about? I just want to hang out. What else am I going to do? Sit around the apartment?"

I felt sorry for the old guy. He just wanted company. And a little Hawaiian tail. Who could blame him? We hit the craft service table for coffee and doughnuts, and I let him regale me with tales of old Hollywood. I had heard or read about many of the stories he told, but it was cool getting them from the horse's mouth. He went through the whole shopping list of ancient gossip. Tallulah Bankhead was easy, Joan Crawford was a bitch, Jimmy Stewart was the nicest guy you ever met, George Cukor was a fruit and tried to touch Scott's dick, Bogie was a good sailor but a lousy fisherman, everybody knew Kate Hepburn was banging Spencer Tracy, from the *beginning,* Mickey Rooney was a horny bastard, Victor Fleming was a hell of a hunter, and John Huston had a sneaky left hook. It was a feast of great dirt for any film buff. This guy had been *there* and done *that.* And then he'd blown it, thrown it all away, as so many do.

In between stories, we worked on his scenes. He'd run lines for ten or fifteen minutes at a time, then get bored with it. That's when he'd get into mischief.

At one point, I was called away to deal with a catering problem. The grips were complaining that our caterer, Eric, wasn't providing enough meat with lunch. Clyde had hired a French chef to cater the show, trying to avoid the food problems he had experienced on his last movie. Now the problem was not one of quality; it was of selection. Crews need protein to get through the day. Eric was providing gourmet-quality food, but he was focusing too heavily on vegetables and pastas and not providing enough meat. After six hours on a set, most of these guys would eat a raw cow if you put it in front of them. Of course, the vegetarians on the crew were very happy. Both of them. I tried to explain the problem to Eric, but he was very upset. He was threatening to quit if he couldn't cook his own way. He had recently catered a show for William Friedkin and couldn't understand why food that was good enough for the director of *The Exorcist* and *The French Connection* wasn't good enough for the crew of *Blonde Lightning*.

In the middle of our conversation, Cambria came to me with a look of concern on her face. "Mark, Scott's in my room again."

"I'm a little busy right now. Can't he just hang there for a while?"

"He's not wearing any pants."

"What?"

"He's not wearing his pants. He's running around in his undershirt and his boxers, and his penis keeps falling out of the boxers. It's making everyone nervous. Nobody wants to change around him."

I bade farewell to the caterer and did a sprint for the wardrobe room. Sure enough, Scott was padding around behind the clothes racks in only his boxers and a tattered T-shirt that barely covered his big barrel chest and enormous beer belly. His penis wasn't out at the moment, but the sight was offensive enough as it was.

"Scott, what the hell are you doing?" I asked.

"I'm just waiting to go to work."

"You're not wearing your clothes."

"It's hot. You should get a better air conditioner."

"But you can't walk around like that. There are ladies present."

"Buncha actresses. Think they never saw a guy in his shorts? C'mon, kid."

"Do me a favor—put some pants on. The director wants to talk to you."

"It's about time."

He went to the rack he had draped his clothes over and started pulling on his slacks. I turned and looked at Cambria and she silently mouthed the words *thank you*. Tears were welled up in her eyes. I don't know if it was out of fear for her chastity or sympathy for the old man.

I went ahead to Clyde to warn him of the situation and get him to give Scott something to do.

Clyde looked at me disapprovingly when he heard the story. "I thought I told you to keep an eye on him?"

"I have been. But I'm doing five jobs around here. I can't watch him every second."

"Tell it to your union boss."

"This is a nonunion show."

"Exactly. Look, just send him to makeup. I'll be ready for him in an hour anyway."

Scott showed up a few seconds later. "You want to see me, McCoy?"

Clyde looked confused for a moment, then caught himself and covered for me. "Yeah, Scott. I just want to make sure you've got your lines down for tonight."

"You worry about your camera, and I'll worry about my goddamn lines, okay, director boy? Who you think you are, Orson Welles?"

"We had some problems yesterday, Scott. I'm running short on film stock, and I don't want to be caught empty-handed tonight."

"I'm not blowing any more takes than any one else on this show. If you could keep the noise down to a goddamn minimum around here, a guy could concentrate."

"I'll try to keep it quieter on the set."

"You do that."

"Mark, why don't you take Scott to makeup and get him ready?"

"Okay."

We worked late into the night. At one point, as I was walking Scott to the set, it struck me how completely wild it was that I was standing next to this guy. He was a direct connection to the movies of my past, the films I had grown up watching and loving. It was guys like him who created the stuff that drew guys like me to this town. I didn't know whether I wanted to hug him or slap him.

Scott had even more problems remembering his lines than he'd had the day before. By coming in so early, he had turned a potentially short day into a very long one, and now he was getting tired. At midnight, Scott looked at his watch and said to Clyde, "You know, I've been here more than twelve hours. Why don't we call it a day? I could come back tomorrow night."

"Scott, I've only got two more shots for you and you're finished."

"I'm tired. You're working me too hard."

"You shouldn't have come in so early. We didn't need you until five."

"I'll come back tomorrow. You're too cranky to keep working."

"I want to strike this set tonight. I need to finish this scene, now!"

"I don't like being yelled at. This is a bad work environment."

"You're just trying to get another day's pay. We can't afford it."

"You saying I'm extorting you?"

"Call it what you want."

"That's it. I'm going home."

Scott turned and walked off the set.

Clyde looked at me and said, "Now look what you've done."

"Me?"

Clyde told everyone to take ten, and he went off in pursuit of Scott. He found him in the wardrobe room, of course. Clyde ushered Cambria and her assistant out, closed the door, and tore into Scott. I couldn't make out exactly what they were saying, but it had something to do with promises they had made to each other in preproduction. I had a feeling Clyde was about to get an old-style Hollywood ass-kicking.

After five minutes of their arguing, the door opened and Clyde told me to get Gary Bettman. Gary went into the wardrobe room, and ten minutes later we were all back out on the set. Scott finished his two shots, and Clyde called a wrap for the night.

I went to Clyde and asked him how he had managed to get Scott back on the set.

"We compromised," Clyde said. "I got Gary to give him five hundred dollars in cash for his 'overtime,' and he promised to finish the night."

"So, the extortion worked."

"It usually does. But he's done now. I don't want to see him on the set tomorrow. No more hanging out, literally or figuratively."

"What if he shows up?"

"Throw him out."

"You want *me* to throw Scott Hewitt off a movie set?"

"You wouldn't be the first guy to do it."

"Yeah, but I don't feel like being the last, either."

"Hayes, did the years riding a desk make you soft, or have you always been gutless?"

"Hey, I'm not afraid of Scott. I just think we should show him a little respect."

"Really? And why's that?"

"He's been around a long time."

"Let me tell you about Scott Hewitt. Back in '48 he was one of the first guys to name names to McCarthy's pack of wolves. This guy sold out his friends to keep working. He'd sell *you* out for a banana smoothie or a peek under the wardrobe mistress's skirt. Respect him all you want, but I wouldn't turn my back on him if I were you."

Clyde went into his office to consult with the first AD about the next day's scenes, and I helped the crew wrap out. I was loading cables into a truck in front of the loading dock when Scott Hewitt and Cambria came out of the dressing room and carried a load of clothes to her car. They piled the clothes into the trunk; then Scott pinched her on the butt. I thought she would slap him, but instead she giggled and gave him a kiss on the cheek. Then, to my amazement, they both got into her car and drove away like a newlywed couple heading for the bridal suite.

After all her bitching and moaning about the old goat, she was giving him a ride. To his place or hers was the big question. And would the ride continue after they got there?

The Cobra had struck again!

chapter twenty

Amazingly enough, Clyde convinced Karen Black to do a cameo in the film, playing Georgia, a woman who has been institutionalized because she was driven mad after our femme fatale framed her for a murder she had committed long before our story ever begins. Vince, following the leads, ends up questioning her twice in the film. Each time with more chilling results. Karen was scheduled for one day of filming and had twelve pages of dialogue she would have to execute while wearing a straitjacket.

Not only was it very cool to have a legend of Karen Black's status working on our little film, but it also brought great happiness to our born-again investors, Tremayne Harris and his twins, Tod and Tressa. Unfortunately, it also brought them out to the set for their first visit. Despite the fact that the twins were "very interested in the movie business," we had not seen any of the Harris clan since they signed their contract and dropped off their investment check. The lure of Karen Black proved stronger than the potential boredom of a film set.

Karen was halfway through her day by the time Tremayne and the twins arrived. She was on our padded-cell set with Clyde and a skeleton crew, which she had requested to keep the heat and distractions down in the cramped space.

I was talking to Gary Bettman when Tremayne walked onto the stage, followed by Tod and Tressa. They approached us, all smiles and happy thoughts.

"Hello, Mr. Harris," I said as I shook his hand.

"No need to be so formal, son," he said. "We broke bread. Call me Tremayne."

"Okay. Tremayne, this is Gary Bettman, our line producer. He's the man actually responsible for bringing the film in on time and on budget."

"I'm familiar with the job description, son." Tremayne shook Gary's hand and said, "Nice to meet you, Gary. I read your résumé, and I know your work. I just want to tell you how happy we are that one of the Sons of Abraham is handling the money on this show."

Gary wasn't sure how to respond to that. It was probably the most insulting and insensitive thing that had ever been said to him on a film set. Which was quite an achievement. The fact that it was said out of complete ignorance and perhaps a touch of insanity kept Gary from responding the way some people might—by punching this sanctimonious jerk in the mouth. Instead he kept smiling and pumping away at Tremayne's hand and said, "Glad to be of service."

It didn't look like Tremayne understood the sarcasm inherent in the statement, because he never missed a beat and said, "Is Karen Black here?"

I jumped back in, hoping to defuse what could become an explosive situation. "She's on the set right now, but she'll have a break in a few minutes. She said she'd love to meet you and the twins. Why don't you hit the craft service table, and I'll come get you as soon as she's free."

Tremayne finally stopped shaking Gary's hand. "That would be swell."

"I'll show you the way." I led them across the stage to the craft service table, which was loaded with every kind of snack imaginable. As we walked, I looked over my shoulder at Gary. His face was bright red, and he was shaking his head in disbelief. Some things are not covered by a weekly salary.

I got Tremayne a cup of coffee, and the twins started munching down on red licorice and PowerBars. Then I said, "Wait here, and I'll bring Karen to you."

I went to the set, waited for the red warning light above the door to go dark, then entered and spoke to Clyde. "Tremayne Harris is here with the twins. They want their audience with the star."

"Aw, jeez. I'm right in the middle of the scene. Can you keep him amused for an hour or two?"

"Sure, but Tremayne already made an anti-Semitic remark to Gary. Who knows what's next?"

Clyde's eyes popped. "You're kidding?"

"No. I think we've got three loose cannons aboard. The quicker they're gone, the better. You wanted me alert to potential trouble. I'm telling you, this is it."

"Okay. Let me think a minute. Where are they right now?"

"Grazing."

He looked at the set. Karen Black was in the corner of the room, wearing her straitjacket. The camera was being moved to get a low-angle shot of her, and the lighting was being adjusted for the change. Most actors would leave the set, take off the straitjacket, and let a stand-in sit for the lighting crew, but not Karen. She wanted to stay on the set and in character, no matter how uncomfortable it might be.

Clyde walked over and talked to Ross, the director of photography. Ross nodded, and then Clyde talked to the first AD. The AD looked irritated for a moment—then he went over to Karen and said, "Ms. Black, can I have you step off the set for a few minutes?"

"Why, darling?" Karen said.

"The guys have to rig an overhead light, and we don't want anything falling on you."

"I don't think they'd let Georgia out of her cell just because they want to change a lightbulb."

"They would if it weighed eighty pounds."

She thought about that for a moment, then nodded. "I suppose you're right. But I'm not taking off my straitjacket."

Clyde walked over and said, "No problem, Karen. I'll walk with you. Maybe we can get some nourishment. Even in the snake pit, people eat."

"Whatever you say, my dear. You're in charge of this asylum."

Clyde helped Karen to her feet, and he led her out of the set. I followed them, at a distance, through the soundstage toward the craft service table. I stayed in the background as he introduced her to Tremayne and the twins. They had a very pleasant conversation while Clyde held a bottle of water with a straw in it under Karen's chin so she could drink. Young Toddy regaled Karen with tales of the first time he saw each of her movies and how each one had personally affected his life. He gushed and blushed, and she took it all in stride, being polite without trying to encourage him.

After ten minutes of this, Clyde said, "We better get back to the set."

Good-byes were said all around, and the Harris clan left happy. No one ever mentioned the fact that Karen had been wearing a straitjacket the entire time. I guess they figured she was a big enough star that she could dress however she wished.

chapter twenty-one

By the end of our sixth day of shooting, we were all more than ready for a break. Fatigue sets in on six-day weeks in a way that does not happen when you work five days and then are off two before the start of the next workweek. And when you have only one day off before the next six-day week begins, that day is usually spent sleeping, paying bills, and doing laundry. I can see it would get old fast. The crew was not happy about the way we had scheduled the show, but it had to be that way because of location concerns and actor availability. Nevertheless, there was quite a bit of grumbling as we were completing our first full week of shooting *Blonde Lightning*.

I hadn't spoken to Tracy in three days. By the time I got home every night, it was way too late and I was way too tired. Of course, she could have called me, too, even if it was only to leave a message. But she didn't.

At lunch, Michelle Kern asked me if I had plans for our day off.

"Sleep," I said.

"Me, too," she replied. She did nothing more to suggest that we could pool our resources for those plans. I wondered what would happen if I made a little effort in that direction myself, but somehow moving this anywhere beyond a set flirtation felt like I would be cheating on Tracy, even though Tracy and I had no specific commitment outlined. I knew she was about as dependable and stable as Charity James had been, and Tracy didn't have the drugs to blame for her instability. Her problems couldn't be cured by joining AA or NA. I wasn't going to encourage Michelle's flirtations, but I wasn't going to discourage them either. Who knew what next week would bring?

We wrapped at four A.M. We were only two pages behind schedule for the week. And the way Clyde was going, I had a feeling he'd catch up with no damage done to the budget.

We were going on location on Sunday, so I had to supervise a mini-wrap of the stage. All the camera and lighting equipment had to be loaded onto the trucks, but at least we didn't have to tear down any of the sets. At any given moment there were at least three sets standing on the soundstage and they were constantly morphing. The art department was already busy changing the asylum set into a lawyer's office.

Clyde came up to me before he left and said, "So far, so good."

"Yeah. I think we're gonna be fine."

"Don't jinx us."

"At least Mace stopped harassing us."

"It's always quietest before a storm," he said as he walked off the stage.

I finished the mini-wrap and got home just before six. The sun was starting to come up, but the good news was I didn't need to be on set for another twenty-four hours. I was beginning to miss being Dexter Morton's whipping boy. The suits have the right idea. Stay in the office and count the money. Production is a lot harder than it looks.

chapter twenty-two

I slept late, then called Tracy and asked to see her for dinner. It was Saturday, so she was home. She worked at the art gallery only on weekdays. The owners had an A team that supervised the place on the weekend, when they did most of their business.

Tracy told me to come down to her house in Santa Monica. The house that she had shared with Adam before she asked him to leave. This was a big move on her part. At least it seemed to be. I had heard about the house, but never been invited there. It was our final taboo.

I arrived at Tracy's during the heart of magic hour. The house was a two-story Tudor, white with green trim in the daytime, but now looking purple with black trim in the dying light. The air was crisp and clean. I could smell the ocean less than a mile away.

Tracy answered the door in a towel, fresh out of the shower. I kissed her, and she led me into the living room and showed me the wet bar. I made myself a drink as she went to get dressed.

I saw her journal lying on the coffee table and was tempted to open it for a look. I wondered what kind of dramas she recorded there, and I was curious to know where I fit into her life. Of course, the best way to enrage a woman is to get caught reading her diary. I steered clear of the coffee table.

Adam had moved out, but you couldn't tell by looking at the place. The living room was still filled with pictures of the happy couple exercising their happiness: skiing in Aspen, surfing in Malibu, partying at Le Dôme.

Tracy came into the living room and caught me staring at the pictures.

"Sorry about that," she said. "I haven't had time to take them all down."

"You two look like you've had a pretty good life together."

"You should know how deceiving pictures can be. You Hollywood types aren't the only ones who know how to put on a show."

We went down to the Third Street Promenade, an area in Santa Monica where the street had been converted into a walkway and devoted to commerce and the good old American hang. It was a half-mile-long block party that went on seven days a week, breaking only when the shops and restaurants and cineplexes closed for the night. Street vendors, working out of portable stands, hawked everything from cinnamon hazelnut cappuccino to embroidered leather jackets. Performance artists entertained the crowds with robot dances and self-mutilation. You could even get the Incredible Psychic Cat, a gnarly-looking white alley cat dressed up to look like Karnac, to tell your fortune. It was a freak show, but a fairly pleasant one.

We ate at the Third Street Café. I had the porterhouse, and Tracy had the lobster special. We exchanged tales of our various adventures throughout the week, and Tracy laughed at all the different ways the production had gone wrong and then righted itself out of sheer luck or determination on the crew's part.

We shared a tiramisu for desert, then walked along the Promenade, taking in the spectacle. We considered going to a movie, but we couldn't find one we both could sit through. We browsed the overpriced antique shops, bought some overpriced designer candy, drank some overpriced cappuccino, then decided to call it a night.

Tracy was unusually silent on the way back to her house. When I pulled into the driveway, she leaned over and kissed me on the cheek. "I'd invite you in, but it's not a good time for me."

"What do you mean?"

"I'm . . . you know . . . it's *that* time . . ."

Considering how long it had been since we slept together, that seemed like a minor obstacle. I said, "I don't mind."

She looked at me like I had broken a family heirloom. Or planned to. "I do," she said. "And I'm getting a headache."

"I'm sorry. You should have told me. We could have canceled tonight."

"It's okay. I'm glad we went out. I had fun."

I walked her to her door and kissed her on the lips. I could tell something else was wrong, but I couldn't ask her what it was. It would just have made her mad. I felt tension coming from her, and I didn't want her to snap and get angry. A hasty retreat seemed in order. I had to hope that whatever it was would work itself out soon and we could pick up where we had left off before I started working on the film. She went into the house, and her porch light was off before I got back to my car.

As the contestants like to say to Chuck Woolery, I had a bad feeling about the way the date ended. I thought about it all the way to the Valley. The pictures of Tracy and Adam in the living room came back to haunt me. I wondered if they would still be there the next time I came to that house.

If I was ever invited back again.

chapter twenty-three

Even though it was Sunday, we had a six A.M. call. Sunday doesn't automatically mean "rest" on a low-budget shoot. It's just another day, and it's often a full day at a location that can't be rented any other day of the week. In our case, it was a restaurant in Hollywood that was normally closed on Sundays. We blacked out the windows with Duvatyne and shot day-for-night until wrap. Luckily, we were shooting interiors all day—it began to rain in the afternoon in intermittent bursts that would have made continuity an adventure on an outdoor shoot.

It didn't take me long to realize that Michelle Kern had figured out what to do with her day off after all. It was clear that she was now involved with our cinematographer, Ross. Her flirtations with me had just been spycraft. She knew how to get the sweetest close-ups on a production, and she had worked out a barter system with Ross while I was quietly lusting after her.

When Vince realized that his co-star was sleeping with his DP, he went nuts. He took Clyde aside and told him that Ross should be replaced because he couldn't be trusted to do his best for everyone involved if he was banging the lead actress. Favoritism would come into play.

Clyde told Vince that he was just upset because Ross had gone where Vince wasn't allowed. He was not going to fire him. But he added that he'd be checking the frames more carefully for the duration of the shoot, just in case. Vince was grumpy the rest of the day. Which was just the right mood for his scenes. I began to wonder if Michelle was perhaps a genius. It was almost as if she were co-directing Vince's performance in the movie.

Michelle said hello to me at the coffee counter between setups. She was friendly, but the flirtation vibe was gone. She acted as if she'd never sent out the vibe in the first place. We were just coworkers again. Of course, it had never been more than that, except in my head.

A little later, Vince was called upon to slap Michelle in one of their scenes. It was supposed to be a stage slap, but he made contact, almost knocking her off her feet. Ross shot out from behind the camera and went after Vince, but Clyde had anticipated everything and got between the two men before they could start punching. He calmed them down, and then checked to see if Michelle was all right.

She smiled and rubbed her reddened cheek. "Just tell me you got it before everyone jumped into the frame."

Clyde looked at Ross, who had been operating the camera, and Ross said, "I think we got it."

Clyde said, "You better have, buddy, or you *will* be off the show. I don't care who you fuck as long as I get my shots. Let's do it again to make sure. And Vince, if you make contact this time, I will not save you."

"Don't worry about me, Clyde," Michelle said. "I can take whatever he dishes out."

Ross walked up to Vince and whispered, "Do it again, and I'll tell them about Reno."

Vince looked at him with horror and hatred. "You bastard."

The shot went off without a hitch. Whatever Ross had on Vince, it made him behave. Clyde printed both takes, and the AD called lunch.

During the lunch break, Clyde took me aside and talked to me somberly. "Mace has surfaced again. He had someone call my cell phone at five in the morning and make death threats. They said they were going to gut me like a pig and drag me down Hollywood Boulevard. It wasn't Mace's voice, but he was behind it."

"How can you be sure?"

"Look, I've got enemies, but no one else who is that stupid. Mace works on a moral and ethical level lower than even the average agent's. He'll do anything to disrupt our lives. He's crazy. And the people who hang out with him are not much better. I'm thinking about hiring a bodyguard myself. Keep your eyes open. You see anyone or anything out of the ordinary on the set, let me know right away."

We ate lunch, and I felt like I was being watched the entire time. The hairs on the back of my neck were standing on end the rest of the day. I was buying into Clyde's paranoia, but after what had happened to Dexter Morton, I realized that watching your own back could be the difference between life and death in this business.

Clyde had been staying sober, but he was working long hours— eighteen to twenty a day, even during prep. He took no days off, and the sleep deprivation was starting to get to him. He was acting fidgety, nervous, almost like a cokehead, but I was pretty certain he wasn't on anything other than natural adrenaline and caffeine. He had just reached that point where sleep was no longer an option and barely a necessity. Insomnia had set in, and now rest was impossible. He had to keep going until the shoot was finished. If he dropped now, he wouldn't wake up for days. His work was steady, but his focus was growing fuzzy. He was beginning to rely more and more on Ross and Vince as far as composition and dramatics were concerned, respectively. Vince didn't seem to mind. I always got the feeling he wanted to direct the film himself anyway. Clyde had made himself a necessary evil when negotiating the deal. But contracts are designed to be broken. Any sign of weakness on Clyde's part was more than welcome by the sharks swimming nearby. Even on a low-budget shoot like this, there were plenty of backstabbers ready to start a palace coup.

We shot out of the restaurant by 4:20. While the crew was wrapping out the location, Clyde sequestered himself with Yuki Nakamura, the production designer, and ordered changes to two of the sets Yuki and his crew had built on the soundstage for the upcoming scenes. Yuki was very upset about the last-minute changes, the most recent of many. After Clyde was out of earshot, he complained to me, "I work twenty-two hours a day on this show, and he's never happy."

"He's happy, Yuki. He just wants to be *happier*."

"He's killing my crew."

"It's almost over. We're past the halfway mark."

"I was beat before we started shooting. I never worked so hard in preproduction in my life. I'm dragging ass."

"Did you tell Clyde that he's working you and your crew too hard?"

"How can I? I work twenty-two hours a day, but he works twenty-three, so I cannot complain. He tries to shame me."

By the time everything was loaded up and returned to the stage, it was almost six. A relatively short day, but we needed it after what could barely be called a day off. Call time wasn't until ten A.M. the next morning, so this would function as a recharge night for the cast and crew after a week of short turnarounds. Except for Yuki and the art department, of course. They would work through the night to make Clyde's changes and take turns catching up on downtime after the sets were complete so someone could still be available on the set while others rested.

One of my duties on the show was to occasionally drive Clyde to and from the shoots so he would be free to work in the car. On our way home that night, he said, "It's early. I'm going to the Nuart tonight to see a screening of *Cutter's Way*. Ivan Passer is going to speak afterwards. Want to go?"

"Sure. I love that movie."

"Yeah. Passer did a good job with that one. He's an underrated director."

"What time do we have to be there?"

"Eight thirty. But I promised Emily I'd meet her for dinner at Viande first."

"She's back in town?"

"Yeah. We worked out a little truce yesterday. The things a guy will do to get a little peace and quiet."

I called Tracy when I got home to see if she wanted to meet us at the movie, but I got no answer at her house or on her cell phone. What's the point of having one of those things if you never answer it? I left messages, but didn't get my hopes up. I had a feeling my future was going to be filled with third-wheel experiences if I tried to stick it out with her.

Halfway through dinner, Emily looked at Clyde with a beaming smile and said, "Aren't you going to tell him?"

Clyde tried to swallow a piece of steak and say "Tell him what?" at the same time.

Emily laughed and punched him on the shoulder the way she liked to when they were being affectionate. He must have had a bruise there that never healed.

"Okay, okay," he said. "Why don't *you* tell him?"

Emily looked at me and said, "We're going to have a baby."

My jaw dropped. I couldn't believe the news. Clyde McCoy—father?

"No kidding? When?"

"Sometime next year. I'm going off the pill this month."

"So you're not . . ."

"Not yet. We're just in the planning stages."

"That's great. Wow, Clyde, I didn't know you wanted children."

Clyde guzzled some water and cleared his throat. "It's Emily's idea. All her girlfriends are having kids. Haven't you heard? They're the latest accessory."

"Yeah? And when was the last time you bought me earrings?" Emily asked. "You're not much of a gift giver. Face it, Clyde—you like the idea just as much as I do."

Clyde picked up a dinner roll and waved it in the air. "Can I just enjoy my bread and water in peace, like a good inmate?"

Emily pinched him on the cheek. "You're going to be a good daddy." She stood up and excused herself, then went down the hall to use the restroom.

I let Clyde chew his bread a bit before I said, "I'm very surprised by this."

"Not half as surprised as I am. She hit me with it yesterday. She told me she wanted to have a baby by the end of next year, and if I didn't want to be the father, then she was going to start looking for another man."

"Jesus, she's practical."

"Yeah. When Emily decides she's going to do something, she does it."

"And you're willing to succumb to an ultimatum like that?"

"Hey, I'm just trying to get along. A lot can happen in the next six months. And a lot might *not* happen, if you get my drift."

We were running late, and the rain was coming down pretty hard by the time we left Viande. We had no umbrellas, so we had to sprint for Clyde's Maserati. Clyde tried the door without using his key, and to his surprise, it opened.

"What the—?" Clyde said. "Who left that fucking door unlocked?"

Emily looked at him sternly and said, "Must have been you. I haven't driven it since I got back."

"Someone left it open!" Clyde's lack of sleep was making him edgy.

I got in the backseat. Emily slid into the front seat and said, "It was probably whatever cooze you had in here while I was away. I can still smell her perfume."

"I didn't have any cooze in here," Clyde said. "Not last night. Not in a long time."

Clyde started the car and pulled out of the lot. Traffic was bad, and we were late for the movie, so Clyde was cursing anyone who got in our way. Most of them were just being cautious drivers, albeit a bit too cautious at times. There were numerous fender benders dotting the rain-slick streets, created by the fear in some motorists of moving forward clashing with the urgent need of others to do so. The movers and the shakers were defining themselves once again.

"No one can drive in this fucking town," Clyde said. "Especially when it rains. It rains, and everybody goes slip-slidin' all over the place. It's ridiculous. It's like bumper cars out here."

We pulled onto the 405 and the traffic got worse, only now there were six lanes to contend with instead of two. Clyde did a lot of weaving and sliding and a lot of stopping and starting. Emily was getting visibly tense. She kept instinctively working invisible brakes on the floor in front of her, and it was adding to Clyde's irritability.

Traffic came to a near standstill as we approached the rise separating the Valley from the city. Then the traffic abruptly cleared in two lanes to the left, and we saw the problem: a multicar chain reaction on the right side of the freeway. Eight or nine cars piled into one another. It looked like it had just happened, maybe thirty or forty seconds earlier. People hadn't even gotten out of their vehicles yet. It didn't look like there were any fatalities, just a bunch of dented bumpers and dazed drivers.

"Jesus," Emily said. "We should stop and see if anyone needs help."

"Fuck that," Clyde said, speeding away from the accident site. "We're late. Half those bastards have a cell phone. We can't do anything for them the paramedics can't do."

"Sometimes you're a real asshole."

Clyde smiled at her. "Only sometimes?"

Emily smiled back. "*Most* times."

"That's my girl."

We were moving along at a pretty good clip by the time we saw the next traffic jam, down near the Wilshire westbound off-ramp. Clyde hit the brakes to slow us down, but nothing happened. He was suddenly pumping the brakes, but the brake pedal wasn't pumping back. It was loose on the floor. The mechanism had fallen apart under his feet.

"No brakes!" he yelled. He threw his right arm out instinctively in front of Emily. Emily shoved his arm away and braced her knees up against the dash. The Maserati had no airbags.

"Just drive!" she screamed.

Clyde swerved the car wildly, trying to avoid traffic in front of us. His foot kept searching for the brake pedal, but there was nothing there. He pulled on the emergency brake, and the car started to slide sideways. He let the brake go and adjusted the wheel, trying to straighten the car out on the slick road. We glanced off the rear corner of a van, crossed over and skidded along the center dividing wall. An eighteen-wheeler was to the right of us, and the concrete dividing wall eased into the lane in front of us in an attempt to funnel traffic from six lanes into five. Clyde could either crash into the truck or bounce off the sloped wall, which might act like a pipe ramp and send us airborne into traffic like we were in one of his old action flicks. He decided to split the difference. He slammed the Maserati against the side of the truck in an attempt to slow us down. We bounced off the truck and were now headed straight for the wall.

"Shit!" Emily yelled. She dropped her feet to the floor and stiffened them and placed her arms on the dash in front of her. Her muscles rippled as she braced for impact.

We hit the wall almost head-on. I was thrown forward with such force that my seat belt snapped and I slammed into the back of Emily's seat. Emily was not there. Despite her powerful arms, the g-forces had thrown her headfirst into the windshield, which spiderwebbed from the impact. Her seat belt had slipped somewhat, but it held and she did not go through the windshield.

The car spun in midair and slammed its rear onto the front of some dude's Mercedes in the next lane over. He freaked and slammed on his brakes. He hadn't been going very fast, but when he stopped, it threw us off the front of his car and we slid onto our side, coming to rest passenger side down. I was upside down in the rear compartment of the car. I could see Clyde hanging from his seat belt, pressing against Emily, who was completely unconscious, blood streaking her forehead. I thought she might be dead.

The guy in the Mercedes must have panicked, because we were suddenly tapped on the bottom of the car, knocking us all the way over. We were upside down on the rain-soaked 405 Freeway, and all I could think of was the eighteen-wheeler we had bounced off a few seconds earlier and how it was now behind us. I was hoping he had better control over his vehicle than the guy in the Mercedes had demonstrated. The trucker's horn screamed, and his air brakes screeched, and his tires skidded as he careened past us. Somehow he had gotten into the other lane, and we were spared what would have been certain death, but it didn't look like we would be making that screening at the Nuart. And no one on the freeway behind us would be going anywhere anytime soon, either.

chapter twenty-four

An ambulance took us to UCLA Medical Center, which was only about a mile from where we crashed. My injuries were relatively minor: cuts and scrapes, pulled muscles, neck strain. Clyde wasn't much worse. He had a bump on his forehead to go with minor lacerations and whiplash. We were lucky.

Emily was messed up. She had hit the front windshield hard and was in a coma. They expected her to come out of it, but Clyde and I were sick with worry as we waited for her to recover. Since we both had head, neck, and back injuries, the doctors wanted to perform a battery of tests on us to make themselves feel better and our insurance companies feel worse. We didn't mind staying. It would keep us close to Emily. We would have been here anyway.

Vince Timlin showed up at the hospital in the morning. He was angry that we were messing up his production schedule. He brought flowers and good wishes, but the subtext of his attitude was definitely, *How could you do this to me?* He asked Clyde if he could direct the rest of the film himself, and Clyde said, "Sure. Talk to my attorneys. I'll be doing backflips before you can get the injunction removed." That was the last time the idea was mentioned.

The shoot was shut down for a week. Vince had a shit fit because we were underinsured and not covered for this kind of delay. It wouldn't matter much. Most of the crew were on daily rates, and they could go off and find fill-in work if they wanted. If they weren't available when we started back up, we'd replace them. Vince and Gary got a waiver from SAG on most of the actors' penalties, and they renegotiated the location schedules and stage rate. The cost of the delay would be under thirty grand. Coffee money on a studio film, but a sizable hit on a movie with a budget this low. I will say this about Vince—he really stepped up during the crisis. He even dug into his own pocket to cover the overages.

Tracy came by every day with snacks and a flask. A little whiskey never hurt anybody. Her visits with me were fairly brief. When she realized that my injuries were minor, she focused her concerns on Emily. I got the feeling that there was something else going on, as well. There was a change in her. Something was missing. Was Adam back? Had he ever really left? She said she was just very busy with work, but we all know what a smoke screen that one can be.

On our third day in the hospital, Emily received a bouquet of black roses. The attached typewritten card read, *From your BIGGEST fan.* Clyde was furious when he saw the flowers. He tried to trace the delivery, but had no luck. They had been dropped off by a young man wearing no identifying delivery-service clothes. Clyde threw the black roses in the trash, then kicked the trash can down the hall, startling the nurses and making them consider sedating him.

On our fourth day, Emily came out of the coma. They had her on a lot of drugs, anti-inflammatories, phenobarbital, Ativan, and God knew what else, but she managed to speak and move all her fingers and toes. Her spinal cord was bruised, but not permanently damaged. I saw Clyde weep at her bedside when they first spoke. It was touching in a quite unexpected way.

After he left her room, he met me in the hallway. "She's gonna get through this," he said.

"That's great."

"Hayes, that woman means everything to me."

I was surprised to hear such an unabashed declaration of affection come out of Clyde's mouth, especially after some of the things he had said about Emily in his more drunken moments. But maybe that had just been the booze talking or Clyde's need to distance himself from showing emotion, and in turn, vulnerability. Perhaps the accident had knocked some sense into him.

Clyde said, "I want to see the car. Are you up for leaving this place?"

"Absolutely."

Against doctor's orders, we checked ourselves out of the hospital and went to the municipal impound lot, where they were keeping the wrecked Maserati. After wading through a mountain of red tape, they let us look at the car. The Maserati was positioned at the edge of a steel graveyard illuminated by tinted mercury-vapor lamps that gave the landscape a creepy yellow glow. The car was one mangled piece of work. It wasn't totaled, but it was close. Clyde opened the driver's-side door, leaned in, and looked around on the floor underneath the brake pedal or where the brake pedal *should* have been. It was lying loose on the floor under the clutch pedal. He wasn't there ten seconds before he stood up and said, "Just what I thought."

He had a small metal cylinder in his hand. He turned it so I could see a tiny hole bored through one end of it.

"See this? This goes through the brake pedal like so—" He picked the brake pedal up off the floor and slid the cylinder through a hole in the end opposite the pedal itself. "This goes through here, then connects with a mate on the plunger that actually presses down the brakes. A toggle pin goes through this little hole to keep the cylinder from sliding out, and the cylinder keeps the two pieces from sliding apart. Someone pulled the toggle pin and turned this car into a time bomb."

"I'm not following you," I said. I actually thought I knew what he was talking about, but I did not want to believe it.

He ducked under the wheel of the car, lined up the hole in the end of the plunger with the hole in the end of the brake pedal stem and slid the cylinder through, reconnecting the mechanism. The pedal now looked fine.

"See, the brakes weren't cut. They did something much smarter. They just pulled the toggle pin. They knew eventually this mechanism would disengage, probably when being pressed on with great force, which, in all likelihood, would mean I would be speeding at the time and needing the brakes."

Clyde pumped the brakes repeatedly, and I watched as the cylinder connecting the pedal mechanism slowly worked its way loose with each pump. Finally the cylinder popped out, and the two pieces of metal disengaged, the brake pedal dropping to the floor.

"Once that cylinder came loose, I had no more brake pedal. The brakes worked fine. I just couldn't push them down. Most cars don't have a connection like that between the pedal and the plunger. It's usually all one piece. But not the Maserati. It's a bad bit of engineering, and these fuckers knew just what to do to make it come apart on us. No one would have figured this out at all if we'd been killed. It would have just looked like an accident. They really got out their thinking caps for this one."

"They who?"

"You know who. Mace and his bunch. One of them got into the car and pulled the toggle pin. They tried to kill us."

"Don't you think you're being paranoid again?"

He looked at me like I was the enemy.

"Maybe the toggle pin just fell apart," I said. "It's a pretty old car."

"It's an '86. Eight years does not make it old." He got out of the Maserati and said, "Look for yourself. If you can find it, then I'll listen to your bullshit."

I slid under the wheel and looked around on the floor. There was some broken glass, but no sign of a toggle pin.

He said, "They didn't have enough smarts to break the pin in half and leave it on the floor."

"This car did flip upside down, you know."

"Yeah, but I didn't notice anything on the floor when I got in at the parking lot, and I guarantee you won't find anything in there even if you search the thing from top to bottom. Our windows were rolled up when we wrecked. If those pieces were in the car, they should still be there. Go ahead. Look around."

I gave the car a quick once-over—no pin—then got out and stared at him. I remembered how Clyde's door had been unlocked when Clyde went to open it outside Viande.

"The door," I said.

"I already thought of that. They got the car unlocked with a bar or something, but they couldn't lock it up. You need the key to lock the driver's door. You can't just push the button down. Keeps you from locking the key in the car. They could have locked it, then crawled out the passenger side and locked *that* door but either it didn't occur to them or they ran out of time. I knew something was wrong the moment I pulled that handle. I should never have started this car."

"How could you have known what would happen?"

"I could feel it. I knew he had been here. I knew Mace had fucked with this thing, but I ignored my feelings. Remember the smell when we first got in? Emily thought it was perfume, but it was aftershave or cologne. Whoever did this had just been in the car. And I started the engine anyway. The thing could have blown up on us if they had planted a real bomb. I'm an idiot. I almost got Emily killed."

I felt a tightness in the pit of my stomach. "They really wanted to kill us?"

"Not us. Me. Emily was a bonus. They could only hope for her to be in the car since she had just gotten back in town, but they couldn't plan on it. You were just gravy. They were after me, but they almost got a three-for-one."

"Why you? I thought Mace hated Emily?"

"He hates *everyone*. I'm sure I moved up a few notches on his hit list after I shoved him in the restaurant. That was a humiliation. I got rough with him, and he didn't get a chance to get rough back. This was his chance. Besides—he gets me, he hurts Emily. And he leaves her more vulnerable to future attacks."

"All this over a stupid commission check?"

"This isn't about money. It's about pride and control. The age-old Hollywood battle. And this bastard is crazy." His face was ashen as he stared into the gloom of the auto yard and contemplated his next move. After what seemed like forever, he cleared his throat and looked at me. His eyes glistened in the dim yellow light. "I'm going to have to do something about this," he said. "Are you with me?"

"Depends on what you plan to do."

"Whatever's necessary."

chapter twenty-five

Clyde called Tracy and asked her to keep an eye on Emily while we were out of town. Tracy forgot to ask Clyde about my well-being. She seemed concerned only with how Emily was doing. I felt the chasm widening.

We caught the red-eye to Las Vegas out of LAX and checked into the Aladdin Hotel. Clyde was a "comp one" at the Aladdin, so his room was free. My room ran only thirty bucks. It was a cheap lure to attract business. Subtle surcharges would be tacked on down in the casino at the tables. I had a corner room on the seventeenth floor, which allowed me to see up and down the strip for miles. It was a great view. And the longer I looked at it, the more money I saved. To leave the room meant certain poverty.

We had gone there to meet a friend of Clyde's named Rick Collonia. Collonia was a Jimmy Cagney impersonator who had a nightclub act that ran in one of the Aladdin's smaller show rooms. It was an old-fashioned Hollywood revue with Collonia's Cagney interacting with a variety of celebrity look-alikes. W. C. Fields, Mae West, Humphrey Bogart, Bette Davis, and Edward G. Robinson all made appearances in the show.

Collonia had blown his fifteen minutes of fame portraying Cagney in a TV movie called *The Star-Spangled Kid,* which did big numbers in the wake of the real James Cagney's death. He did a follow-up a year later, *The Man Who Thought He Was Jimmy Cagney.* It was about a guy who survives a plane crash, but his face and his memory are messed up. They rebuild his face, and he looks just like James Cagney. Since he has only vague memories of his past life, and some of those memories include famous scenes from James Cagney movies he had seen before the crash, he makes the logical assumption that he *is* James Cagney. Mirthful mayhem ensues.

Unfortunately, the audience didn't embrace that one with the same enthusiasm as *The Star-Spangled Kid.* Collonia had hoped it would serve as a pilot for a weekly series; instead it was a one-way ticket to Has-Been Land. He had taken those lemons and made lemonade. He had a show at the Aladdin and made guest appearances at mall openings and boat shows to fill in the gaps in the income. Then there were the commercials for local auto dealers. He had spots running late night in Vegas and L.A. The only guy I saw hawking cars more often than Rick Collonia was Cal Worthington, who seemed to have at least three TV spots running during every commercial break on every local channel in L.A. after two in the morning.

Clyde had met Rick Collonia down in Mexico on the set of *The Man Who Thought He Was Jimmy Cagney* while doing a quick polish on the script, and a solid friendship had grown out of the experience. Collonia liked knowing a writer who could toss him free material for his act from time to time, and Clyde liked Collonia because he was connected. And he didn't mean to the film industry. No, Rick Collonia was connected to the mob. He had ties that ran deep into one of the big New York families. Collonia wasn't an active member or a made guy, but his friendships gave him a sense of job security in Las Vegas, even with all the big corporations moving in and crowding the mob out. It would take a lot more than roller coasters and animal acts to get "the boys" out of the town they had built out of sand. Collonia would always be able to find a casino that would offer him space for his ten shows a week.

It was too late to find Collonia by the time we got settled into the hotel, so we hit the blackjack tables and played until five thirty in the morning. I lost about six hundred bucks, but Clyde was winning when last I saw him. He was up two grand, and they were changing dealers on him. I was still punch-drunk from the car crash and the more recent ass-whipping at the blackjack tables, so I said good night and went up to my room.

I slept until noon and woke then only because of a loud knock at the door. It was room service delivering a full breakfast that I had not ordered. Bacon, sausage, ham, eggs Benedict, English muffins, toast, coffee and milk. A feast fit for a king. Not a guy who blew his last spare change on the quarter slots at six in the morning. I was told by the bellhop the meal was compliments of Mr. McCoy in room 1801. I assumed that meant Clyde's luck had held.

I ate like a starving man, showered, dressed, and went down to the casino. Clyde was at the same table he had occupied the night before. He had a five-o'clock shadow going, and I realized that he had never gone to bed. His stack of chips was roughly the size it had been when I went upstairs to my room.

"How's it going?" I asked.

"I'm up. I'm down. I can't get any traction."

"Maybe you should take a break."

"I plan on it. I spoke with Rick. He's going to meet us for lunch at two o'clock."

"I just ate breakfast."

"Fake it."

chapter twenty-six

We met Rick Collonia at the Hard Rock at two sharp. He was as impressive looking in person as he had been in his films. Rick Collonia *was* Jimmy Cagney, and not just because that's what it said out on the marquee. He had Cagney down: the same features, same height, same build, same body language, same mannerisms, and same facial tics. How much of it he was born with I did not know. Much of it had to be an act, but if you told me he was James Cagney's son, I would have believed it. If you had shown me black-and-white film of him and told me he was Cagney himself, I wouldn't have argued with you. It was uncanny. He was a dead ringer for Cagney, and he seemed to delight in casually invoking Cagney's spirit twenty-four hours a day. If he had ever been anything but an exact duplicate of James Cagney, that original creation had long since vanished. His current incarnation was that of the early 1940s Cagney. Luckily Cagney had a long life and a long career, so Collonia could alter his act as he aged to match that of his doppelgänger. He was immediately very friendly to me in the cocky sort of way Cagney often was to the new kid in the gang.

Clyde explained what he perceived to be the situation with Mace Thornburg, from the first fateful meeting between Thornburg and Emily, through the deals and broken deals, real and imagined, the extortion attempts, the libel campaigns and acts of fiscal terrorism, climaxing the story with the possible sabotage of the Maserati and our near-fatal accident on the 405. As Clyde spoke, Rick Collonia's happy elfin Cagney face slowly transformed into the rock-solid, hard-as-nails, kick-ass son of a bitch who burned the screen down in *White Heat.* I could tell the cogs were spinning in that street urchin's brain of his.

"Meet me at the show tonight," he said. "Ten o'clock. I'll tell Carmine to be there. He'll know how to handle this."

chapter twenty-seven

The ten o'clock show was extremely entertaining in that Las Vegas way where you think it's going to be a big drag but the show just gets better and better until you suddenly realize you are having the time of your life. A lot of cool and unusual entertainment awaits those who look past the tables and slots in Vegas. The show took place in one of the smaller stages in the lower depths of the building. Debbie Reynolds and Donald O'Connor were kicking up sawdust in the main theater upstairs. The *real* Debbie Reynolds and Donald O'Connor. Look-alikes had to work the basement of the Aladdin.

After the show, Collonia, Clyde, and I went to the restaurant upstairs to sample the $1.98 prime rib dinners. Just as we were ordering, we were joined by a man roughly the size of a gorilla. He could easily have stepped out of the Siegfried & Roy animal show. He was a beast.

This was Carmine C., one of Rick Collonia's very best friends. Carmine didn't offer an explanation of what the *C.* stood for, and no one at the table pressed him for the info.

Clyde once again recounted the story of Mace Thornburg and Emily Woolrich, from the very beginning when Mace assumed his management role in her career to the car accident that almost claimed our three lives. He told the story without embellishment and left all his suspicions out of the telling, allowing Carmine to draw his own conclusions.

After he heard Clyde's story, Carmine C. leaned forward and said, "From this point on, you call me Gerry."

"Gerry?" Clyde asked.

Carmine, who was now Gerry, nodded solemnly. He pulled a ballpoint pen out of his jacket and scribbled the name down on a cocktail napkin and slid it in front of Clyde.

"With a *G,* huh?" Clyde asked.

Gerry nodded again and wadded the napkin up into a little ball and stuffed it into what was left of his au jus. I suppose this signaled he was finished with dinner and wanted to get down to business.

"Something like this happens, you got no choice," Gerry said. "You gotta take the guy out."

"Whoa," I said. "We don't want anything like that to happen." I looked at Clyde for confirmation.

He just stared at me.

"Do we?" I asked Clyde directly.

"No, of course not," he said. "We just want to scare him off."

"It's a mistake," Gerry said. "Guy came at you, you come back at him and don't finish the job, he's gonna get serious. You may not have another chance."

Clyde said, "Can't you just talk to him? Threaten him a little?"

"Sure, but I'm telling you that may tip him off. Some of these guys, they don't listen so good. Sometimes it's just better to take care of it permanently. He tried to kill you, right?"

"We can't be totally sure of that," I said.

"So you're saying you're not serious about this?"

"No. It's not that. We just don't want anyone getting hurt."

"Someone's already hurt," Clyde said. I could see his anger growing. I knew he was thinking of Emily lying in that hospital bed with her head wrapped in bandages.

"Sounds like all three of you got hurt," Rick Collonia said. "Sounds like you could have been killed."

"But we weren't, and we don't want to go to jail," I said.

"Look," Gerry said, "you let me handle this, and believe me, you won't go to jail. And you'll be able to sleep at night, too. Trust me."

"Just talk to him, okay?" I said. "Let him know we're serious, but don't hurt him. Can we at least try it that way first?"

"Hey, it's your play," Gerry said. "You fuck it up, and it will be your asses. The one thing I've got to know is, no matter what happens, will you hold your mud?"

"Excuse me?"

"He wants to know if things get hot will we talk to the police about his involvement," Clyde said.

"Oh. Of course not," I said.

"You get this, Rich?" Gerry said to Collonia. "I'm supposed to go on 'of course not.' "

Collonia broke into his best Cagney grin. So close to the real thing, it was spooky. "That's funny," he said. But he did not laugh.

"I'm going to need more than 'of course not,' " Gerry said.

I sat there looking confused.

"What would make you comfortable?" Clyde asked.

"I need something on you. On *both* of you. Something I can use in case you turn on me."

"That will take some doing," Clyde said. "I don't think Mark's exactly the criminal type, are you, buddy?"

"What do you mean?"

"He wants info on you. On something you've done and not been caught at. You know. Something illegal. Stealing ideas doesn't count."

"I haven't done anything illegal," I said. Nothing anyone could prove, anyway.

"See that?" Collonia said. "The kid's a straight arrow. He's a good kid."

"That's the worst kind," Gerry said. "They squeal quickest and loudest."

"I'm not a squealer."

"We'll come up with something," Clyde said. "Nobody's completely clean. Not even young Hayes here."

chapter twenty-eight

I was supposed to meet the team down at the blackjack tables at noon, but I decided to go down early and try my luck. It was running pretty good. Clyde had floated me five bills until we got back to L.A., and I was up three hundred bucks after only half an hour, which cut my previous losses by half. I decided not to push it. I took my winnings and wandered around the casino.

I ran into Rick Collonia and had to work hard to keep from laughing. There was something hysterically funny and wonderful about meeting James Cagney in the casino of the Aladdin Hotel. He was dressed to the nines, ready for work, and looked even more like Cagney during the day than he had at night, if that was possible.

"You seen Clyde?" he asked through that cocky Cagney grin.

"No. I've been at the tables."

"And he wasn't there?"

"No."

"He must have gone to another casino. You can't pry him off these tables when he's in town. He's a sick one. A complete degenerate." Collonia never lost his grin. I guess he was putting me on. Although the thought did occur to me that he might be more right about Clyde's degeneracy than either of us would care to admit.

We drifted through the casino, drawing stares from the gamblers and their significant others. Cagney was in da *house*! Collonia went to one of the pit bosses and handed him some passes for the show. The boss would distribute the passes to the high rollers as the day progressed.

"You know, they're closing this joint soon. It's going under the knife. A complete overhaul. It's gonna be a big deal. But I bet it ends up looking like every other swank joint on the strip. Get your fill of the old Aladdin now, 'cause it won't be around much longer, and they won't be making 'em like this anymore. All the new casinos look like amusement parks and shopping malls."

"It's too bad," I said. "I like this place. It's got charm."

"You said it."

We walked a bit more, Collonia handing out passes whenever he spotted someone he thought worthy. He seemed sad. Maybe he thought the end of the old Aladdin would be the end of his stage revue.

"Comin' to the show tonight?" Collonia asked me.

"I don't know. I'm just kind of trailing behind Clyde."

"Keep a close watch on him. I think he's going to need all the help he can get."

"What do you mean?"

"Hollywood thrives on iconoclasts, but they kill 'em regularly, as well. If you're his pal, you'll make sure nothing bad happens to him."

"Something bad already happened. To all of us."

"Believe me, that's nothing. You guys got lucky. This will get worse before it gets better."

"I think we should just go to the police."

"And say what? You think they'll believe you? The way things are nowadays, you make accusations like that against a scumbag like Mace and you'll end up getting sued. It's not like the old days when you could settle things out in the street like men. Nah. Let Carmine handle it. But until he does, watch your back. And Clyde's back, too. He's a good guy. Loyal as the day is long. He may have a temper, but he doesn't lie."

Clyde and Gerry approached us. Clyde and Rick Collonia gave each other a warm hug and traded good-natured insults. We went to the bar and had a few drinks and played some keno. None of us won. I've never won at keno in my life, and I don't know anybody who has.

Clyde and Gerry seemed to have worked something out, because Gerry was flying back with us on the four-o'clock plane. Gerry said he had business in L.A. and that he could help us out while he was there. I had the feeling the trip was all about Mace. I wasn't privy to the deal, but whatever was going to happen was going to go down fast.

We grabbed a quick bite to eat and then hit the tables for the last round of gambling. I lost back the three hundred and gave the casino two hundred of Clyde's loan for good measure. They didn't build the place by letting suckers like me walk away with their money in my pocket. Disgusted, I went upstairs and packed.

chapter twenty-nine

Clyde and Gerry made no mention of whatever their plan was on the cab ride to the airport or on the flight back to L.A. We left Gerry at the LAX Avis counter, and he simply said he'd be in touch when "the thing" was done. Whatever that meant.

I didn't really want to know, but I had to ask. I waited until we were on the 405 headed north. Clyde didn't seem forthcoming with info, so I had to grill him.

"So, what are we doing?"

"Going to see Emily."

"Okay. And what is Gerry doing?"

"He's going to talk to Mace. He'll straighten him out."

"Just talk, though, right?"

"Right. I made it very clear that we only wanted to threaten him, not hurt him."

"Good."

We stopped at the hospital to visit Emily. Like any athlete with her conditioning, she was making a remarkable recovery. The doctors were shocked and amazed. They had been prognosticating with severe pessimism from the moment she was admitted to the hospital. She was making liars out of them by the hour. Now they were saying she might be able to go home within a week. It wouldn't have surprised me if she got up and slapped them all on the way out.

chapter thirty

After we left the hospital, we drove to a warehouse in Van Nuys where Clyde had installed his editor, Bill Shaffer, an assistant editor named Sally, and a full Avid nonlinear editing system. The location of the editing facility had been kept a closely guarded secret from everyone in production, including Vince Timlin. The secrecy of the operation was one of Clyde's stipulations for making the deal with Vince and his producers. After the last debacle where he had his picture taken away from him before he could edit it, he was taking no chances. He said he'd burn the film before anyone else cut it this time. To ensure there was no interference in this part of the process, Sally picked up the video dailies of the film from the lab every day and brought them to the warehouse. Clyde himself had been picking up reels of negative whenever he had a chance and securing them in a completely different—and even more secret—

location. Bill Shaffer was assembling a cut of the movie as quickly as we could shoot it. The plan was to have a good rough cut ready three days after the last footage was shot and a director's cut five days after that. Due to the shooting gap presented by the accident, Bill was all out of new material now and nervously awaiting Clyde's comments on what he had done so far.

We watched fifty minutes of assembled footage. It was a little clunky in spots, but overall quite effective. The photography was excellent for a picture with this small a budget. Clyde's crew had pulled off a miracle. The film looked better than it had any right to look.

As we watched the footage, Clyde made very specific and detailed suggestions for trims and replacement shots. Sally took diligent notes, and Bill actually made many of the changes as we went, using the superfast Avid, but as the evening progressed, I could tell he was getting perturbed. Nothing he had done seemed to satisfy Clyde. I thought the cut was very good for a first pass, but Clyde was being picayune about every detail, every nuance. *Directors.*

When we were finished, Clyde said, "Not bad, Bill. Not bad at all."

"Gee, Clyde," Bill said with a frown, "don't get all gushy on me. We've only been putting in eighteen-hour days to stay on your crazy schedule."

"You're making a noble sacrifice. You will be remembered come Oscar time."

"Very funny."

"Do you have a copy of the assemblage? There were a couple of things I think I missed. I'll look at it at home and call you with changes."

Bill handed him a VHS tape marked CLYDE.

"Assemblage is right," Bill said. "That's who you should have hired, an assembler, not an editor."

"Now, now, Bill. Are you saying I've got a heavy hand?" He did not sound apologetic.

"Heaven forbid."

"You'll still get the solo credit."

"Oh, joy."

"I think you need a break. After you make the tweaks, you should take a few days off. We're not going to have new footage until Tuesday or Wednesday anyway."

"Great. I can check in at the house and see if my wife has left me yet."

"Speaking of credits, the transparencies come back from the title house yet?"

"Yeah, I've got the main titles over here. They're holding off on shooting the end roll until you finalize the list."

We followed Bill across the room to a table that had a lightboard built into the surface for the easy viewing of slides and film. He picked up a large envelope that lay next to the illuminated glass and handed it to Clyde, who opened it and began placing sheets of black film over the light stand. The opening titles of the movie were burned into the black film in white letters. When the titles were photographed later, any color could be added to alter the white if so desired. The lettering was done in a classic film-noir-style font. He positioned the main title card in the center of the light stand and stepped back to get a better look.

BLONDE LIGHTNING

"What do you think?" Clyde asked.

"Looks good," I said.

"A little retro for my taste," Bill said.

"I suppose you'd rather it be something more *Saturday Night Fever*?"

Bill blushed. Seems he had a *SNF* fixation that went back to his teen years. "What can I say? It changed my life."

"Well, this ain't *Saturday Night Fever*."

"You can say that again."

Clyde gave him a nasty look and continued flipping through the transparencies, double-checking to make sure the title house had spelled everybody's name correctly. Bill turned away and stared off into the distance.

Clyde stopped flipping through the title cards, looked at me, and said, "Prepare yourself." He moved the main title card off the light stand and put a new one in its place. The card read,

ASSOCIATE PRODUCER
MARK HAYES

I stared at the card, slack-jawed. There it was in transparent black-and-white. My first official credit on a film after fifteen years of toil in the trenches. Sure, it was only a little straight-to-video quickie, and it was only an associate producer credit, but the credit was mine, and it was single card, which meant that for a few seconds of screen time there would be nothing else to look at up there on the silver screen (or more likely on the TV screen). I had expected to be listed somewhere in the end credit roll like most flunkies. Clyde had really done me a solid with this gesture.

"Like it?" Clyde asked.

I was too choked up to respond.

"What's the matter?" Bill asked. "Lettering not big enough for you?"

"N-no, it's fine," I sputtered.

As we drove home, Clyde asked me what I thought of the rough cut.

"Looks good," I said, remembering how I had been scolded in the past for criticizing his work.

"No, really, what did you think? You can be honest."

"I think it's good, considering what you had to work with."

"What's *that* supposed to mean?"

Suckered again! I tried to save face. "I mean, for the budget you've got, and the cast you've got, and the locations you've got, I think you've got the best movie there that you could possibly have."

"Those are some hellacious qualifiers."

"I don't mean it that way."

"I know it's not up to your big-time studio standards. . . ."

"On the contrary, I think it's better than a lot of the big-budget stuff I've been involved with in the last few years."

"Damn straight."

"I really think you've got something there."

Clyde smiled. "Yeah. Maybe this one will work out."

He said it with a mixture of hope and desperation that was almost heartbreaking.

Gerry was waiting in the Viande parking lot when we got back. Clyde invited him into his apartment for a brandy.

Once we got settled in, Gerry got serious. "The problem—it's not a problem anymore," Gerry said.

We both sat up with a jolt. That sounded more final than we expected.

"What do you mean?" Clyde asked.

"You want details?"

"Of course."

"Sometimes the less you know, the better."

"What did you do, Gerry?" I asked. "You didn't hurt him, did you?"

"You tell me to hurt 'em?" Gerry said, offended.

"No."

Gerry looked at Clyde sternly. "I never let you down before, have I?"

Clyde said, "No."

I thought, What the hell?

Gerry settled back into the sofa and sipped his brandy. This was his chance to be raconteur. He was going to milk it for all it was worth. "So

I drive over to their house, and I park a block away. I dumped the Avis rental and got a big red Caddy with tinted windows from Rent-A-Wreck, so it's a scary fucking sight if they look out their window. And the muffler's fucked up, so it sounds like a rocket ship rolling down the street. I call 'em up on the cell, and the broad answers. I say, 'Put your man on the phone,' and she says, 'Who's calling?' and I say, 'Put your piece-of-shit boyfriend on the phone,' and she hangs up on me. I call back, and she picks up and I say, 'I'm staring at your house right now. Hang up on me again, and there's gonna be blood and silicone all over your living room.' She drops the phone and runs to get the asshole.

"He gets on the line, and his shit is scared already. I lay it out for him. 'You been fucking with a lot of people in this town, and they want you to stop.' He says, 'I don't know what you're talking about,' and I say, 'You know exactly what I'm talking about.' He asks me who I am and shit, and I tell him, 'Tony. That's all you got to know,' and I say if he fucks with one more person in town, I'm gonna make him and his whore girlfriend rest in *pieces.*

"Thinking he don't believe me, I tell him to look out his window and check it out. I see the curtain open and close real quicklike, and I ask him if he likes the car. He says it's real nice, and I tell him he's gonna get to ride in it one day if he's not a good boy. In the trunk. Then he's got the balls to ask who I 'represent.' I told him he don't want to know, and he better keep his nose clean in general. That we'd be watching him. Then I pulled out real slow and did a funeral pass in front of the house."

Gerry took a sip of brandy and grinned at us. I got the feeling he lived to tell stories like this.

"That's it?" Clyde asked.

"You said not to get too specific with the guy."

"Did he sound scared?"

"They both had to change their drawers when it was over."

"Think it's going to work?"

"This guy's a chickenshit. I think he's gonna take a long vacation until whoever is mad at him cools off."

"You did good, Gerry. Thanks."

"Hey, that's what I get paid for."

He put his brandy snifter on the table, stood up, and straightened his suit. A fair-size temblor suddenly rocked the apartment. Gerry's eyes went wide. He ran and stood under the doorway between the living room and the kitchen, bracing his arms against the frame. Glasses rattled in the cabinets, and a potted plant Emily had bought Clyde fell off the top of the television. Clyde and I just sat where we were and rode out the vibrations. We were used to this. We'd ridden out thousands of aftershocks since the Northridge quake. Gerry looked completely freaked out. His eyes bugged out wildly, and he was shaking twice as fast as his surroundings were.

When it was over, Gerry wiped sweat from his forehead and said, "I hate those goddamn earthquakes." He was still vibrating.

"That was an aftershock, not an earthquake," Clyde said.

"What's the fucking difference? The earth starts shaking and shit falls over—that's an earthquake to me!"

Clyde posed no argument. Gerry straightened his suit again and tried to regain his macho bluster. "I'm going back to the hotel. I'll be in town for another week. The guy so much as sneezes your direction, give me a call."

We shook hands, and I was reminded of Gerry's massive strength. I guess the only thing a guy like him is scared of is something he can't strangle. Like an earthquake or an atomic bomb. I felt like I was shaking hands with a hybrid of King Kong and the Devil.

chapter thirty-one

It didn't take a week for Mace to sneeze. The very next day he called Clyde and Emily separately and threatened them over the phone. He accused them of hiring a hit man to kill him and said he would be going to the police. After his call to Emily's hospital room, she instructed the switchboard to block all her calls. She was in no mood for his threats. She grilled Clyde pretty hard about the accusations, but he lied like a rug and eventually convinced her that it was just Mace being Mace.

Clyde made a few calls to other people he knew who were on Mace Thornburg's enemies list and found that they had all received the same call. Mace obviously didn't know who the true instigators were, and he was using the shotgun approach, hoping to bluff someone into confessing. The grapevine was buzzing with Mace's latest paranoid rant. No one was sure whether a hit man had been hired or not, but a lot of people were giving lip service to the fact that it was a pretty good idea.

Instead of slowing Mace down, the event seemed to light a fire under him. He launched a citywide fax campaign libeling Emily, Clyde, and six other people, naming them all in the conspiracy to kill him. I don't know if he actually called the police, but if he did, they must not have taken him very seriously, because no one Clyde knew got a visit or a call from them.

Clyde told Gerry about Mace's actions, and Gerry took it as a personal insult. The threats had not frightened Mace enough to silence him. This made Gerry look ineffective. Clyde begged Gerry to go back to Vegas and let the situation cool off. Gerry told him to relax. He would handle it. At least this was how Clyde laid it out to me, but I was beginning to doubt the veracity of Clyde's stories. He was, after all, a writer and a director—a lethal combination of creativity and ego. I felt his grasp on the truth was tenuous at best. The whole affair was making me nervous. I didn't like getting involved with characters like Gerry. He was some kind of Z-grade throwback to Richard Widmark pictures. He was Sonny Corleone without the style. He was a loose cannon, and I had a feeling that dealing with him wasn't going to be much better than dealing with Mace himself. I tried to impart this wisdom to Clyde, but he waved me off and assured me that he had things "under control." That was the director in him speaking. But the real world isn't a movie set. Mobsters don't cut anybody slack just because they can make a motion picture.

chapter thirty-two

We resumed production on *Blonde Lightning,* and all went smoothly for the next three days. The crew had gotten more than enough rest during the break, so they were like fresh horses. Most of them returned to the set, not having found new jobs in the interim. Gary Bettman had to find a few replacements lower in the ranks, but all the department heads were still with the show, so we managed to pick up right where we left off, as if nothing had happened.

The problems with Mace seemed to have disappeared, the threatening calls ceased, no power lines attacked anyone, no cars were sabotaged. I began to believe that Gerry had been just the right tonic to cure ourselves of Mace after all.

We were back on the soundstage for the rest of the shoot, but Clyde and a skeleton crew would be stealing some street location shots with a few of the actors whenever the schedule permitted.

I was sitting in the stage's production office not long after lunch on the third day back when the call came in.

It was Emily, phoning from her hospital room. "Where's Clyde?" she asked, sounding very agitated.

"Emily! How are you? How are you feeling?"

"Angry. Where's Clyde?"

"On the set."

"Get him."

"I can't, Emily. It's a hot set. He's way behind schedule, and he doesn't want to be bothered."

"Oh, he's going to be bothered. I'm going to bother the hell out of him."

"What's wrong?"

"Mace is dead."

I immediately lost all my wind. I couldn't breathe, I couldn't speak, but I knew if I didn't get something out, I would incriminate myself. "Wh-wha—" was all I could manage.

"He's dead. The police found him in an alley behind the Formosa last night. He was stabbed to death. It's all over the news."

"Jesus . . ."

"Go get Clyde."

"Okay."

I put her on hold and went to the set. The red light was on outside the stage door, indicating shooting was in progress. I knew it would go off at the end of the take, so I waited. No use making the entire crew suspicious by ruining a shot. I stood there for almost a full minute contemplating the abyss. We were fucked. Truly fucked. It had to have been Gerry. He would get caught and bring our names into it, and it would go down in Hollywood history as a murder for hire. My producing career was about to end before it began. And my freedom would end with it.

The red light went off, and I barged onto the set before Clyde could start another take. I was lucky. They were moving the camera. That meant a lighting change and at least a twenty-minute break. I found Clyde consulting with Jackie Taylor, the script supervisor.

Clyde saw me coming and immediately knew something was wrong. "What's up?" he asked.

"We've got a scheduling problem for tomorrow. I need to talk to you about it. Alone."

"Okay. Jackie, just print the last two."

"I thought you liked take one also?"

"Oh yeah. For the outtake reel. That was nice and embarrassing. Print that, too."

She nodded, and Clyde and I walked away from the main stage. We had to find a place far enough away that none of the sound mixer's microphones would pick us up. I didn't want to confess on tape. Not yet anyway.

Once we were properly secluded, I dropped the bomb. "Mace is dead," I whispered.

"Say what?"

"Stabbed to death. They found him behind the Formosa."

A smile slowly spread on Clyde's face. "That's great."

"Great? Don't you get it? We are in big trouble."

"Why? *I* didn't kill him. Did you?"

"No. But I know who did."

It took a second for Clyde to comprehend what I was suggesting. "He wouldn't have. . . ."

"Who else?"

"Mace has got a lot of enemies."

"Not like Gerry, I bet."

"You're jumping to conclusions."

"I'm not the only one. Emily's on the phone. She sounds mad."

"Don't panic. We don't know what happened. If we act like we do, we're sunk. Who knows? Maybe you're wrong."

"I don't think so. You better talk to Emily. I left her on hold."

Clyde's eyes got wide, and he headed for the office. I towed along, desperate to see how he handled this one. By the time he got to the phone, he was perfectly calm. He fielded questions from Emily and acted properly shocked and completely surprised. He feigned innocence and sounded truly insulted by her accusations. When Emily was finished yelling at him, Clyde hung up the phone and his face dropped.

"We're through," he said gravely.

"What happened?"

"She didn't buy it. She said she's had it with me. She doesn't care what happened. She's washing her hands of me."

"She's said that before."

"I think she means it this time." His expression changed to one of optimism. "It's okay. It's better this way. Now she won't be in the way."

I didn't like the sound of that.

chapter thirty-three

We finished the day in a bit of a panic. Clyde called a wrap at exactly twelve hours, causing the production team some concern. They liked to work the crew a few extra hours each night. This was a nonunion show. The crew was being paid a daily wage, and overtime didn't kick in until we exceeded fourteen hours of shooting. Even though they had contracted for a twelve-hour day, it was understood that we could go to fourteen without penalty. Whenever we went to fourteen, the crew grumbled. If we didn't go to fourteen, the producers grumbled. Someone was always grumbling.

When we got to the Viande parking lot, we were horrified to find Gerry waiting for us in his Caddy. We knew then that our fears had been warranted. The bastard had killed Mace. Not wanting to speak out in the open, Clyde invited us in to his apartment for drinks. Once we were inside, he did not offer the promised libations.

"What happened?" he asked Gerry angrily.

"The guy got smart with me and pulled a piece," Gerry said. "I had to cut him."

"We didn't want him killed," Clyde said. "We were very specific about that."

"Ah, come on. You're glad he's dead, aren't you?"

"That's beside the point."

"I don't think so."

"Trust me. It is. This is bad, what you've done. I don't want any part of it."

"Any *part* of it? You *are it,* completely. I wouldn't even be in L.A. if not for you guys. I'd be in Vegas."

"I thought you had other business here?"

"I just said that to make you feel better. No, Clyde, you *were* my business. I was here to specifically take care of your problem. It is now taken care of."

"So, why are you here now?"

"I need money."

"I paid you already."

"Not for the whole job. Not for what I had to do."

"That was unauthorized. It was your own idea."

"I told you it could come to this. I warned you when we first entered into our agreement. And I told you there might be additional expenses as we went along."

"Listen, I am not going to pay you for killing that guy."

"Well, someone is gonna to have to. I'm going to Hawaii until the heat dies down, and I need dough to go."

"That's not our problem."

"It'll be your problem if you don't get me some cash."

"How much are you looking for?"

"Fifty K would just about do it. I'd ask for more, but I know you're a *writer*. I want to be realistic."

"Man, I don't have that kind of money. I'm livin' hand to mouth around here."

"Get it from your girlfriend."

"I'm not going to hit Emily up for fifty grand in blood money."

"Why not? She's the one who benefited the most, isn't she?"

"She doesn't know anything about this bullshit. If she did, she'd kill us all."

"Let me explain something to you," Gerry said, pulling his jacket aside so we could look at the .38 revolver he had clip-holstered to his belt like he was a homicide cop or a nasty pit boss. "Ain't no kung-fu bitch gonna kill *me*. She comes at me, and I'll put her down."

"It was a figure of speech. She is actually a very peaceful person."

"Yeah. So am I until someone crosses me. Then it's not pretty. Dig up fifty K quick, and I won't have to do no demos."

Gerry walked out of the apartment, leaving Clyde and me staring at each other, trying to figure out what to do.

Finally Clyde asked me, "Got fifty grand I can borrow?"

chapter thirty-four

Clyde and I went to work the next day and acted like nothing unusual had happened. The crew had seen the reports of Mace Thornburg's murder on the news, and there was much joking around about how happy Clyde must be, along with cheerful speculation about how he could manage to stab Mace to death while maintaining his busy schedule. The time of Mace's death had been established at approximately ten thirty the night of the murder. Clyde was on set at that time, working. Fifty witnesses could attest to that. He had the perfect alibi. Until you looked in his Rolodex and found Carmine C.'s Las Vegas phone number.

Clyde had a very good day on the set. He got all his setups with no delay, and he even caught up on two scenes that he had dropped earlier in the shoot when he was falling behind schedule. He seemed invigorated by his situation. There was no sign of panic on his countenance. Everything was cruising along nicely until we neared wrap time. Then Gerry showed up.

I don't know how he found out where we were shooting, and I was certain that asking him would just anger him. I asked him to wait in Clyde's office while Clyde filmed the martini shot (as the last shot of the night had long ago been nicknamed by alcoholic crew members) but he insisted on standing at the edge of the set, watching the proceedings.

Clyde was shooting a close-up of Michelle, and she was required to cry. He had been pushing her hard all day, so she had no problem turning on the waterworks. Clyde got it in one take and called a wrap. It took a while for Michelle to quit sobbing.

I couldn't tell if Clyde had spotted Gerry hanging out in the shadows of the stage. If he had, it didn't seem to rattle him. There was no panic in his movements. Only complete professionalism. Clyde was averaging forty-two setups a day. A stark contrast to the work ethic of the last director I had seen in action, Charles Jacobs, the helmer of *Maelstrom*. He was lucky to get three usable setups a day. The difference was that Charles's movie would break a hundred million at the box office and Clyde's would go straight to video. Clyde was right. The relative skills required to make a low-budget film and a big-budget one were directly inverted, and so were the rewards.

The crew began wrapping out the set. We were done with that one, and a new one would be in its place by tomorrow. The art department swing shift was already hard at work building it. Out with the old; in with the new. I went to Clyde and drew his attention away from Vince, who was asking him how his performance was for the fiftieth time that day.

"We've got company," I said.

"I know. I saw him."

"How'd he know where we were?"

"Don't let his lack of social skills fool you. He's not a dummy."

Clyde walked over and shook hands with Gerry, treating him like he was just another potential investor or business associate.

"How are you, Mr. Parker?" Clyde asked Gerry.

I assumed Clyde used the fake name just in case anyone was listening. Gerry went right along with it. He didn't even flinch at having an alias for his alias. I doubt anyone had called him by his birth name (whatever it was) in a long, long time.

"We need to talk," said Gerry.

"I'm bushed. It's been a long day. Can't it wait until later?"

"Nah, I'm having a timetable problem. I'm going to be leaving town earlier than I thought. Let's have a cup of coffee."

"Okay. Mark, can you bring us up some coffee? We'll go into the conference room upstairs, where we can have some privacy."

"Okay," I said. Then I went to the craft service table to get two cups of coffee and the fixings. Clyde had remained calm, but I could tell a mixture of anger and fear were battling it out beneath his cool exterior.

I took the coffee to the conference room upstairs. No one was allowed on that floor, as it had been cordoned off by the stage manager. Clyde had a key and permission to use the space only when absolutely necessary. This meeting qualified. By the time I got there, they were already at each other's throats.

Clyde was saying, "This is so stupid, I can't believe it, not even from you."

"Don't get rude with me, fuckface," Gerry said without emotion.

I closed the soundproof doors, set the tray down, and handed Gerry his coffee. I left Clyde's on the tray so he wouldn't be tempted to throw it at anyone.

"Rude? How can I be rude to you? You don't hear anything I say!"

"Listen, Clyde. Here's how it is. You're involved in a murder. Both of you are in it up to your shit-eating grins. That was *your* enemy I killed. I didn't even *know* that guy. I was doin' you a favor. Shit got out of hand. I didn't want to kill him, but *you* wanted him dead. You put this action in motion. It's practically a contract hit."

"That's such bullshit," Clyde snarled. "You're a fucking psychopath! We didn't want anybody to get hurt. We said that over and over again. This is all your fault, and I'm not taking the heat for you!"

Gerry suddenly brought his hand up and slapped Clyde across the face. It was a solid, meaty slap, equivalent to a punch from a smaller man. Clyde was rocked, almost knocked off his feet. He shook cobwebs from his head and went red with anger. He balled his hands into fists, but Gerry put his hefty left hand against Clyde's chest and made a threatening fist with his right.

"Don't make me knock you out, Clyde. That won't do us any good."

Clyde tried to calm himself. He stepped back and touched the welt on the side of his face.

"I don't like being called names, Clyde. You know that."

"Sorry," Clyde said insincerely.

"Just get me my money. I've gotta lay low while the cops bounce around on this. Hate to have to spill everything to 'em, but if I get caught, you boys will be turned over like bad cards."

"What about the code of loyalty?" I said.

"Fuck you talkin' about? I'm just telling you straight. I'm not going to jail on a murder I didn't want to commit. This is your beef. Both of you. I go down, and I got to have leverage. You're it. I'll cut a deal. Now wouldn't it be easier to get me some dough and let me skip on out of here?"

"Yeah," Clyde said. "I'll see what I can do."

Gerry patted Clyde's swollen face gently. "See that," he said. "I knew we'd come to an understanding."

chapter thirty-five

Clyde and I drove straight from the stage to the airport. We were in Vegas by midnight, and we went immediately to the Aladdin. Clyde called Rick Collonia on the house phone, and he told us to come up to his room.

Collonia was freshly showered and dressed, his hair still wet, slicked back on his head like Cagney in *Public Enemy.* The room was nice, but no nicer than the one I had inhabited on my last trip to the Aladdin.

He offered us coffee from his room-service tray. It was after midnight, and he was just now having dinner. We sat and drank coffee while he devoured a New York strip and a baked potato. After some small talk, we got down to business.

"I need help with Carmine," Clyde finally said. "He's gone nuts on us."

"Things didn't work out with that guy you wanted him to talk to?"

"They worked out *too* well."

"I see. That can be a problem."

"Now Carmine's changing the terms of our contract and being ridiculous."

"Whatever you do, I don't want to know nothin' about it, see?" Cagney through and through.

"Sure," Clyde said. "I just wanted your take on it."

"You're a big boy. You got a problem, you got to handle it."

"I just didn't want to upset you."

"He's my friend, but if he's out of control, he's out of control. I understand the fix you're in, but you started this yourself."

"I know. So you're saying I should pay him?"

"I can't tell you what to do. You think you owe him something, you should pay him."

"I paid him what he wanted, but now he's shaking us down for more, and I don't have it. I don't think he's going to go away."

"I've talked to him, and I can tell you now that I can't talk to him. He's not listening to me."

"You talked to him? When?"

"This afternoon. He didn't get into details. He just said you were being a bad boy."

"Really? Me? *He* threatened *us*. He even threatened Emily."

"Hey. That's what he does for a living. You knew that going in. That's why you hired him in the first place. I told you not to get on his bad side."

"He fucking killed a guy."

Collonia leaned in and motioned for Clyde to move closer to him so he could whisper. "Don't ever say something like that again. Not if you know what's good for you. I'm serious. You're my friend, but don't push it. Nobody did no such thing, and I don't like talk like that. Understand?"

"Yeah. I'm sorry."

"You better be. You got a mess. If I were you, I'd find a way to clean it up."

"You got any suggestions?"

"All I can tell you is 'When in Rome, do as the Romans do.' "

"That's what I've been thinking. But I wanted to talk to you first. See if you approved."

"Hey, what am I now, the Godfather? You come here for *permission* or something? I got nothing to do with that kind of business, you know that."

"It's just that you've known him for so long. . . ."

"He makes his own bed. And so do you. I can't give you permission to be a man. You gotta do what you gotta do. I just don't want to be any part of it. I've already heard too much. And said too much."

"I understand. I'm sorry."

They stared at each other for a very long moment.

Then Collonia broke into his "happy" Cagney grin and gave Clyde a tap on the cheek with his fist. "All right, then—let's hit the tables!"

chapter thirty-six

We played a few hands of blackjack, then made the early flight back to L.A. We were in the Viande parking lot before dawn. As we got out of my car, I said, "So much for sleep."

Clyde shook his head and said, "It's overrated."

We headed for our respective apartments, but as I was fumbling with my keys, I saw movement out of the corner of my eye. Something large suddenly darted out from behind the bushes lining the brick wall of the parking lot. It was Gerry, and he was rushing toward Clyde, who was standing in his own doorway, his key half in the doorknob.

"Clyde!" I yelled, but it was too late. Gerry slammed into Clyde full force, shoving his face into the door. Gerry held him against the door and patted him down quickly, checking to see if he had a weapon on him. Finding nothing, he peeled Clyde off the door, spun him around, and punched him in the stomach. Clyde doubled over, gasping for breath. He never got a chance to say a word.

"You went to fucking *Vegas* to talk shit about me to Richie?" Gerry snarled. "You *motherfucker . . .*"

He straightened Clyde up, hit him in the chest, and threw him across the sidewalk into the bushes. I moved forward to try to stop

Gerry, and he pulled his .38 out from under his jacket and shoved it in my face.

"You want this? You want to help your boyfriend here fuck me over, I'll give you this!"

I stood frozen, staring down the barrel of the gun, thinking how different it was to have a real gun aimed at my face than the prop guns we used on films. A squeeze of the trigger, a flash, and I'd be gone. There was a finality to it that I had never grasped until now.

Gerry sneered at me and shoved me aside; then he leaned down next to Clyde. "Listen, cocksucker. Get me that money by tomorrow night or I'm going to take you apart. Ain't nobody gonna help you on this one. Nobody here and nobody in Vegas, so don't be fucking around like that again. You're not here with my money tomorrow night, I'll find that cunt girlfriend of yours on one of them movie sets and stick a tripod up her ass and open it."

Through a frightened, battered haze, Clyde still managed to look up at Gerry with hostility.

It just made Gerry madder. He smacked Clyde across the face with an open palm. Blood dribbled out of Clyde's mouth. "Don't fuckin' look at me like that. You ain't no tough guy."

Gerry stood up and looked at me.

"I ought to kick your ass, too, but I'm fucking tired. I been doin' squats in those bushes all night."

I just stared at him, trying not to move a muscle or say anything that would further agitate him. He had such a hair trigger, I had the feeling that if I twitched, he would blow my brains out.

"Take care of your butt buddy, and make damn sure my money's here by nine tomorrow night or I'll fuck *you* up, too."

He pocketed the gun and walked down the sidewalk into the dark. I bent down next to Clyde to see if he was still alive. He looked pretty smashed up, but his eyes were starting to gain focus.

"Can you move?" I asked. "Or should I call the paramedics?"

"Just help me up," he grumbled.

I helped him to his feet, and we went to his door. As I turned the key that had been left in the doorknob, I heard a rumble not unlike the earthquake that had torn the city apart those long months ago. It was Gerry, cruising by on Morrison Street, still driving the big red Caddy with the fucked-up muffler from Rent-A-Wreck. He stared daggers at me as he passed the apartment complex, establishing crystal-clear communication. If we wanted to stay alive, we had to get him his fifty K.

chapter thirty-seven

Clyde was staring into his bathroom mirror, working on his eye with a cotton ball dabbed in hydrogen peroxide. There was a small cut over the eye, and the area around it was swollen, but it hadn't turned black and blue yet.

"Rotten fucker," Clyde said. "He's gonna regret this breach of etiquette."

"We better call the police."

"And get ourselves arrested? No way."

"He's crazy. I think he'll kill us if we don't do what he says. Or worse, he'll turn us in."

"He'll never get the chance."

"What are you going to do?"

"Just what Rick Collonia told us to do."

"And what was that? I don't remember him getting too specific."

"He said 'When in Rome,' right?"

"So?"

"Well, you know, in Rome they once had a rat problem, so they brought in cats to eat the rats, then they had a cat problem, so they brought in dogs to eat the cats, then they had a dog problem, so they brought in lions to eat the dogs."

"Your point being?"

"When in Rome, do as the Romans do. If you're having mad dog problems, get a bigger, badder dog."

"What the fuck are you talking about?"

"I know some guys who can take care of this jerk."

"Let me get this straight. You want to hire some guys to kill the guy you hired to kill some other guy?"

"I didn't hire Carmine to kill Mace. That asshole improvised."

"You knew it could go that way. That's why you contacted him. You wanted Mace to disappear. You just didn't want to dirty your own hands."

"I'd be careful throwing speculative talk like that around."

"You going to have me killed, too?"

"Don't be ridiculous."

"*I'm* being ridiculous? Listen to you. We're already implicated in one murder—now you're suggesting a second murder to cover the tracks of the first one. It's insane!"

"You got a better idea?"

I just stared at him. He had me there. I didn't have a clue how we should proceed.

"I didn't think so. Maybe you like being threatened by Cro-Magnons, but I don't. I am tired of eating shit, and I'm not going to take it from the likes of Gerry or Carmine C. or whatever the fuck he wants to call himself."

"What about his people? If something happens to him, won't they come after us?"

"Are you kidding? Carmine is so *un*connected, it's pathetic. They tossed him out three years ago for skimming."

"I didn't think they did that sort of thing. I thought once you were in, you were in—unless they killed you."

"That's the movies, kid. Carmine's sister is married to a made guy back East, so they let him do bag man shit over the years, but he got sticky fingers. They made him pay the dough back, roughed him up a bit, but they don't kill anyone unless they have to. It's bad PR. Something happens to Carmine, believe me there will be a list of suspects longer than Dumbo's dick. We will be very low on the list."

"But Rick Collonia will know."

"Rick doesn't give a damn about Carmine. He won't get in the middle of this. *No one* gives a damn about Carmine."

chapter thirty-eight

Clyde was a lot calmer about the situation than I was. I felt downright vulnerable. I had a mobster on my ass trying to extort money for a hit he felt Clyde and I had commissioned (even though I had not been privy to the details of the deal and I had not personally paid him anything), and for all I knew, Mace Thornburg's associates could be lurking in the alley waiting to cut the brakes on *my* car to avenge his death. Also, someone had thrown a rattlesnake over my balcony wall a few months earlier, and I still hadn't figured that one out. On top of all that, my lady love had started to sound distant when we spoke on the phone and made herself conveniently unavailable when I wanted to see her in person. Her estranged husband wanted to kill me, but he hadn't been around in a while, so I had a feeling he was visiting with her instead of me. I couldn't win for losing on that one. And Emily was due to be released from the hospital any day now. If she were to come into contact with Gerry, the whole twisted ball of twine would unravel very quickly and we would all be dead or in front of a grand jury.

I shaved and considered cutting my own throat to save the world the trouble. Not having the requisite nerve, I dressed and prepared for another long day on the set. It was time to check in for work alongside my murderous neighbor.

Clyde wore some very subtle makeup to cover his new bruises, and no one seemed to notice the blood in his eye as we began our final day of filming *Blonde Lightning*. Red, white, and blue had been the colors of Clyde's eyes from the beginning. There was just a little more red in one of them than usual, courtesy of his good friend, Gerry. If anyone noticed, they probably attributed it to our recent car accident.

The day was uneventful and productive. We even wrapped an hour ahead of schedule. Somehow Clyde had done it. He had shot an entire feature film in twelve working days (with a little breather in the middle for a hospital break) despite the various external pressures and bizarre circumstances surrounding the production. If anything, Clyde seemed to thrive on the confusion.

Vince Timlin was ecstatic. Even though we were slightly overbudget, he felt he had done some of his best acting in years and he thought the film would sell well to cable. He was so happy, he said he'd spring for a wrap party up at his compound sometime next month. Everyone was invited. A wrap party is a standard event on most films, but for one with this small a budget, the crew is lucky to be furnished with wrap beer on the last night of filming. A party is a luxury. Vince thanked Clyde heartily before driving off with his latest temporary fiancée, one of the extras we used in a crowd scene three nights earlier. I considered asking the crew if any flashlights had gone missing, but then thought it better to just save the wisecracks for the state penitentiary.

As we were wrapping out for the final time, Clyde took me aside and said, "I bought another day."

"What?"

"I called Gerry and bought us another day."

"How?"

"I promised him we'd have his money by tomorrow night. I told him that I sold my points in the picture and they were going to pay me tomorrow. He went for it."

"Good. It gives us time to pack."

"We're not going anywhere. I've got a plan."

"Oh, good. A plan. Finally. Want to tell me about it?"

"I know a couple of guys, grips I used to work with back in the eighties. Tough fuckers. I would have used them on this show, but they've got steady gigs on *Baywatch*. I talked to them, and they're willing to straighten this shit out for us. We're meeting them later at Residuals."

"You're certifiable. This is just going to sink us deeper."

"Why don't you relax and let me handle this? Just come along for the ride. If you don't like where we're going, you can bow out."

"I already don't like it."

"Just have a beer with us, and let's talk it out. C'mon. One beer. What can that hurt?"

"Okay," I said. "One beer."

postproduction

chapter thirty-nine

We met Doug and Muana, the killer grips, at Residuals, a sports bar in a strip mall on Ventura Boulevard near Universal where actors and stuntmen like to hang out while waiting for work. Anyone who got a residual check in the mail for less than a dollar could bring it in and trade it for a free drink. The check would then be proudly displayed on the wall with hundreds of others. We bought two pitchers of beer and four shots of Jack Daniel's to give the brew some backbone. The four of us downed the Jack and slammed the shots onto the table. I took a quick hit of beer to ease the burn tearing down my throat. Muana and Doug grinned at me.

"Too hot for ya?" Doug asked.

"I'm thirsty," I said.

The two grips looked at each other knowingly. They were tanned and leathery from their years of dragging cable and hauling equipment through the sand on *Baywatch* and other outdoor adventure shows. Doug was the larger of the two, but Muana had more tattoos, I guess to compensate for his lack of size. He also had more teeth that were not chipped or cracked. Doug had a grin that advertised he could take a punch. And *had* . . . often.

"Doug's a second-degree black belt," Muana said out of nowhere. "He's a badass."

"Shut the fuck up," Doug said with a snaggletoothed smile.

"What style do you study?" I asked.

"Shotokan and Jeet Kune Do," Doug said.

"That's Bruce Lee's shit," Muana said. "That Jeet Kune stuff . . ."

"I know."

"You a Bruce fan?" Doug asked.

"Who isn't?" I replied.

"Tell 'em your Bruce Lee story, Doug," Muana said.

"Nah."

"C'mon, tell me," I said.

Doug looked very serious for a moment, trying to decide if I was man enough for the secret knowledge; then his voice got low and he told me about the moment that changed his life forever.

"When I was a kid, I went to see *The Chinese Connection* at the Strand duplex. I was only thirteen at the time, and my grandmother had to take me to get me into the theater, because it was rated R, but I'd been seeing those spots on TV with this crazy Chinaman kicking everybody's ass, and I had to see that fucking flick, so I convinced her to take me into town and get me into the movie. She didn't want to watch it, so she went to the theater next door and watched *The Legend of Boggy Creek*. The Strand was the first theater I ever saw that was split in half to make two theaters. I thought it was cool back then. I didn't know they were gonna do it to every theater in the country until there was nothing but dinky screen multiplexes all over the place. Anyway, I watch this flick and I couldn't believe my eyes. This guy was amazing. He was a god! You ever see *Chinese Connection*?"

Everyone at the table nodded solemnly.

"Then you know what I mean. We were in the middle of the kung-fu craze. Carradine had his show on ABC, and all the chop-socky flicks were comin' to town, and I'd seen a couple, *Five Fingers of Death* and *Lady Kung Fu*, and they were pretty good, but they were nothing like *Chinese Connection*. Bruce Lee was the real deal! He'd already had *Fists of Fury* released here, but somehow I missed that one, which is okay 'cause it's good and all, but it's no *Chinese Connection*. That fucking movie was *it*!"

"Tell 'em about the cabdriver," Muana coaxed.

"I will, just let me tell it my way," Doug said. "So, my grandma gets out of *Boggy Creek* and wants to go home, and I beg her to let me stay and see the flick again. She finally says okay and gives me cab fare to get home. Then I watch *Chinese Connection* for a second glorious time, and I swear to God that I am going to see every movie Bruce Lee ever makes and one day I'm gonna be just like him. An iron motherfucking movie star! Not one of these faggots we're always working with, but a piece of fucking *steel*. Steve McQueen is the only American movie star in the last thirty years who actually had balls. Him and maybe Lee Marvin."

"How about Mitchum?" Muana interjected.

"Okay, yeah, Mitchum had balls," Doug said.

Muana snorted. "Mitchum had a cluster of balls!"

"Yeah. But he was basically a nice guy. Lee Marvin and Steve Mc-Queen and Bruce Lee, they were *mean* motherfuckers. They'd kill you if you fucked with them. Mitchum would probably just beat you up a little, buy you a drink, and hope you'd go away."

"Yeah," Muana said. "And while you were drinking that drink, he'd fuck your wife and your daughter, then slash your tires so you couldn't follow him."

"Ain't that a fact?" Doug said, high-fiving Muana.

"Finish the story," Clyde said impatiently.

"Oh yeah, anyway, I watch *Chinese Connection* a second time, and I woulda watched it a third time, but that was the last show. I get a cab, and while the guy's driving me to my grandmother's house, he asks me what flick I just saw. I tell him all about the movie and this amazing fucker Bruce Lee, and the cabbie says, 'Hey, one of them kung-fu guys died today,' and I go, 'What?' and he says, 'Yeah, one of them martial arts guys died today. I think it was that guy on the TV show,' and I say, 'You mean David Carradine?' and he says, 'Yeah, I think it was that guy.' And suddenly I got totally depressed 'cause I knew it wasn't David Carradine. I *knew* it was gonna be Bruce Lee who was dead. I knew it just as sure as I knew that fucking cab was yellow. And sure enough, I get home and turn on the TV and there it is on the news, 'Asian Superstar Bruce Lee dead at 32,' and I cried like a baby. It was like my blood brother had suddenly died. I'd only known the guy for three hours watching that movie twice, but I just fell apart."

"How'd you know in the cab it was Bruce who died and not David Carradine?" I asked.

" 'Cause nothin' good lasts on this fuckin' planet. And Bruce Lee was just too good to be true. Just my luck he dies on the day I discover him. It was only later that I realized he had been Kato on *The Green Hornet*. He was the best thing on that show, too. You know he was supposed to be Kwai Chang on *Kung Fu*? It was down to him and Carradine, and the asshole producers went with Carradine because they said Bruce looked too 'oriental.' Can you believe that bullshit?"

"Carradine don't know squat about martial arts," Muana said.

"That's right," Doug said. "That's why they always had to slow the film down when he was doing his kung fu, 'cause he didn't know the shit and it looked ridiculous at full speed."

"They sure as fuck wouldn'ta had to do that with Bruce in that role," Muana said.

"That's the fact," Doug said. "They mighta had to slow it down just to see what the fuck he was doin' to the bad guys, but they sure wouldn't need to trick that shit out 'cause he didn't know his stuff. Bruce Lee was the real deal—that's the fact. The real fucking deal!"

"They killed him, you know," Muana said.

"Now they've done killed his son," Doug added.

"Motherfuckers . . . ," Muana muttered.

"It's a terrible thing," Clyde said. "But can we get down to business?"

"We already talked it out," Doug said. "We're ready to help."

"We got a couple of ideas we want to run by you," Muana added.

So they laid it out, right there in the middle of Residuals, a plan as nuts as they were. It was so ludicrous that even if we were heard over the din of the other losers in the place by some passing waitress, she would have just thought we were working out the plot of a bad TV movie. It was sick and degenerate, and when the conversation was over, we were all in total agreement. We would go through with the crazy-ass plan, and if we were lucky, by midnight tomorrow night, Gerry would be a dead man.

Somewhere along the way, I went from thinking this was the last thing in the world I wanted to be a part of to believing it was the only way we could escape the clutches of Gerry, formally known as Carmine C. Guilt slipped further away with every drink.

We drank hard the rest of the night and closed the place. Instead of taking the party to some after-hours joint, we all agreed to go home and get a full night's rest. Two A.M. is late enough to party on the night before you commit murder.

chapter forty

Tracy surprised me by bringing over breakfast early the next morning. I hadn't seen her since my hospital stay, and I had been missing her, despite the nasty business that had been keeping me occupied. I tried to get her to crawl into bed with me, but she had serious news to deliver with my bagel and cappuccino.

"I see you've recovered enough from your near-death experience to go drinking," she said.

"Clyde's a bad influence."

"I know. I've been telling Emily that for years."

She wasn't having anything to eat or drink, so I took that to mean she had an ulterior motive for coming by so early. "Something's wrong, isn't it?"

She took the old pregnant pause before saying, "Adam wants to see me."

"About what?"

"He wants to reconcile."

"So?"

"I'm considering it."

"Um . . ."

"We've got a lot of history together."

"Yeah. *Bad* history."

"Not all of it was bad."

"Oh shit, I can't believe I'm hearing this. What about *us?*"

"Look. I'm just going to talk to him. He deserves the courtesy. I'm not going to decide anything. I'm not going to do anything rash."

"Things were just going too smoothly, weren't they?"

"What do you mean?"

"You're getting bored. There's not enough drama in the air for you, so you want to go back to the turmoil."

"Don't be ridiculous."

"You go back to him again, and I'm not going to be here for you the next time it all falls apart."

"I know that."

"And you don't care?"

"It's not that. I *do* care. But I can't expect you to keep waiting for me."

"It sounds like you've already decided."

"No. I'm just going to talk to him. But if I can't even talk to my husband without you flipping out, I don't think we have much of a future anyway. I think maybe I just better be alone for a while."

"Maybe so." Like that was going to happen.

She got up and walked out of the apartment.

I took another sip of cappuccino and lay back down. The day had started on a bad note. Hard to believe things were going to get worse, but I was almost certain of it.

I passed out again and slept until noon, then showered and shaved. I almost threw up in the shower when I remembered the pact we had all made the night before. It was sick, and now in the harsh light of day and the blinding glare of a hangover, I knew I couldn't go through with it. I planned on putting a stop to the scheme before it went any further.

After dressing, I went down to see Clyde. I knocked on his door but got no response. I was certain he was in there. He just didn't want to talk to me. I went back upstairs and called him on the phone. He did not pick up. I sat in the hammock, watching the parking lot, waiting for him to come out of his apartment. I contemplated our options, but couldn't come up with a better solution than the one we had agreed on last night. It was vile, but it was probably the only way we were going to get out of this jam alive and free. If that was at all possible.

After about an hour, Clyde came out the back door of Viande. The guy had been over at the bar drinking lunch! I guess he was officially off the wagon again. Now that the movie was over, he was back on the sauce. But one would think that even Clyde McCoy would understand that the plan for the night called for focus.

I stood up so he could see me on the balcony. "Hayes," he said cordially, but he did not slow down on his beeline for his front door.

I scanned the area to see if anyone was around. The coast seemed clear. "Can I talk to you for a minute?"

"I'm kind of busy," Clyde said. "Can't it wait?"

"Not really."

He frowned and went to the entrance of the vestibule. I had to go down to unlock it. He stepped in, and I closed the door behind him. We stood at the bottom of the stairwell, and I whispered, "I think this whole thing is a bad idea."

"Okay. I'm listening."

"What?"

"Tell me *your* plan. What should we do?"

"Uh, I don't know."

"That's what I thought. Well, that leg-breaker is going to be here in a few hours. If you don't want to go through with it, come up with a better idea. Otherwise, it's *on*."

He opened the door and walked out. I went upstairs and paced the floor. As the day progressed, my nerves grew more frayed. I considered getting in the car and driving to Reno to wait out the next few days. Maybe they would all kill one another like in *Yojimbo,* and I could go back to my job hunt. I was ready to give up on show business. I wanted to work somewhere nice and sane. Like a meatpacking plant or Area 51.

A little after four, my doorbell rang. I opened the side window in my living room and looked down at the doorway. It was Clyde. I ran down the stairs and let him in.

"I need to talk to you," he said. He looked like an undertaker who had forgotten to take his Prozac.

We went upstairs and sat in the kitchen.

Clyde said, "I want you to sit it out tonight."

"What?" I was shocked, startled, and relieved all at once.

"You're nervous. And you should be. But this requires calm action if the plan is to work. We don't need any nervous Nellies fucking up the works. One mistake, and the operation comes apart."

I was immediately insulted, and suddenly I wanted back in. It was a completely irrational impulse, but I went with it. "That's nonsense," I said. "I can do my part."

"You just come up with your share of the dough, and we'll call it even. Okay?"

I almost argued with him further, but then I realized what I was doing. I was trying to convince him to let me actively participate in a murder. I decided to relent and let him have his way. "Okay," I said, feigning hurt feelings. "If you really don't trust me."

"It's not that. It's really more of a space thing. My apartment is going to get crowded. Too many cooks, you know?"

"Sure. Okay. Whatever you want."

"Good man," Clyde said. "This will all be over soon. You *could* do one thing for us, though."

"What's that?"

"We're gonna have a talk with the man. If things don't work out, it might get loud down there. I've already swept the neighborhood to make sure we're not under any kind of surveillance for that other thing, but I want you to keep an eye out, make sure there aren't a whole bunch of people around. Especially cops, if you know what I mean."

"You want me to function as a lookout while you commit a murder?"

"It's going to be self-defense."

"How can self-defense be premeditated?"

"With careful planning."

"Do you hear yourself? Doesn't it bother you that you are preparing to kill a man?"

"I'm hoping it won't come to that, but you see how Gerry is. He's *dangerous*. If things get out of control, I'd just like to know that you're there for us."

"I guess it's the least I can do."

"Your words, not mine."

"You know that story you told me about the Romans and the rats and the dogs and the lions and all that shit?"

"Yeah."

"Was that true?"

"I don't know. I might have seen that bit in a movie. Sounded good, though, didn't it?"

I went to my bank and withdrew one thousand dollars. I put it in an envelope and knocked on Clyde's door. He opened the door and took the envelope. I wanted to say something but couldn't find the words. Clyde smiled wickedly and closed the door in my face.

I stood there, thinking about what I had just done. A thousand dollars. Blood money. My share of a two-thousand-dollar murder-for-hire, a hit to be carried out by a couple of showbiz day laborers. How in the hell had I come to this place in my career?

chapter forty-one

I turned the lights off on my balcony and sat there in what could only be described as the gathering gloom. Rock music was coming from Clyde's apartment. Not loud enough to disturb the neighbors, but loud enough to drown out sounds of struggle if need be.

At eight o'clock, a white van pulled up and parked on Morrison Street. Doug and Muana got out and opened the back of the van. They pulled out a long, fat roll of carpet and carried it to Clyde's apartment. The door magically opened before they could knock, and they disappeared into the place.

Growing more nervous, I went to my fridge and got a beer. Clyde had said he was going to try to talk some sense into Gerry, but I suspected that wasn't going to happen. They had mapped out the original plan the night before at Residuals, and talk was not part of the proposed scenario. The plan was simple: Gerry (aka Carmine C.) would enter the apartment and demand the money. Doug and Muana would be hiding in the bedroom. While we distracted Gerry, Doug and Muana would jump him, disable him, kill him or at least knock him unconscious, then wrap him up in the roll of carpet that they would have earlier spread out on the living room floor so no blood (if there was any) would get on Clyde's own carpet. They would then take the mobster-laden carpet and dispose of it. Where, I did not know. They said that detail was unimportant, and knowing too much could only get me in trouble.

They were probably spreading the carpet out over the floor right now. Laying the trap. This was murder most premeditated. I wondered if Clyde had handed them my envelope and one of his own with matching funds as soon as they walked through the door or if he was actually going to try to talk to Gerry and pay the blood money to the two grips-cum-assassins only as a last resort. The price to be paid to Doug and Muana was quite reasonable for such a grave matter, but my end of the deal nearly wiped out my savings. I was broke now, but I probably wouldn't be needing much money where I was going. I was certain we would all end up in jail or worse. But Clyde and his boys had no such concerns. They were all so damned calm about it. Like it was just the cost of doing business. I wondered if one day I might pose a similar problem to them and have to be dealt with as simply and effi-ciently. They did not seem concerned about me keeping my silence, but *I* was. If the cops asked me what I knew about the murder of Mace Thornburg or the disappearance of a minor mob figure once known as Carmine C., I had a feeling it would not take much to make me crack.

I began to hope Gerry would not arrive. Then I began to pray, which is a pretty big move for an agnostic. At nine o'clock sharp, the ambigu-ity of my religious beliefs was reinstated as I heard the throaty rumble of Gerry's Cadillac coming down the alley. He parked in the Tower Records Annex parking lot, got out of the car, and adjusted his shirt sleeves, which were poking out irregularly from under his sport coat.

He looked up at my balcony, and I shrank back, hoping he hadn't spotted me lurking in the darkness. I heard him tread the sidewalk under my ledge and stop in front of Clyde's door. At least I hoped he was in front of Clyde's door and not mine. I had no contingency plan for getting rid of Gerry, no grips waiting in my apartment with guns or knives or pipes, preparing to separate him from this mortal coil. That would be in apartment 3. Please go there.

Nothing happened for almost a full minute. I was going crazy with suspense, wondering what the hell Gerry was doing down there. Was he looking through Clyde's window, suspecting a trap? Was he checking his firearm, preparing to kill whoever he found in the apartment? Or was he just hitting the Binaca so his breath would be sparkling fresh? I didn't know, but I dared not look over the railing. He would spot me for sure.

Finally, he knocked on Clyde's door. There was no response. He knocked again, and I heard the door open.

"What you doing in there?" Gerry said. "You didn't hear me knocking?"

"I was sleeping," Clyde said in an exhausted voice. The fucker was putting on a show.

"I told you I'd be here at nine," Gerry said in astonishment, like his word was Gospel.

"Oh yeah, sorry," Clyde said. "C'mon in."

The door closed, and I heard the music go down a notch. It was Cream playing "Born Under a Bad Sign."

I went nuts. I sprang to my feet and scoured the parking lot for cops, stragglers, make-out artists, drunks. I couldn't see anyone. Then I moved to the other side of my balcony and looked down the alley. Not much was happening. Luckily, it was a Tuesday night, a light traffic night for the area. There was a little action out on Ventura Boulevard, but that was beyond hearing range of the apartment building. Unless there was gunfire, of course.

Gunfire? What was I saying? Oh, Christ, yes, they were about to kill a man down in apartment 3, and I was the lookout. How could I forget?

I ran down the stairs and stood on the inside of the vestibule doorway, listening for sounds of struggle. I couldn't hear anything other than the stereo in Clyde's apartment. I opened my door a crack to hear better. "Strange Brew" was now playing. Clyde must have had *The Best of Cream* on the CD player. The music suddenly went up two notches, and I jumped back like I had been slapped. It was *happening*. It must have been. They were *killing* Gerry. Or maybe he was killing them. It was impossible to know. I tried to close my door as quietly as possible, but in my state of panic, I practically slammed the damn thing. I ran up the stairs and hid in my bathroom, wedging myself under the sink, trying not to hear the immaculate guitar riffs coming from Eric Clapton's ax, Jack Bruce's throbbing bass, and Ginger Baker's textbook drum fills. As a lookout, I made either a great plumbing fixture or a lousy rock critic.

The perverse mutant strains of Clapton's lead guitar on "Politician" drifted up through the floorboards, and I clasped my hands tightly against my ears—to no avail. I could still hear the music and, worse, could still imagine the scene playing out in apartment 3. The music suddenly went down in volume by half. Something had been decided on the battlefield.

I heard the door open downstairs. I rushed out of the bathroom like a madman and ran to the balcony. I must have looked completely insane. My hair was wild and my eyes wilder.

Doug and Muana were loading the roll of carpet back into the van. The carpet roll now looked lumpy and a good 280 pounds heavier. The grips were straining, but they managed to shove the carpet in with a minimum of fuss. They were *grips* after all.

Clyde was standing in front of his apartment, smoking a cigarette, like he was just taking a break from his writing or carpet laying. He looked up at me and smiled, then flashed me a thumbs-up sign, like we had all performed a job well done. I tried not to show my panic, but something on my face must have told him that I was losing it. He watched Doug and Muana close up the van and pull away; then he went to my door and knocked.

I went downstairs and opened the door.

"Get your keys," he said humorlessly. "We need to take a ride."

We drove down Ventura Boulevard in my car, not saying anything. I felt like I was going to burst. I wanted to yell at him. Slap him. Beat the hell out of him. But I was sick to my stomach from the thought of what had just happened. Clyde sat quietly, rolling one of those damn cigarettes. He was as cool as a morning breeze.

I took Beverly Glen up to Mulholland Drive and cruised along the winding snake of a road until I built up enough nerve to speak.

"How did it go?" I suddenly blurted.

"Fine." He said it like I was asking about a weather report.

"I can't believe we did that."

"*We* didn't do anything. Doug and Muana did."

"It doesn't matter. We're all responsible. We've got blood on our hands."

Clyde held his hands up for inspection. "I don't see any blood."

"C'mon. We killed Gerry. Carmine. Whoever the fuck he is . . . was. We *had* him killed. It's the same thing."

"Hey, he said, 'Something like this happens, you can't fuck around. You got to take the guy out,' didn't he? We just took his advice. We did what we had to do. He would have done the same thing if he was in our shoes. He was *doing* it. He came over tonight to collect or kill. This was self-defense, pure and simple."

"This is sick, man. I never wanted to be part of anything like this."

"You wanted to be in the film industry, didn't you?"

"Yeah."

"You want to make an omelet, you got to break a few eggs."

"What does committing murder have to do with making movies?"

"Making movies is all about problem solving. We just solved another problem."

"That's bullshit. This is way out of control. We're going to go to jail."

"Not if you don't freak out. Trust me, you have no prosecutable connection to any of this. And if you don't snap and start running your mouth, neither will I."

"I guess I'm next on the hit list. No witnesses, right?"

"Don't be an asshole. Just hold your mud, and we'll be fine. I trust you. You showed me you got balls by standing watch like you did. Just don't go pussy on me now that everything's working out."

I neglected to bring up my sojourn under the bathroom sink. "Working out? We're responsible for two murders!"

"You're getting hysterical."

"The cops will connect the two deaths and follow the trail back to you, and that will lead them to me."

"You greatly overestimate the police department and their need to resolve these kinds of crimes. They don't care about guys like Mace and Carmine. They'll put an old-timer on each case, let him work it until he's retired, then they'll stack the files in Unsolved Homicides. The investigators will probably never even link the two of them together. Hell, they probably won't even *find* Carmine. No body, no investigation. No crime."

"You've been writing movies for too long. That's not how the cops work. I've dealt with these guys. They had Dexter Morton's murder solved in about ten minutes—then they let everyone stew for months while they worked the case until they compiled enough information to put Alex away for life."

"That was a slam dunk. The vic was rich, and your buddy didn't have a plan."

"So you condone Dexter's murder?"

"I've got to admit, Dexter getting killed like that was pretty inspirational."

"You've really lost it, Clyde. You've crossed the line and dragged me with you."

"Hayes, I did what I did out of self-defense. I took care of Mace because I wanted to protect Emily. I took care of Carmine because he gave me no choice. I had to. I did it for you every bit as much as I did it for me. You were on the hook, too, and you didn't resist very much along the way. If you really thought what we were doing was so wrong, you should have stopped it when you could."

"I couldn't stop you. You were going to do what you wanted no matter what I said."

"You never know what a cool voice can achieve in the heat of conflict. If it bothered you that much, you should have said something."

"I did. I asked you to stop. I wanted you to stop."

"Did you?"

I stared at him for a moment, assessing my involvement in what had happened. I may not have been the instigator, but I certainly had gone along for the ride. I finally said, "I probably could have been more forceful."

"Look, you're having a little crisis of conscience. It's natural. Shows you're human. But I want you to do something tonight. I want you to swap places with Mace and Carmine for a few minutes. I want you to put both those bastards in your shoes. They're alive and you're dead. They killed you. Mace killed you in that car crash or Carmine strangled you to death in your living room when you didn't pay him his extortion fee. You think about that tonight and ask yourself one question: Do they feel bad because they killed you? Do they feel guilty? You think about that, and if you truly believe that they would give a damn if they were responsible for your death, I'll consider going to the police with you and telling the whole story to them. We can get all moral and shit."

"Oh, God, I don't want to do that. Are you crazy, man?"

He smiled a devil's smile. "A little bit. Sure."

"Well, I don't want to go to jail. And I don't want you to go to jail either."

He slapped the dash of the car triumphantly. "See there? We've been working off the same page all along. I knew you were a good Joe. And think about it. At the end of the day, isn't the world a better place without Mace and Carmine?"

Sure, Clyde. Whatever you say. You're certainly one writer I don't want to piss off. I don't feel like being the main ingredient in a carpet tortilla.

chapter forty-two

I was beat. All I wanted to do was climb into bed and pass out. I started to unlock the door to my apartment and suddenly realized it was already open. Had I neglected to secure it when I left? Visions of Clyde finding the door to the Maserati unlocked minutes before we crashed flashed in my head. Who was in my apartment? Had Carmine come to life in the back of that van, killed the two grips, and returned to do me in? Or was it one of Mace's associates looking for a little revenge? Or the cops, come to pick me up after a long night of surveillance? I considered bolting, just running for my car and driving until I hit Canada. Then I heard a soft voice call my name from above.

I climbed the stairs and found Tracy on the balcony waiting for me, half-asleep in the hammock. She had used the key I had given her. The one she refused to put on her key ring. I was surprised but happy to see her. I was also immediately concerned. I had a feeling she was not bearing good news. I kissed her and crawled in beside her in the hammock.

I put my arm around her shoulders, but she didn't snuggle up. She didn't pull away, but it wasn't exactly like old times either.

"How are you?" I asked.

"Not so good."

"What's wrong?"

She didn't answer, but I could feel her tremble with nervousness under my embrace.

"You're going back to him, aren't you?"

"Yes."

I got out of the hammock, angry that she had led me on. At least that's how I felt. Led on. Deceived. She had known this morning that she was going to go back with him. The dog and pony show just added insult to the injury.

"Goddammit, then why are you here?" I asked.

"I just wanted to tell you in person. I didn't want you to hear it from Clyde."

"You're all heart." I went into the apartment, but left the front door open. She could either come in and continue the drama or leave. I didn't really care anymore. I was tired of being jerked around.

I pulled a beer out of the refrigerator and went into my bedroom. I leaned against the headboard, drank my beer, and stared out the window at the big neon marquee across the way currently advertising the Gap on the electronic display board in the center of the sign. This night was turning out to be a real winner. First a murder, now *this*.

After a few minutes, Tracy appeared in the doorway and said, "Don't sulk."

"I'm not sulking. I'm drinking and trying to wind down."

"I think you're sulking."

"You have a right to your opinion."

She sat on the edge of the bed. "You know what I liked most about you?"

"What's that?"

"You're not a whiner like most of the guys I meet. You seem to accept things the way they are."

"That's because I lack true ambition."

"That's the only thing I *don't* like about you."

"I was being facetious."

"But it's true. You *do* lack ambition. You have a lot to offer, but you don't seem to have the drive to do anything about it. I know it will probably never work out with Adam and me. Not forever. You're right about that. And he may not be an artist or a big success, but at least he's *trying* to make something of himself. I find that rather romantic."

"And you don't find me romantic?"

"You're romantic. God, yes. You make me feel like I'm on cloud nine when we make love. You make me forget everything. But I know that won't last, and then we'll hit the bad times. You'll get over your obsession with me, and then you'll see my deformity, and you'll either hate me or feel sorry for me or both. I've already been through that with Adam, and now he accepts the way things are. He loves me despite my flaws. You might not be able to get past it when you really see me for what I am, and then I would hate us both."

"Don't put this on me. Your only deformity is your own image of yourself."

"That's not true. You've seen the scars. And you know it runs deeper than that. Adam said you won't love me anymore when you find out who I really am."

"What a wonderful thing to say about your wife."

"I believe him."

"And you don't think he's got a vested interest in that statement? He wants to keep you down so you can't be free."

"I think it might have already happened. I think deep down you want me to give you an easy way out."

"That's horseshit. You know how I feel about you. If you want to stop seeing me, make sure you understand that it's *your* idea—not his, not mine."

"This is all your fault, really. You left me alone so you could go off and make that movie with Clyde."

"One minute you complain I'm not ambitious; the next you complain I'm working too much."

"Working to make other people's dreams come true is not a sign of ambition."

"It's a means to an end. I have to work if I'm going to get anywhere."

"Work is one thing. But that was ridiculous. I was completely alone. I can be alone with my husband."

"You couldn't have just waited a few weeks?"

"You think it's easy for me to do this?"

"It must be. Or you wouldn't do it."

"What's that supposed to mean?"

"You always take the easy way out. You just go with the flow. Whoever made the best play for you last gets the brass ring. I'm tired of playing rotation with you and that fucking guy."

"That *fucking guy* is my husband."

"That didn't mean much when you were in this bed. Were you thinking of him then?"

She was silent, which was an answer in itself, and I could feel my blood pressure rising. I had asked the wrong question.

"Why don't you just leave?" I said.

She got up and walked out of the room without saying another word. I heard her close the front door, and I was suddenly seized with panic. I got up and ran through the apartment, hoping to catch her before she got to her car. When I opened the front door, I found her standing at the railing of the balcony, staring down at the parking lot. I was completely embarrassed. I was chasing after her like a schoolkid. I didn't care. I threw my empty beer bottle across the floor and kissed her passionately. Her eyes were wet with tears, and I knew I had done just what she wanted. She needed one more melodramatic scene for her journal. One more passionate lay before she went back to her husband. If that's the way she wanted to play it, I would give her something to write about.

I carried her to the bedroom, kissing her all the way. We made love half-dressed, then again completely naked. The passion was tinged with hostility. Extreme sexual tension gave way to complete abandon, and we rutted like rabid dogs under a full moon. It was a night I would remember for a long, long time. I would have to, because there weren't going to be any more like it.

Afterwards we lay in bed half-asleep. She covered her scarred chest with a sheet, and I thought about what she had said. *Was* my attraction to her just a novelty that would wear off eventually? Was I so shallow that I could one day look at her as if she weren't a complete woman? I didn't believe that. But who knows what time (and familiarity) could bring?

She fell asleep for a few minutes, then startled herself awake. She rummaged through her purse and brought out a pack of cigarettes and lit one up. Considering her medical history, I was stunned that she was smoking, but I didn't say anything.

"I'll miss this," she said.

"What? The sex?"

"Um-hmmm."

"So will I."

"Who knows, maybe we could stay fuck buddies?"

"I'm not interested in sharing you with anyone."

"You're greedy."

"Hey, if it doesn't mean more to you than sex, it's not worth the hassle. We can both get laid anytime we want. But that's not what I'm looking for."

"What *are* you looking for? A wife? Kids?"

"I just wanted to be with *you.* I hadn't thought much past that."

"I did. One day you'll want children. And I can't give them to you."

"If that happened, we could adopt."

She sat up abruptly. "We're having this conversation again. I've got to get out of here. You're like the devil. You cast a spell on me, and I forget what I'm doing."

"Maybe it's because this is what you *should* be doing."

"This was a mistake. I'm sorry."

"Ah, shit." I got up and went to the refrigerator for another beer. I went back to the bedroom and stood in the doorway looking at her. She had wrapped herself with the sheet again, and she was resting her eyes. She looked angelic. I stared at her and sipped my beer.

She opened her eyes and was surprised to see me standing there, watching her. "Why are you staring at me?" she asked.

"Just trying to embed you in my memory."

"Don't be so dramatic. I'll be around. We can still be friends."

I laughed, almost snorting beer out of my nose. "That's not going to happen. You think I can stand around and be your pal while some other man has you? No, Tracy. If this is it, then this is it."

"If that's the way you want it."

"That's the only way it can be."

"Do me a favor?"

"Sure."

"Go in the other room while I get dressed."

It wasn't what I thought she was going to ask as a favor, but not much went as I planned when I was around her. I turned and walked out of the apartment onto the balcony so she could get dressed, safe from my prying eyes, as if I hadn't already fondled, studied, and made love to every inch of her body for hours on end. We were suddenly strangers again.

She came out of the bedroom a few minutes later, looking wide-awake and completely refreshed. The psychodrama had been good for her. She may have had Damaged Goods Syndrome, but in her case Nietzsche was right—what didn't kill her made her stronger. She'd probably bury us all and dance on our graves.

Tracy took a sip of my beer and said, "I guess I better be going."

"Okay."

She went to the head of the stairs and hesitated, waiting for me to make another dramatic move. One last embrace, one last kiss. Or maybe a good hard shove down the stairs? *Kiss of Death* sans wheelchair? I decided to disappoint her for a change and not give her the soap opera moment she craved.

"Drive carefully," I said.

She stiffened as if cold water had been thrown on her. She had her back to me, so I couldn't see her face. I didn't know if she was crying again or not, and frankly I didn't care. I had had my fill of her shenanigans.

"Take care of yourself," she said; then she walked down the stairs and out the vestibule door. She must have parked on Morrison Street, because I didn't see her go into the Viande parking lot. After a minute or so, I heard her car start up and drive away.

I sat out on the balcony, staring at the parking lot and thinking about all she had said. She was right. More right than she could possibly know. I had no future. No plan. And I probably didn't need one. The way things were going, I had the distinct feeling that I was headed for prison. I wasn't even sure what I had done, but I knew I was guilty of something. I had participated, with varying degrees of involvement, in two murders. Even if my participation had primarily been my silence and a little blood money. I would be very surprised if the whole thing didn't blow up in my face in the next few days.

But maybe I was wrong. The cops never even came by to question Clyde about the death of Mace Thornburg, despite his presence high on Mace's enemies list. And we had heard through the grapevine that Monique Eden, Mace's girlfriend, was so frightened by his sudden demise that she had fled to Europe, which meant she wouldn't be around to hurl accusations Clyde's way. Maybe Clyde would slip through the fingers of the law. And maybe I would, too. But then I thought about that cockamamie story of his about the Romans and the rats and the cats and the dogs and the lions. After they brought in the lions to get rid of the dogs, what did they do to get rid of the lions? Clyde's story stopped short of that answer. And we now had at least two new lions on our hands.

chapter forty-three

A week went by and then another, and no one came to arrest or kill me. Gary Bettman and I spent the two weeks wrapping out the show: organizing paperwork, finalizing the cost reports, supervising the returns, paying off the vendors, claiming our deposits. Even a low-budget film has a million details that must be attended to. Most of the department heads were finished within the first three days of post. After that, the office was reduced to an army of two. Gary and me. Vince dropped in from time to time to check on our progress, but he was already in prep on his next film. Despite our hard work, Vince didn't offer either of us a job on his new project.

Clyde never set foot in the production office again. He was ensconced in the editing room, and he was trying to avoid Vince, who was desperate to see an assemblage of the movie. Vince tried to get the location of the editing room out of me a number of times, but I kept telling him I had no idea where it was. He did not believe me.

Clyde also had no interest in encountering me. The few times I saw him getting in or out of his rental car in the Viande parking lot, the expression on my face gave him no comfort. It was hard for me not to remember what we had done and feel guilty when I was around him. We did not speak, but I could tell he was worried that I would not be able to keep my mouth shut about the "complications."

The budget allowed only two weeks of post/wrap for me. From that point on, Gary Bettman would be working from home, but at half his previous salary due to the limited amount of work he would have to do until Clyde delivered a final print of the film to the distributors. My last official duty was to help Gary shut down the office. Then I returned to the land of the unemployed.

When I got home that last day, I noticed that the Maserati was parked in Clyde's old spot once again. I walked around the car twice, checking out the new paint and bodywork. The job was meticulous. The car looked like it had just rolled off the assembly line. It's amazing what seven grand in insurance money can do for a machine. Too bad Charity James wasn't a car. Oh, they put her back together. Painted a smile on her face, powdered her nose, sewed everything up nice and tight for the funeral. But she was a machine that would never run again.

Now that Tracy was gone from my life, my thoughts had once again drifted to Charity James. The daily onslaught of O. J. Simpson news didn't help matters any. Nicole was just another in the series of tragic blondes who had marked this town since the invention of peroxide, but at least she was putting blonde power on the map. Her force had been so strong that it had to be extinguished. Even in death she would haunt her killer, even if he escaped the hands of the law. Charity James wielded no such power. And she had not been struck down out of a rage to control her. She had dissipated away under a cloud of apathy and neglect. Her death had not been mourned by millions, but only by a select few.

After having a sandwich, I looked outside and noticed the Maserati was gone. I decided to visit Clyde in the editing room. The original editing schedule had evaporated as Clyde kept finding more and more things wrong with the movie. Gary and I had heard reports from Bill Shaffer's assistant that Bill had been reduced to a nervous wreck as

Clyde had him assemble, disassemble, and reassemble scene after scene, trying to make it all work. Clyde had even gotten into the habit of giving Bill long stretches of time off so he could be alone with the footage. It was during one of these periods that I found him, staring silently into the monitor of the Avid. A series of shots of Michelle Kern firing a gun filled the little boxes on the monitor. I stood watching Clyde for a long time, not saying anything for fear of disturbing a stream of thought he may be working on. I didn't think he had even noticed that I had come into the editing bay.

Finally he looked up at me and said, "You know it's not just about the shots on either side of the cut, it's what's *between* the cut that really makes it fly."

"I don't think I'm following you." As far as I knew, there was nothing between a cut in film but a straight line, which, when projected, would not be any more visible than the lines between the frames.

"There's a mystery in there. It's what makes the great films work. Two frames come together, two shots come together, they may be completely different shots, but if the cut works, they make a third thing when they meet. A feeling between the frame. And I just can't get it to work on this movie. I can't find that third thing."

I looked at his eyes. They were so bloodshot, they looked like he had been punched in both of them hard.

"When was the last time you slept?"

"Huh?"

"Sleep. Remember it?"

"Yeah. Sure. I slept Monday. I think."

It was Wednesday.

"I saw your car in the parking lot this afternoon. Didn't you sleep last night?"

"I just came by to shower and get clean clothes. The body shop called yesterday and said it was ready, so I wanted to dump the rental."

"Why don't you go home and get some rest?"

"I've got to get this done."

"It's not going to get done if you're so tired you just stare at the screen."

"There's a cot in the back. I'll take a nap in a little while. But let me get back to it."

"Fine. Kill yourself. It will save them the trouble."

"Yeah. Whatever."

"You know, Vince is going crazy. He wants to see the film."

Clyde looked at me with eyes that would have frightened Count Dracula. "He'll see it when it's ready. Now get out."

He went back to staring at the screen, and I left the building without saying another word. I wondered if Clyde's lack of sleep was completely work related or if he saw such horrible things when he closed his eyes that it was better to just leave them open.

chapter forty-four

I didn't see Clyde the next day. Or the day after. On the third day, I realized that not only had I not seen Clyde, but I hadn't seen his car either. I went down to his apartment and knocked. No answer. I looked through his bedroom window. It was dark in there, but I could see that most of his dresser drawers were open and askew. The place looked ransacked. I went back and tried the door. It was locked.

I drove out to the editing room. The door to the warehouse was unlocked. I stuck my head through the doorway and called out, "Hello." The word echoed back to me in a way that gave me a chill. I sensed an emptiness in the room that had not been there before. I stepped into the large room cautiously. There were no lights on, but enough sunlight filtered through the skylights overhead that I could tell the room was in disarray. As I approached the editing bay, I heard what sounded like sobbing.

The editing bay was trashed. Nothing was in its proper place. Tapes were on the floor, and papers were strewn everywhere. As I approached the Avid, I saw that Bill Shaffer was sitting in the corner of the room, his face buried in his hands.

"Bill? What happened?"

He dropped his hands and looked at me through wet, red-striped eyes. "They took it. They took it all."

"Took what?"

"The film. The dailies. The cuts on the Avid's memory. Everything. There's nothing left. It's been wiped clean. They even took the external hard drives. They took everything and left me with nothing."

"Who took it?"

"I don't know. I came in here this morning, and everything was gone."

"When were you here last?"

"Last night. We've been working on it day and night. We were getting close. It was almost finished!"

"Have you seen Clyde?"

"No. I called him, but I couldn't get hold of him. He warned me something like this might happen. He told me to be on the lookout for strangers. He's going to kill me when he gets here."

"I wouldn't worry about that happening." I turned and started to walk toward the exit.

"What the hell does that mean?"

I didn't want to share with him my thoughts on the matter, but I figured that either Clyde had stolen the film elements himself or he had been abducted by someone—Carmine's people or maybe even people working with Vince Timlin staging a coup. If that was the case, then they got the director to go with the film. A complete set. Either way, I did not think Clyde would be visiting this building again.

Bill Shaffer stood up and yelled at me, "I said, what the hell does that mean?"

I exited the building without answering him. He was having a breakdown. He had worked hard, and now that work was gone. Vanished. A building fire would have been more merciful.

By the time I got my car started, Shaffer was out the door and running toward me. He had snapped. He wanted answers, and I was not interested in trying to supply them. I had no answers. Only suspicions.

I hit the gas and left him choking on my dust.

chapter forty-five

I drove down to Emily's house in the Palisades. I didn't call first, so I didn't know if she was home, or if she would even welcome me if she was there. Clyde had sent me down there a few weeks earlier to drop off the last of the things she had left at his place, so I had no trouble finding her house. I rang her doorbell and waited. There was no car in the driveway, but the garage was closed, and considering her recent history, I assumed that she would keep the car protected from the public when she was home.

I heard movement from inside the house, and I called out Emily's name. Then I heard nothing. I saw a shadow move behind the peephole. Someone was in there, looking at me standing out on the doorstep. I assumed it was Emily and she didn't want to accept my call. Then I started to get that creepy feeling again. What if it wasn't her? What if it was Carmine's friends? Maybe they were inside the house, waiting for Clyde to show up? And if that was true, what had happened to Emily?

I turned and walked slowly toward my car, trying not to show any sign of panic, not wanting to alarm any potential captors or killers.

The door opened behind me, and I quickened my pace just a bit. Could I make it to the car before they got to me?

Then a female voice called out to me, "Mark?"

I turned and saw Emily standing in the doorway, wrapped in a robe. "What do you want?"

I walked toward her. She looked good. It was hard to believe she had been at death's door only a month or so before. She had a scar on her forehead, but it was healing well. Luckily, her roles did not call for her to play the sexpot. In her line of work, the scar would just add character. "I'm looking for Clyde. Is he here?"

"Hell no. I haven't seen or heard from him in weeks. We're finished. You know that."

"That's what I heard, but I've heard it before. I thought maybe you guys had made up."

"You thought wrong."

I stopped in front of her, and she made no move to invite me inside. "He's disappeared, and so has the film."

Her eyes showed no surprise.

"Well, you've come to the wrong place. We're through. And this time I mean it. I love Clyde, but he's not going to make it. He's going to end up dead or in jail, and I have no intention of joining him in either place. If you've got any common sense whatsoever, you'll stay clear of him, as well."

"I want to find him."

"Why?"

"I want to know why he did it."

"He's Clyde McCoy, that's why. It's what he does. Self-destruction is his special talent."

chapter forty-six

I returned to my apartment and spent a restless night, tossing and turning. Every car coming down the alley was a Mafia-mobile. Every rustle of the trees was a hit man moving toward my door.

I finally hit REM state come daybreak. Things were getting good in dreamland—I was having a rather luscious encounter with a woman who bore more than a passing resemblance to Emily Woolrich, which was surprising considering the variety of erotic images my subconscious could have drawn from as of late—and then a frantic ringing echoed throughout my apartment—the doorbell! I rolled out of bed clutching my heart. They were here. They had come for me!

I thought about going for my old hiding place under the sink in the bathroom, but I gave up on that, realizing that it was effective only if absolutely no one entered the apartment looking for me. If they did breach the doors, my cowering form under the sink would just inspire laughter on the part of my attackers. No. It was time to face the music. I had nowhere to go.

I went to the window overlooking the front door. I considered dropping my TV on the mafiosi if they were out there, but that would just prolong the inevitable. Someone would just take their place. I was slightly surprised to find Vince Timlin standing at the door, directly beneath my gaze. Not surprised by the fact that he was paying me a visit, but that he was up and about so early. It wasn't even eight yet. Usually an indication Vince had been up all night.

"Vince?"

Vince looked up. "Hayes. Let me in."

"Be right down."

I went downstairs and opened the vestibule door. Vince looked furious.

"What's up?" I asked.

"What's up? You know what the fuck is up. Your partner has made off with my movie."

"He's not my partner. And come to think of it, it's not really *your* movie. Clyde wrote and directed it."

"Yeah. And *I* paid for most of it. My money, my movie. Where is he?"

"I don't know."

"Listen, I can have both of you in jail by tonight if I want. That movie is *my* property. Stealing it is grand larceny. I want my movie back."

"I'm telling you I have no idea where either Clyde or the movie is."

"You know *something*. You told Shaffer not to worry about Clyde showing up."

So that was it. Bill Shaffer had reported to Vince, and Vince had drawn the obvious conclusions.

"That was just an assumption on my part. Not an informed statement."

"I think you know where he is, Hayes. And even if you don't, I think you can find him. I advise you to do so, unless you want to burn in his place. I'll give you forty-eight hours."

"You mean like in the movie with Nolte and Murphy?"

"No, like in 'I'm turning your smart ass into the cops day after tomorrow if you don't produce results.' "

"Vince, I'm not his babysitter. How did I suddenly become responsible for the whereabouts of the director and the film?"

"You're the associate producer? Right?"

"Yeah."

"And you're McCoy's best friend."

"I wouldn't say that."

"That's the way I see it."

"Well, he doesn't have that many friends."

"That's right. And you were given instructions at the outset of this project: Keep an eye on the director. You've failed your mission. You have a fiduciary duty to the producers of this film, and I'm holding you legally responsible if it all goes into the toilet."

"That's not fair, and you know it. No court of law will buy that."

"I'd check your contract before you assume such things. The bottom line is, Clyde has made off with my property. I consider you a co-conspirator. You've got an investment in this film, as well, small as it may be. You might not think turning him over to us is the right thing to do, but trust me, it is. We plan on recouping our investment on this picture, with or without the director's approval. Save yourself. Convince Clyde to return the film and tape elements to us, and all will be forgiven."

There was no reasoning with this guy. This is what happens when you let actors produce. "I'll see what I can do."

"Good boy." He turned and walked away.

chapter forty-seven

Two more weeks passed. Still no sign of Clyde. The good news was that no one else came by either. Vince's threat seemed to have been an empty one. Either that or he was having attorneys draw up legal papers before he approached me again.

I put out some job feelers with the studios. I was shocked to discover that I was no longer the guy-who-may-have-murdered-his-boss. I was now known as the guy-who's-so-desperate-he-works-on-low-budget-movies. That was my new pigeonhole. They have a million excuses for not hiring you in Hollywood. And if those aren't good enough for you, they'll make up number one million and one.

While having coffee on my balcony one day, I noticed a black Cadillac in the parking lot facing our apartment building. Two men were sitting in the Caddy. They just sat there, staring at the building, making no move to get out of the car. I didn't know if they were looking at my apartment or Clyde's, but it didn't really matter. It was clear who they were and what they had come for. They were Carmine's pals, come looking for their friend. Or for the people who made their friend disappear.

I acted like nothing was wrong and drifted back into my apartment. I checked on them through my curtains every now and then. They were out there for a long time. I couldn't see them very clearly, but they had big silhouettes. They were cut from the same cloth as Carmine had been. And that was a mighty large cloth.

I made damn sure my doors were locked, and I started packing my bags. If they took a dinner break, I was getting the hell out of there.

Around five I checked again, and they were gone. This was my chance. I took the two suitcases I had packed and put them by the front door. Then I sat down and had a beer. I was being paranoid. If those guys were after me, they would have come to the door and kicked it in, wouldn't they? How did I know who they were? And if Clyde had been abducted by Carmine's associates, why would a new team be parked out in front of our apartment building? Unless he had talked. I convinced myself that flight would be foolish at this time. Besides, where was I going to go? And how would I get there? I was almost broke.

I decided to sit still and see what happened. I killed the lights and turned on the TV to see how O. J. Simpson was doing. Jury selection was to begin soon. An army of talking heads were feasting on the carcass of this murder case, and they were giving the defense, in particular, a big forum so we could all jump in and play armchair jury. The "Dream Team" was dominating the airwaves with complete bullshit. Johnnie Cochran was so indignant that you would have thought O. J. Simpson was Nelson Mandela fighting apartheid, not a guy accused of hacking two people to death with a Rambo knife. The trial hadn't even begun yet, but the "blackwash" campaign was in full swing.

I looked outside around nine o'clock and was shocked and horrified to find that the black Caddy was back. The men inside were now just menacing shadows. I had blown my window of opportunity. Of course they wouldn't kick my door down in the middle of the day. They were waiting until dark!

I grabbed the phone and dragged it over to the corner of the room that was above my downstairs entrance so I could listen for them. If they were going to break in, I'd at least be able to call the cops before they made it up the stairwell to the next set of doors. I sat like that the whole night, but I fell asleep after a while. I woke myself with a start a little before dawn. My neck was stiff, and my body was cramped up from my awkward position on the floor. I sat there for a few minutes listening to the sounds in the alley. And listening to the sounds in my own apartment, wondering if the creaks and groans of the wood settling were actually the footsteps of men come to kill me. Finally I sneaked a look out into the parking lot. The Caddy was gone again.

Maybe they were looking for Clyde after all. They didn't seem interested in me, and I was now certain they weren't just parking in the lot to make out. They were staking out Clyde's apartment. I considered briefly that they might actually be the cops, but I dismissed that notion quickly. The Caddy was the giveaway. The cops didn't go on stakeouts in Caddies. Mobsters did. Carmine loved a good Caddy, too.

Even though I was feeling optimistically less threatened, I still thought the wisest move I could make would be to leave town. I decided it was high time I visited my folks in Boca Raton. I called my father around ten o'clock his time and discussed the matter. He said they'd love to see me, but they were heading down to Key West for a fishing trip in a few days. Could I wait until they returned? I told him

I was thinking of driving out and that I was going to take my time doing it. I'd see them when they got back.

I went about the business of preparing for an extended vacation. I grabbed all my bills and cut checks for them. When I was done, there wasn't much left for me to take out of the bank. Luckily I had credit cards. I'd do a large cash advance if that's what it took to survive the next few months.

I was preparing to leave the apartment when the phone rang. I wasn't about to pick it up. I let the answering machine get it. The last voice I expected to hear was the one that came out of the speaker. It was Clyde McCoy.

"Hayes? Hayes? Are you there? Pick up!"

I snatched the phone out of the cradle. "Where the fuck are you?"

"Well, hello to you, too."

"Clyde, goddamn it, where the hell are you?"

"Are you alone?"

"Yes."

"I'm not going to talk to you on this phone. I'm going to give you a number, and I want you to call me back from a pay phone. Make damn sure no one is around when you make the call."

"Okay."

He gave me a number. It was long. "Bring lots of change," he said. Then he hung up.

The phone rang again almost as soon as I put it in the cradle. I instinctively picked it up, thinking it was Clyde calling back. It wasn't.

It was Vince Timlin. "Well? Where the fuck is my movie?"

"Vince! I thought you were going to sue me or have me arrested?"

"There's other ways of dealing with guys like you."

"Oh, now you're going to threaten me? That's good. You have no idea how funny that sounds."

"There's nothing funny about your predicament."

"Hey, Vince, there's been something I've wanted to say to you for some time now."

"What's that?"

"Fuck off."

I hung up the phone. It rang again a moment later. Not only did I not want to talk to him, I didn't want to hear a message from him or anyone else in this shitty town. I grabbed the phone and the answering machine and yanked them both right out of the wall.

It felt good. Real good.

I snatched up the coffee can that I always threw my spare change into, checked the parking lot for Cadillacs, grabbed my two suitcases, locked up the apartment, and walked down the stairs.

I put my suitcases in the trunk of my Camaro, then walked to the pay phone next to Viande, keeping an eye out for the boys from Las Vegas. Or Chicago. Or New York. Or wherever it was that they grew men like Carmine C.

I dialed the many digits Clyde gave me and was instructed to deposit three dollars! The phone didn't ring on the other end. It beeped or buzzed—I wasn't quite sure what you'd call the sound.

After quite a few of these alien noises, Clyde picked up the other end of the line. "It's about time. For a minute there, I thought you weren't going to call back."

"That was an option I considered."

"So, how's it going in the old U.S. of A.?"

"Everything's great here. Vince Timlin and his investors are threatening to break my legs, and it looks like a couple of Carmine's friends are watching our apartment building. Of course, they could be friends of Mace's instead."

"Naah. Mace didn't have friends. And his *associates* have moved on."

"You sound very sure of yourself for a man on the lam. Some people were beginning to think you were dead."

"That would be wishful thinking on their part."

"Let's quit fucking around. Where are you, Clyde?"

"Are you sure it's safe to talk to you? They don't have you, do they?"

"They who?"

"Any of they."

"No. I'm alone. And on my own recognizance."

"Prove it."

"How?"

"Take the phone from your ear, look around, and say, 'You're a guinea cocksucker.' "

I took the phone from my ear and did as I was told. There was no one around to hear the insult, but from the Starbucks across the street I must have looked like a madman talking to his invisible rabbit.

"How's that?" I said.

"Okay. I have to assume you would have gotten a slap or a kick from someone for that if you were being held captive by the boys from back East."

"Why is it you believe I might be a kidnap victim?"

"I knew the vultures were circling."

"Nice of you to warn me three weeks later."

"They're not after you. They want me. Or the film. I finished it, by the way."

"What?"

"You heard me. I finished the film. I want you to come down and pick it up."

"Where?"

"Mexico."

"Mexico? You want me to fly to Mexico?"

"No. I want you to drive. I'm not that far south of the border. You can be down here in three or four hours. Meet me tomorrow, but make damn sure no one follows you."

"Why don't you just bring it up here? Or at least meet me halfway?"

"I'm not crossing that border again. I'm done with America. Are you going to do this or not?"

I had to think about it. I had an investment in *Blonde Lightning*. Of both time and money. Even more important, I wanted to *see* it.

"Tell me where you are."

"Don't write it down. Don't write anything down."

"Fine. Just give me directions. Can I reach you at this phone number?"

"No. It's a pay phone. There aren't a lot of home phones around here."

He gave me brief, rough directions and told me to stop by around two in the afternoon of the following day. He finished with, "I think you're really going to like the movie." Then he hung up.

I stood there, looking at the receiver, thinking that it had better be the best damn movie ever made.

chapter forty-eight

I wasn't sure what to do. Should I travel a few hundred more miles for this madman or should I just head for fun in the sun in Florida and come back after they had all killed one another? Whoever "they" were. What would I lose if the film burned in Mexico? Fifteen grand? Better than losing my life. Once I was in Mexico, Clyde could silence me with impunity. Was he just laying a trap for me, thinking I would one day turn him in to the police? He sounded pretty paranoid on the phone. Beyond his normal level of paranoia, that is.

I drove down to Emily's house again. This time she let me in. The news that Clyde McCoy had surfaced was enough to earn me a cup of coffee. I told her about the phone call, and the next thing you know I was telling her more than I should about our recent activities. I explained to her about how we had hired Carmine/Gerry to warn Mace off and how it had escalated beyond our control, but I stopped short of telling her how we had dealt with our accidental hit man. I didn't know if she'd turn us in for putting Mace's demise in motion, but I was sure that the direct commissioning of a follow-up murder would send her straight to the cops. She sat there looking at me stony-faced, her blood boiling. But nothing I had said had come as a big shock. She had suspected much of the story as it was unfolding around us. When it was over, she rubbed wetness from one of her eyes, doing her best to avoid tears.

"You two certainly make a fine pair."

"I didn't mean for things to get out of hand like this. I don't think Clyde did, either."

"Clyde never lets anything happen unless he wants it to. He's developed a freakish ability to control events and make things go his way, even if it appears they're not. He played you, Mark. He'll keep on playing you as long as you let him."

"Do you think he wants to kill me?"

"He could have done that anytime he wanted. I think he's run out of friends and he's down to you."

"That's flattering."

"Hey, at least *you* have one friend, too. That's one more than you had when we first met you."

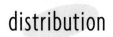

distribution

chapter forty-nine

It was dark by the time I left Emily's house. As angry as she was, we still ended up spending the entire afternoon talking about Clyde McCoy. She told me things about his past that I could never have guessed, and when she was done, I think I understood him a little better. Better, but not enough to forgive him for making me an accomplice to murder. He had seen more than his share of tragic loss, but it didn't justify his current behavior. Nothing could.

Emily had no sympathy for me whatsoever, and she said that if I saw Clyde, I should tell him to never, ever contact her again or she would turn his ass over to the police. She said that as long as we kept her out of it, she would not rat us out, but that if the police came after her, she would not cover for us. I'd keep that last bit to myself. I had no idea how far Clyde would go to save his own hide.

As I drove toward the 405 Freeway, the thought of heading north began to frighten me. What kind of scene would be awaiting me at my apartment? Who would I have to encounter first? Wise guys from back East come to find out what happened to their buddy Carmine? Vince Timlin and a couple of killer attorneys ready to work on me with wrenches, screwdrivers, and lawsuits until I talked? The police, finally having put together a solid case against me in the murder of Mace Thornburg or the disappearance of Carmine C.? Or maybe my own killer grips wanting a bump in pay? I didn't feel like talking to any of them, so I did what any self-respecting outlaw would do: I headed south for Mexico. I was an unlikely Ahab in search of the white whale that had done me wrong, but it was better than sitting around waiting for the hammer to fall.

The night was cool and, once I was south of LAX, the traffic was light, so the ride was quick and painless. I stopped at an ATM in San Diego, withdrew the last available eighty dollars in my checking account, and crossed the border into TJ just before midnight. So much for the nest egg. So much for my dreams.

Tijuana was an even bigger shithole than I remembered. A crumbling wasteland, packed solid with ill-behaved tourists and poverty-stricken hustlers. A treacherous landscape of thieves, corrupt cops, drunken college punks, and angry sailors on leave from the nearby naval base. I shot through the place as quickly as I could on the murderous route through town, a road so poorly planned and maintained that it managed to claim more lives annually than all the roads in San Diego combined.

I went another twenty miles south and hit Rosarito Beach. There are basically two ways through Rosarito and its neighboring environs. The relatively safe and modern toll road and the incredibly rough and dangerous *libre* road, which was so bumpy and pothole ridden that you didn't really need two cars involved to make an accident, but the number of speeders and drunk drivers on that strip of broken two-lane blacktop made every trip along it a dangerous adventure. I jumped off the toll road on the north end of town and cruised through Rosarito proper. It was after midnight, and the town was relatively quiet. It took all of five minutes to drive the length of Rosarito. I kept going, and then parked in front of Rene's Sports Bar on the southern outskirts of town.

I got stinking drunk at Rene's, fell in with some expats from Arizona who thought my being from Hollywood was a "hoot," and spent the night drinking cheap liquor on the beach. The next morning I checked into one of the fleabag motels a few miles south of Rosarito. My funds would allow for only a two-night stay if I wanted to continue to eat and drink at my current voracious pace, which I did. The thought of seeking out Clyde McCoy danced occasionally in my head, but I kept putting it off.

I showered, then wandered around Rosarito and took in the sights. I hadn't been to Mexico in more than three years. Things hadn't changed much. The place was under continuous construction. Most of the side streets in town were still dirt. Aside from the bars and the hotels, Rosarito's primary commerce is generated by the tourist booths and shops, most of them selling the same things at various low prices: hats, Mexican blankets, outdoor fireplaces, handcrafted trinkets, and mass-produced junk. You can also buy Chiclets on just about every corner. I picked up a straw hat and a blanket (for a combined grand total of seven bucks) on the theory that I might eventually need to set up shop out on the beach. Perhaps my next move would be to join the world of the homeless. My inevitable pursuers would never find me down here—that's for sure.

I stopped at a little food stand called Paco's Tacos and had the carne asada. It tasted a little odd, and I noticed the local dogs and cats were giving the stand a wide berth, which can be cause for consumer concern in Mexico. When I asked the owner of the stand what kind of *carne* was in the carne asada, he just shrugged and replied, *"Carne es carne."*

No shit. *Carne es carne.* I had to come a long way to find this philosopher, but he sure put things in proper perspective. Thanks, Paco.

On the way back to the motel I saw a large gathering of people on the side of the *libre* road in front of a strip of run-down houses painted in a variety of pastel colors. I pulled over to have a look and found that they were circled around the body of a child. He looked to be about five or six. He was lying flat on his face, and he wasn't breathing. Half the people in the crowd were crying, the other half just staring at the body. It took me a while to piece together what had happened. The boy had run into the road and been struck by a car. The driver never stopped. I don't know how long the boy had been lying there, and I don't know if there had been any hope of resuscitation, but it didn't appear that a lot had been done to help him. I went forward and looked closer at the boy. I touched him, and the crowd murmured, like I was doing something forbidden. I lifted him up a little and expected to see his face crushed in or some sign of trauma to his body, but he looked perfect. There wasn't a mark on him. He just wasn't breathing and he was cold as ice. I let him lie flat again, and a woman nearby wailed. Someone said the woman was his aunt. I stood and looked at the crowd. Some of them looked back at me angrily; others just stared at the child. I wondered where the ambulance was and why it hadn't gotten there yet, and then I remembered Paco's words and realized it didn't matter when the ambulance would arrive.

Carne es carne.

chapter fifty

I drove south in search of the place Clyde told me about. Twelve miles of rough road later, I saw Puerto Nuevo on my right. Rancho Reynoso was supposed to be only another mile to the south. I kept going, my nerves starting to jangle at the prospect of facing Clyde McCoy. My very own Mr. Kurtz.

I came to a group of homes behind a stretch of metal fencing that was designed more to create the *illusion* of a gated community than to provide actual protection. A weathered sign near the entrance proudly proclaimed RANCHO REYNOSO. I pulled onto the cobblestone road, which was so uneven that it made the ride on the *libre* road seem like a cruise on a superhighway by comparison. I bobbed and rocked through the property in search of any sign of Clyde.

The place had been laid out as a simple grid. Long ago, the Reynosos had purchased a large plot of beachfront property and were selling it off in lots. Houses dotted the landscape, punctuated by empty lots that had either not been sold or not yet been developed. Some of the houses were quite nice; others were in disrepair. They were retirement homes or weekend retreats for expatriate Americans who couldn't afford beach property in their homeland. Being a weekday, the population on the streets was scarce. The weekenders were at work in the United States, and the retirees probably didn't want to venture out into the heat of the midday sun. There was no one in sight on the property. It was like a ghost town. I drove up and down each street, looking for Clyde's car, thinking about what these streets would do to the undercarriage of his Maserati. On the last street, the one closest to the beach, I finally spotted his car, tucked under a carport next to a small hacienda with an attached guest cottage.

I parked and got out and looked around. The quietness of the area was eerie. I was not used to not seeing people everywhere I looked. A cool wind blew in off the ocean, and I could hear faint music drifting in from somewhere, probably all the way from Puerto Nuevo. I went up to the door of the house next to the carport and knocked. There was no answer.

I walked over to the bluff and looked out at the ocean. Small waves curled into shore. Seagulls and pelicans were making a spectacle of themselves in the shallows. The feeding was good here.

I saw a figure down on the beach in the distance. It looked like it might be Clyde. He was ten yards offshore, standing *on* the water, casting a fishing line out into the ocean. A dog was running through the surf nearby, chasing the seabirds at an unbelievable speed.

There was a flight of winding stairs fifty feet to the south of where I stood. I took them down to the beach and walked toward the figure in the distance. I looked to the north and saw a pack of dogs running down the beach, heading my way. They were of all sizes and breeds, although there didn't appear to be many purebreds among them. I stopped and watched them, trying to discern if I was in any danger. They surrounded me quickly and appeared to be a very happy bunch. At first I thought they meant me no harm. They were sniffing me, licking my hands, jumping up to say hi. They just seemed happy to see someone they could play with.

But then I realized that I was getting a little nip every now and then. They weren't just licking me, they were tasting me! And *testing* me to see if I could be overwhelmed. The smaller dogs were gathering behind me, and the larger dogs were jumping up and pushing on my chest, trying to make me trip over the little dogs behind me. They were like a pack of schoolyard bullies with sharp teeth. Except that if they managed to topple me over, I think these bullies planned to eat me.

The snapping and pushing got more serious, and I had to start pushing back. Finally I started kicking the dogs away from me. It didn't do much good. They never growled or snarled, but their intentions were clear. I was going over, and they were going to chew on me for a while. I began to panic. Had this been Clyde's devious plan? Had he lured me down to Mexico so that I could be eaten by his new canine hit squad? I started yelling at the dogs and shoving them into one another, but it just seemed to inspire them to pump up the volume. I was beginning to lose my balance in the sand when I heard a loud whistle. The dogs immediately stopped messing with me and ran down the beach toward the figure fishing out on the water.

I looked at my pant legs. The dogs had put quite a few holes in them, but I didn't seem to be bleeding underneath the fabric. Not enough to notice, at least.

The dogs were running and tumbling through the waves, chasing the seabirds, dancing around the man with the fishing pole and saying hello to the dog that was already out there. As I walked closer I saw that it was, indeed, Clyde McCoy. He was tanned and smiling, dressed in white shorts and a Hawaiian shirt emblazoned with various colorful alcoholic beverages. He had on a pair of Wayfarers and a San Diego Padres baseball cap. Typical Dodgers fan. He leaves town for a month and switches alliances to the nearest home team. Clyde still appeared to be standing on the water, but he was actually on a sandbar thirty feet offshore. He gathered his tackle and his bucket and started walking toward me. At a certain point he sank to his knees.

He walked in out of the surf and met me at water's edge. "Howdy, neighbor," he said with a smile. A lot had happened since he had said those same words to me at the pool hall those many months ago.

"How's the fishing?"

He showed me his empty bucket. "It's great if you're a pelican."

The dogs started jumping all around us. Every now and then one of the larger dogs would make a smaller dog roll over and spread their legs to demonstrate subservience. When the ceremony was complete and the larger dog moved on to other business, the smaller dog would then find an even *smaller* dog and inflict the same treatment, thus regaining a little self-respect and reenforcing the pecking order. It was like watching a studio commissary.

"I see you met the pack," Clyde said.

"I thought they were going to eat me."

"They were just playing."

"They play rough." Two of them jumped up and put their paws against my chest and tried to lick me happily as if to say "We were just joshing you." I pushed them off me and pointed my finger at them sternly. They looked embarrassed for a moment, then rejoined the mayhem.

"They haven't eaten anybody in weeks," Clyde said.

"Are they yours?"

"Are you crazy? They're just a wild dog pack. They don't belong to anyone. Gringos come down here and leave their dogs. If they're lucky, they find one another. It's better to hunt in numbers."

"They seem to like you."

"I guess I'm just another lost dog."

We started walking toward the stairs.

"How'd you end up down here, Clyde?"

"I've lived down here on and off for years. I rent a place from a couple of lady cops who moved down here when they retired. They've got a guesthouse that they rarely use, so I rent it when I need to get away from America for a while. It's cheap. Four hundred bucks a month to live on the beach."

"But why'd you split like that? Without telling anyone?"

"I had to get out of town. I knew someone was watching me. I didn't know if it was Carmine's people or someone from Vince's company trying to find out where I was keeping the negative, but I didn't want anyone fucking with me or the film. Not when I was so close to finishing. I grabbed all the elements and got out."

"Why didn't you tell me?"

"It could only have led to trouble."

"You left me holding the bag."

"If you're going to let people like Vince freak you out with empty threats, you really ought to go to Florida and become a real estate salesman. Threats are like pennies in this business. You'll find a few in your pocket every night, but they're not worth collecting."

"You're the Confucius of B movies."

"Got to have a philosophy."

"What did you do with the movie?"

"I made a deal with a Mexican video company. They gave me access to their editing room and their lab in exchange for the Mexican video rights."

"Can you do that?"

"Mexico is one of my territories. I can do with it as I please. It was worth the trade-off. I finished it a few days ago. They've been striking a final answer print. I hired two guys to fly the print up here when it's ready. They should be here tomorrow or the next day. I'll give you the print, and you can take it to Vince. He'll know how to handle it from there."

"What if he tries to recut it? You won't be there to stop him."

"He won't have any of the other elements. It will be pretty difficult for him to fuck with it. He could chop into it maybe, but at least he won't be able to load it up with extra close-ups of himself. They're all in a vault in Mexico City."

We walked up the stairs. The dog pack no longer seemed interested in us. They were chasing birds and tumbling through the sand, snapping at one another. As we walked toward Clyde's guesthouse, I heard more barking ahead of us. When we rounded the corner, I saw a medium-size dog barking and growling at a Mexican man who was pressed up against a fence, too afraid to move. The dog was of indeterminate mix, and while she was not very large, she was making up for it with intimidating fierceness. I thought it might have been the dog that had been running near Clyde when I first arrived, but I wasn't sure.

"Emily!" Clyde yelled at the dog. "Get the fuck away from him!"

The dog acted like she didn't hear Clyde. She kept pressing forward toward the frightened man, who looked at Clyde and raised his hands in the air in a "what can I do" gesture. Clyde walked over and took the dog by the collar, opened the gate in front of the guesthouse, dragged the dog through the courtyard, into the house, and closed the door.

He came back and looked at the Mexican. "You've been throwing rocks at her again, haven't you, Jorge?"

"Just little ones, to keep her off my truck."

"Little ones, huh? She's going to rip your nuts off one of these days." Clyde looked at me to explain. "Mark, this is Jorge."

I shook Jorge's hand. He was tall and lean, his skin darkened by years out in the sun. His grip was like steel. His smile was similar. He had many gold and silver teeth.

"He's the ranch handyman. Every time I go off for any length of time, he starts fucking with my dog. When I come back, she tries to get revenge."

"Your dog?"

"Yeah. She adopted me when I came down here last month. She was part of the dog pack, but she decided she wanted to live with me, and she hung out on my front porch until I relented. My landlady thinks I must look like someone who fed her at some time. The weekenders come down and feed the dogs and play with them for a few days, like they're doing them a big favor or something, then just abandon them again when they go home. It's a form of torture. If you take a dog in while you're here, you should make the dog your responsibility for life. We're partners now."

"You named her Emily?"

"It's an homage."

"Emily's not too happy with you. The human one, I mean."

"I bet. Want a drink? You can update me on my hate mail."

I nodded. He opened the gate, and I stepped into the courtyard.

"Behave, Jorge," Clyde said as we entered the guesthouse.

The dog was standing at the window, growling as she watched Jorge walk down the cobblestone street.

"Chill out," Clyde said to her as he swatted her on the butt. "Emily's part coyote, or so the vet said."

"What's the other part?"

"Whatever the coyote caught."

Clyde poured drinks, and we sat out in the courtyard and caught up on things. I told him everything I knew about the men in the black Caddy, the threats from Vince about legal action, and Emily's request that he never contact her again.

He took it all in very stoically. "I warned Emily that she would hate me one day. She never believed me."

"You worked hard to prove your point."

"We all have to make our own destinies. She backed the wrong horse. But she's a strong person. She'll get over it."

"I think she already has."

"See? Good for her. Emily's better off without me around."

"I don't think you'll get any argument there. From anyone."

"I know that."

Maybe he did care for her after all. Maybe he had taken himself away from her because he knew it was the only way to protect her. But then again, Emily warned me herself about ever attributing Clyde's actions to a higher cause than his own self-interest.

We talked through two drinks. He told me of his adventures in Mexico. How he had first come to this place while working on *The Man Who Thought He Was Jimmy Cagney*, which filmed for two weeks in nearby La Misión. How he had always come here when the air got too thick in L.A. How he spent almost a year down here after America embraced *Pretty Woman*, feeling his own country had lost all sense of its values. It was hard for me to hate him, even though I knew I should. His selfishness and paranoia had destroyed everything I had worked for my entire life. And the probability of going to jail now weighed heavily upon my brow.

"You know what they're all going to say about you now, don't you?" I asked.

"Nothing I care to hear."

"They're going to say they were right about you. You're not to be trusted."

"Do you think it matters? I'm done with the film business. *Blonde Lightning* will be my swan song. That's why I've gone to this trouble to protect it. I wanted there to be at least one film that was mine."

"You've quit before."

"You get a certain age, and people start to take your retirements seriously."

"I don't understand. You seemed to have a good time making the movie. And it looked like you did a pretty good job. But then you had to shoot yourself in the foot. I think you're self-destructive."

"How observant. Bottom line is, I don't have anything worth saying that enough people would want to hear to justify the time and money it takes to say it. So I'm just going to shut up and fade away."

Sounded logical to me. We finished our drinks. Clyde stood up and started gathering his fishing gear. "Well, it's time to get back to work. I need to catch my dinner for tonight. Drop by tomorrow night and pick up the print. It should be here by then."

"Okay. I'll see you tomorrow."

We walked out of his yard, and his dog followed him toward the beach. I went to my car and drove slowly out of the compound, trying not to scrape bottom on the rough cobblestone roads. I waved at Jorge, who was picking up trash with a nail stick and stuffing it in a big plastic garbage bag.

When I got to the *libre* road, I had to wait a while before an opportunity to join the fray presented itself. A steady flow of speeding traffic was dominating the uneven blacktop. I finally had to haul ass along the dirt shoulder to get enough speed going so I could jump onto the raceway. I had barely gotten into the northbound lane when I saw a big black Cadillac rip past me going south, two large men riding in the front seat.

I watched in my rearview mirror as the Caddy pulled off the road at the entrance to Rancho Reynoso. I looked for a place to turn around, but there was too much opposing traffic. I tried to slow down, but the move was answered by blaring horns behind me. I finally saw a decent turnout to the right, and I pulled off the road and waited for a big enough gap in traffic in both of the lanes so that I could perform a quick, hair-raising U-turn. I floored it back toward the ranch.

I pulled back onto the cobblestone lot and blew my horn, hoping to warn Clyde if it wasn't too late already. Sparks flew as I bottomed out on the cobblestones, but I'd have to worry about oil leaks later. As I came around the corner, I could see a very large, overweight guy in a suit holding Jorge against the wall of the hacienda and waving his finger in his face. The black trash bag and the nail stick were on the ground at their feet, trash scattering everywhere in the wind. The other man who had been in the car was nowhere to be seen. I hit my horn again and the fat man turned and looked at my approaching vehicle.

Jorge took advantage of the distraction and picked up the nail stick. As the man turned back to Jorge, Jorge shoved the nail stick into his stomach and chest, quickly and repeatedly.

The fat man stumbled backwards, grabbing at his wounds, a flabbergasted look on his face. Red stains were quickly spreading on the white shirt under his jacket.

I slammed on the brakes, got out of the car, and ran over to the bleeding man. He reached under his coat and clumsily pulled a pistol out from a concealed shoulder holster.

I stopped in my tracks and thought for a moment I was about to be shot, but the man fell forward onto his face and made a variety of rude sounds from the various openings—both natural and artificial—of his body. The gun clattered on the cobblestones and came to rest a few feet in front of me.

I yelled at Jorge, "Where's the other one?"

Jorge pointed in the direction of the beach.

"Is Clyde still down there?"

"*Sí.*"

I tried to think through my panic. It was time to make a stand. I scooped up the pistol and looked at it. It was a .38-caliber Smith & Wesson. I had fired a number of .38s while testing weapons with the special effects guys on *Blonde Lightning*, but they were using quarter-load blanks, not real bullets. Still, the weight of the gun in my hand boosted my confidence to an unreasonable level of calm.

I ran toward the beach. When I reached the edge of the bluff, I saw that Clyde was back at his fishing spot on the sandbar. Another man in a black suit was walking down the beach toward him. Clyde's back was to both of us, and he seemed completely unaware of the approaching danger.

I raised the pistol into the air and squeezed the trigger.

Nothing happened.

I looked at the gun, found the safety on the side, and clicked it off. The leg-breaker was getting closer to Clyde now.

I pointed the gun into the air again and pulled the trigger. It fired, but it didn't exactly sound like a cannon over the roaring surf. Still, it did its job. Clyde turned and looked over his shoulder, spotting Carmine's clone. Unfortunately for me, the mobster also turned at the sound of the gunshot and saw me standing on the bluff.

Clyde stuck his fishing pole into the sand and dived out into the ocean. It looked like he was going to try to swim to Hawaii. The mobster turned back and saw that his quarry was departing in a way he did not wish to emulate. He turned back to me and did the quick math that told him that something had happened to his partner. I was his enemy. He began running toward the bluff. He was another one of the thick types, but considerably slimmer than his partner. He was moving fast, and he looked like he could do some serious damage if he got his hands on me. I had to decide: flight or fight. If I ran, I probably couldn't get to my car and get out of the compound before he shot me. He still hadn't pulled out a gun, so I thought maybe I could shoot him in the leg and slow him down long enough for both Clyde and myself to get far, far away. I aimed at his running form and fired. Sand kicked up such a distance away from him that I wasn't even sure it was my shot that made it dance. My aim was laughably off. But the man was not laughing. He looked furious. He picked up the pace and was sprinting hard for the stairs.

I fired again. I hit the ground closer to him this time, but still no cigar. I was beginning to think I had made a mistake. Running would have been smarter. But now I had even less of a head start. The proximity of the second shot must have made the guy think I actually could be some kind of threat, because he stopped and pulled out his own gun. He aimed and fired at me, but I hit the ground before he got the shot off. Still, I could hear the bullet whiz over my head as I tasted dirt. He was a lot better at this sort of thing than I was.

I started crawling backwards, not wanting to stand up. The man began running again. I heard a barking sound and saw Clyde's dog racing across the sand. I have no idea where she came from. She tackled the gunman and tore into his arm. He spun around, trying to dislodge her, but she held tight. He brought his knee up and kicked her in the stomach, sending her flying. She immediately got back on her feet and charged him, but he aimed and fired his gun at her. She yelped and dug her face into the sand. She rolled around in her own blood, howling with pain. I couldn't tell where she was shot, but she was out of the game.

I aimed from my sprawled position and fired at the man's legs again. Again I missed. I had discharged the weapon four times. The gun had six chambers. If they were all loaded, I had two more shots. They had to count. The man turned and fired at me again. And again I heard the shot whiz overhead. He began to walk slowly toward me now. He knew he was dealing with an amateur, and he was no longer worried about my shitty gun handling. He was determined to get an angle on me and blow my brains out.

I tried to steady my shaking arm. It was time to think movies. I'd seen a million scenes like this on the screen over the years. I needed to find a way to make this scene play out properly—with the good guy vanquishing the bad guy. And *I* needed to be the good guy.

I lined up the front sight of the gun with the man's approaching legs. I decided to go for the left leg. He was no more than sixty feet away now, almost to the stairs, but I still had the advantage of being above him, and now that I was flat on the ground, my arm had some stability to it. I squeezed the trigger.

I guess I had wanted it too badly. I hit him, all right. But not in the leg. The man doubled over, shot in the stomach. He went down to his knees and looked up at me. Out of desperation and anger, he fired his pistol at me repeatedly until it was empty.

I covered my head with my hands as the bullets flew overhead. One of them bit into the ground a few feet from my face, scattering dirt over me and making me think for a moment that I may have been hit. The firing stopped, and I looked up. The man was keeled over on the beach, lying back on his knees, staring straight up into the sky. His chest was heaving. He was still alive, but his shirt was a crimson mess. I slowly got to my feet, keeping an eye on the man at all times.

Jorge came up on my side and looked down at the dying man on the beach. Jorge smiled and gave me the thumbs-up sign. I wondered where he had been hiding while the actual shooting was going on.

Clyde dragged himself out of the surf and studied the scene, trying to figure out what had happened and wondering if he was safe now. He spotted his dog lying near the fallen man. She had stopped howling, and from my angle she looked like she might be dead. Clyde ran across the beach to her.

Jorge and I started down the stairs. By the time we got to Clyde, he was sitting by his dog, stroking her face. She was breathing shallowly and appeared to be in shock. Her right front leg was a bloody mess. I couldn't tell if the bullet had hit her in the chest or the leg, but she was losing so much blood, it didn't look like she'd be alive much longer, no matter where it had struck her.

Clyde looked at the gun in my hand, then looked over at the man in the sand twenty feet from us. "Who the fuck is he, Hayes?"

"I have no idea. I think they're the guys who were watching our building in L.A. I saw them pull into the compound as I was leaving, and I just had a bad feeling about it."

"Them?"

"There's another one up by the house. Jorge stabbed him."

Clyde looked at Jorge, and Jorge smiled innocently and shrugged.

"Goddamn it, Hayes, you led them right to me." Clyde got up and walked over to the man I had shot.

I followed him, but Jorge stayed with the dog, who whimpered as Clyde left her side.

The man had not moved from his original position. His legs were pinned under him, and he was staring straight into the sky. He was still breathing, but his eyes were losing focus. Blood was turning the sand around him into wet clay. He looked like a gymnast who had really messed up a routine.

Clyde bent down and looked at the man's face. "Who the hell are you, friend?"

"Get me a doctor," the man wheezed.

"Fuck that if you don't tell me what I want to know first. Now, who are you? Or better yet, who sent you?"

"Sal the Pro."

"Sal the Pro? Why the fuck did he send you after me?"

"He didn't. We been looking for Carmine C. on account he owes Salvatore twenty-six large. Richie Collonia told us Carmine was out visiting you in L.A."

"This ain't L.A., amigo. How'd you find me down here?"

I got a jolt at the thought that the dying mobster was about to confirm that he followed me to Mexico.

"We kept going by your place in L.A., but when you never showed, we called Richie and he told us you had a place in Mexico. We thought Carmine might be holed up down here. Took us fucking forever to find it."

"And Sal the Pro's not looking for me?"

"Why the fuck would he be looking for you? Get me a fucking doctor or I'm gonna bleed to death. I can't feel my legs already."

"That's cause you're sitting on 'em, fuckface."

"You got no reason to talk to me like that. . . . You guys shot an innocent man, here."

Clyde stood up and looked over at his dog. "Dude, you came to this place uninvited. And you shot my dog."

Clyde stared at his whimpering dog, contemplating the predicament. One dead mobster up in the compound. Another one dying on the beach. What to do, what to do. Neither of us was looking down at the man. We both suddenly heard a click. We looked down at him and saw that he had pulled his pistol up out of the sand and aimed it at the back of Clyde's head. He had pulled the trigger, hoping there was something left in the chambers or just having forgotten that he had emptied it my way or just working on dying instinct, doing what came natural.

Clyde's eyes bugged out when he realized what the man had tried to do. He grabbed the .38 out of my hand and took two steps toward the man, who clicked on another empty chamber.

"You have so had it now, motherfucker," Clyde said. "Mexico is no place to push your luck."

Clyde fired the .38 point-blank into the man's forehead. The back of his skull blew out onto the sand. I jumped two feet into the air, startled by the abruptness of the action and the sound of the blast. The gun sounded much louder when fired at the ground.

The guy's face had disappeared under a wash of gore. His mangled expression, what could be seen of it, looked stunned and stupid. There was no spark in his one visible eye to indicate that a sentient human being had been present only a moment before.

Clyde looked up at me without emotion. "Looks like I'm going to have to head farther south now. My landladies will not approve of this situation. Not at all."

chapter fifty-one

Clyde went back and looked at his dog. She was breathing steadily now, but not wanting to move. He brushed her coat back, looking for the wound.

"I think it hit her in the upper part of her leg," he said. "Maybe we can save her."

I shook my head in disbelief. "She's lost a lot of blood."

"What do you think I should do, just let her lay there and die?"

I had no reply. Clyde took off his shirt and wrapped it around the dog. She yelped in pain as he lifted her up, and for a moment I thought she would bite him out of blind rage, but when she realized it was Clyde picking her up, she relaxed her head and let him carry her.

We went up the stairs, and Clyde put Emily in the passenger seat of the Maserati.

The three of us walked over to the guy that Jorge had stabbed and looked down at him. He had the same vacant expression on his face that his partner was presenting down at the beach under a mask of crimson. There was just more of it.

"Damn, Jorge, you really fucked this guy up." Clyde didn't sound very distressed about it.

Jorge grinned shyly again.

"Clyde, don't you find it troubling?" I asked.

"What's that?"

"The growing body count."

"Once you start something like this, it's kind of hard to stop. It's become a self-perpetuating situation."

"Where will it end?"

"Don't put this on me. These guys were just down here for a visit. You two jumped to conclusions and killed them. I was minding my own business, fishing down on the beach."

"I thought they had come to kill you."

"Getting a little trigger happy in your old age, aren't you?"

"I just fired in the air to warn you. Then he came after me. I had no choice. I just wanted to wound him, not kill him. Matter of fact, I *didn't* kill him. You did."

"Don't be so modest. That guy was gut shot. Down here that's a slow, painful death. There's no way he could have been saved at a hospital. If he didn't die today, it would have been tonight or tomorrow. Having him talk to the *federales* would have just put us all in jeopardy. And what do you think would have happened if he *had* pulled through? You think he would have let you walk after shooting him? You think Sal the Pro would have just said, 'Thanks for just killing *one* of my guys'? I finished him off, but he was dead the moment you shot him. You get credit for the kill. You can't shirk your responsibility on this one."

He had me there. I let it sink in that I had finally joined the official ranks of murderers. It brought my mood down a few notches. "I guess you're right."

"Well, at least you can say you killed a man down in Mexico. Not many junior executives can honestly claim that."

"Yeah, I've got *that* going for me."

"My landladies are coming down here tonight to prepare for a party they're throwing tomorrow night. We gotta get this place cleaned up quick before they get here or someone else decides to take a walk on the beach and they spot that dead whale down there. I'm going to take Emily to her vet and see if he can save her. You guys get rid of these bodies and clean up the blood."

"Say what?"

"You heard me. It's like fishing. You killed 'em—you clean 'em. Jorge, go get your truck and haul these guys up to the dump. That place is so washed out from the storms, you ought to be able to find a good hole to toss 'em into."

Jorge nodded and walked down the cobblestone street to fetch his truck. He didn't seem to be in a very big hurry.

"There's a hose behind the house. Use it to wash away that blood."

"What if someone catches us?"

He sneered at me as he backed toward his car. "Do what you do best. Kill 'em."

By the time Jorge pulled up in the rusted old truck, I had dragged the hose from around the back of the house. Jorge went to the supply shed and got some sheets of heavy black plastic. He spread one of the sheets on the bed of the truck, and we tried to pick up the fat guy. He was probably only a little more than three hundred pounds, but it felt like we were lifting five hundred plus. It was *dead* weight. As hard as we tried, we could not get all of him up onto the back of the truck at once. An arm and a leg, two legs, his head and shoulders, but not all of him at once. We just could not manage to lift him high enough into the air for his whole body to clear the back of the truck's gate.

There was a winch on the front of the truck. Jorge pulled the cable from the winch and dragged it over the top of the truck, over the bed, and down to the dead man. He wrapped the cable under the man's arms and secured it with the tow hook. Then he found two two-by-fours in a pile of lumber nearby and leaned them against the tail of the truck, creating a ramp. He went back to the winch and threw the lever. I helped guide the man along the two-by-fours as he was slowly dragged up the ramp. Once he was all the way up onto the bed, I yelled, *"Alto!"* and Jorge pulled back on the lever. The winch stopped. Jorge got into the bed of the truck and unhooked the cable.

I turned the hose on and attempted to wash away the blood on the street. A lot of it had congealed on the cobblestones, and it wasn't going away easy. For a moment I panicked as I realized that I was taking a relatively small amount of blood and diluting it as if it was a concentrate, creating a red river that was flowing down the cobblestones in front of all the neighbors' houses. But the longer I let the water run, the less red the river became. I was diluting it to the point that it looked no worse than rust-colored water. I set the hose down and let it run while we went down to the beach to get the other guy.

The second man was much lighter than the first, but still too heavy for us to carry up the stairs. We dragged him through the sand and brought him to the base of the bluff. Jorge moved the truck, repositioned the two-by-fours, then rappelled down the hill using the winch cable. He tied the cable under the man's arms and hauled him up the side of the bluff, right up onto the bed of the truck. The body left a trail of blood in its wake.

I used a shovel to spread the bloody sand where the man had lain all across the beach until it was so dispersed that no one would have any idea that someone had been killed there.

By the time I got to the top of the bluff, Jorge had the hose and he was washing down the side of the hill.

I got up into the back of the truck and went through the men's pockets, stripping them of anything that could identify them. They were both carrying thick wallets. The fat guy's name was Tony Boden. The slimmer man, the man I had killed, was Martin Leone. Tony and Marty. At least that's what their driver's licenses said. Who knows what names they had been born under? And where they were going now, it didn't matter what we called them. There would be no markers on their final resting places.

The men were carrying a sizable amount of money as well as a dozen credit cards between them. Tony had more than four hundred dollars in his wallet, and Martin had a little less than a grand. Jorge came over and looked at the money in my hands. I looked at his face and thought about how it would be almost as easy for him to bury three bodies as two; then I extended the money his way. He looked at it in my hand but did not reach for it.

"Go ahead. Take it," I said. "I wouldn't feel right keeping it." As if I could if I wanted.

Jorge took the money and rifled through it, getting a rough count. He smiled at the windfall, then he looked at me, and I could see in his eyes that thoughts similar to mine suddenly occurred to him.

"Why don't we split it?" he said with a suddenly remarkable command of English.

I reached out and took a fifty-dollar bill. Not enough to rile him, but enough to ease his mind. "For expenses," I said.

"Yes," he said. "For expenses."

We covered the men with more of the black plastic, tucking it under them so it wouldn't blow away, and drove up into the mountains, passing tourists and locals alike with our dead cargo. Jorge took a winding dirt road off the beaten path until it ended at an area that had been turned into a makeshift dumping site due to the irregularities of the land. Erosion had created natural pockets in the ground. The land was pockmarked with deep grooves where runoff from the mountainside had bored out soft ground and moved it down into the flats. People in the know had begun to fill these pits and valleys with their garbage. The place reeked of spoiled meat and rotten fish. Vultures hovered overhead, waiting for us to leave so they could return to their business. A few bold ones eyed us from perches nearby.

We walked along the rocky ridges, looking down into the holes at the variety of busted appliances and bagged trash that were collecting down below. Jorge stopped at a hole that contained two busted microwave ovens and a large amount of discarded food that looked like the refuse of a restaurant. The food had been contained in plastic bags, but predators had done their work picking through it, so now it appeared to be a sea of rotting fruit, beans, cheese, and of course, *carne.*

"This is good," Jorge said.

I wondered what language he was speaking, because the word *good,* as understood in English, certainly had no place in this conversation.

Jorge backed the truck along the ridge, being extremely careful not to slide over any of the edges of the ground. He got as close as he could to the hole, then parked. We climbed into the back of the truck and stripped the men out of their clothes. They stank bad, but it was nothing compared with the stench rising out of this amateur landfill. We dragged them off the back of the truck and rolled them into the hole. They hit the rotting garbage with a splat and a thump. At which point, I tossed Clyde's drinks out of my stomach right in after them. Jorge took all the plastic out of the back of the truck and let it float down and cover the bodies. He took the men's bloody shirts and tossed them on top of the plastic, saying nothing about my gagging and wheezing.

"Shouldn't we cover them up with dirt or something?" I asked, trying not to puke again.

"No. The animals would just dig them up. Better to leave them out. There won't be nothing left in the morning."

That did it. I retched again and purged my stomach of all substances. Jorge barely noticed.

We went back to the truck and drove cautiously down out of the mountains. When we got to Rancho Reynoso, Jorge went to the black Caddy and found the keys still in the ignition. He popped the trunk, and we saw two black suitcases filled with clothes waiting for us there.

He ran the hose on what was left of the men's bloody suits, then wrung them out, put them on top of the suitcases, and closed the trunk.

"What are you going to do with the car?" I asked.

"My cousin has a body shop. He'll give me five hundred dollars for this car, and it will disappear forever."

"What about the clothes?"

"I have *many* cousins."

After Jorge pulled away in the Caddy, I looked for any trace of blood left on the cobblestone street. The sun had burned away all the water and diluted blood. There was no indication a murder had taken place on the site less than three hours earlier. I went down to the beach and looked for the spot of my first official kill. The wind had blown the sand about so completely that I wasn't even sure where the exact spot was that the man had fallen. Nature was quite an accomplice down here.

I walked back up the stairs and saw that Clyde's car was now under the carport. I went through the gate and walked through the courtyard to the front door of the guesthouse. I looked through the screen door and saw that Clyde was inside making coffee. I knocked and opened the screen door.

"How's your dog?" I asked, a bit afraid of the answer.

"The vet said she'll probably pull through. He had to take the leg, though. Good thing she's got three more."

"You can rename her Tripod."

Clyde looked up at me. "You think that's funny?"

"Sorry my humor isn't up to your standards. It's tough to come up with good material after going on a body dump."

"I don't want to hear anything about it. I assume Jorge knows what he's doing. But I don't want to know details."

"Yeah. You should keep your hands clean."

"Hayes, I'm just doing what it takes to survive. Are you going to be okay about this or are you going to go on one of your guilt-trip freak-outs?"

"Don't worry, Clyde. I'm all over feeling guilty about anything. Long as we don't get into double digits on this whole murder thing."

"Someone comes at you, you better be ready to deal with it."

"That's what Carmine said about Mace. Right before the bodies started to pile up."

"He was right. And you better learn to embrace that philosophy. I'm not going to be with you when you get back to L.A. If you don't know how to conduct yourself, you won't last long."

"They're going to keep coming after us, aren't they?"

"They who?"

"Those mob guys."

"Sal the Pro's guys? I doubt it. How will anyone tie us to those two wise guys unless you go shooting off your mouth? I'm not about to say anything, and Jorge doesn't know anything about you."

"What about Collonia?"

"He may end up thinking I have something to do with those guys disappearing, but he wouldn't suspect *you* had the balls to pull this off. He won't even think of mentioning you to anyone who comes asking about their whereabouts."

"I don't think I want to take my chances on that."

"Hey, do what you have to do. Like the song says, 'Be Happy.' "

chapter fifty-two

I watched the sun set from the beach across the street from my motel, then walked down the street to the liquor store. I stopped in the dirt parking lot near the entrance and stared down at a tattered, mummified-looking human arm, severed at the elbow. Pieces of dead flesh clung to the bone in a few spots like parchment, but most of the meat was gone. The hand was intact, but skinless, the bony fingers curled as if they were still trying to clutch something. The middle finger was almost straight, as if this long dead hand was reaching out of the grave just to flip me the bird.

I went into the store and reported my discovery to the rotund man behind the counter. He said, "The rains. They wash up the dead."

Okay, then.

I bought a bottle of Cuervo Gold, a bag of ice, and two limes, then went back to my room to party. As I left the store, I saw a dog running down the street with the arm between its teeth, its head darting from side to side on the lookout for competition. The middle finger still jutted up at the end of the hand. The mutt was flipping off all of Mexico.

I rinsed out a paper coffee cup and got the ball rolling. I was a third of the way through the bottle before I had to go into the bathroom and puke my guts out. I turned the air conditioner all the way up to drown out the sound of the beating waves and the speeding traffic on the *libre* road, then slept restlessly through the night, visions of dead bodies and evil friends contaminating my fevered dreams. I had to throw up only two more times before my stomach was completely purged.

chapter fifty-three

I felt so good in the morning that I didn't even want a drink. I lay in the darkness of the cool room, listening to the air conditioner and hoping the last few months had all been just a bad dream. But when I tried to stand up on my wobbly legs, I realized that it had been no dream. Or if it had, the nightmare was going to continue. I opened the blinds, and the harsh sun of Mexico jolted me the rest of the way awake.

I showered, put the bottle of tequila in my trunk, then went into town. A large wreath was planted at the exact spot on the side of the *libre* road where the little boy had been the day before, and it looked like a million flowers and candles had bloomed around the wreath. He must have been very loved.

I wasn't due at Clyde's until nighttime, so I killed the day in town, watching the natives trying to convince the gringos to part with their spare change. Then I went to the Rosarito Hotel and drank until the sun gave up out over the ocean. It was all coming to an end. One way or another. I stayed far longer than I should (which happens to a lot of people in Mexico) and then headed down to Rancho Reynoso.

I pulled up near Clyde's house and got out of the car. A cacophony of voices and music floated from the courtyard, which was lit up like it was New Year's Eve. As I approached and looked over the fence, I saw that the courtyard had been transformed into party central. Ten tables now crowded the grounds, and more than fifty senior citizens were drinking, eating, and chatting around those tables. More people were mingling inside Clyde's guesthouse and the main house. A banner spread between the two houses read

HAPPY 60TH, ETHEL—
From your friends at the Orange County Sheriff's Department

Clyde was tending bar in the center of the courtyard, an apron wrapped around his waist emboldened with a couple of giant red lobsters snapping at each other. He saw me standing by the gate and said, *"Hola!"* Then he looked at one of the ladies at the table nearest to the gate and said, "Nonie, that's my friend I was telling you about."

The lady said, "Get him a drink and tell him to join the party."

Clyde came over, opened the gate, and welcomed me, giving me a big hug, which allowed him to whisper into my ear, "Ix-nay on the old urder-mays."

I patted him on the back roughly. "No shit-ay. Asshole-ay."

We laughed like we had just shared a joke and didn't hate each other.

"Hey, man, come have a drink. Nonie and Judy are having a reunion for all their friends from the sheriff's department. There's plenty of booze."

"I'll need all of it."

We walked through the sea of tables toward the bar. The partygoers seemed oblivious of my presence.

"Who's Ethel?"

"The lady over in the corner in the wheelchair. It's her birthday, too, but that was just a coincidence."

I looked over and saw a tough-looking broad downing shots with some friends in the corner of the courtyard.

"She looks pretty good for sixty. Why's she in the chair?"

"She got thrown down the steps of the courthouse by a felon she was escorting. Been on disability for fifteen years. But, man, can she shoot. Even from the chair. She's almost as good a shot as you are."

"You really are a sadist."

"Hell, I'm just trying to lighten your spirit. You're always so down."

"I wonder why that is?"

"Have a margarita. You'll feel better."

"Fine."

He started mixing the drink in a high-speed blender. "I can tell you what your problem is, but you don't want to hear it."

"Sure I do."

"You take everything so damn seriously. It's why you never made it in the film business. You're like the poster child for Right Guard—*before* the guy uses the deodorant. Everybody can see you sweat."

"I think that's a little unfair, considering what you've put me through."

"What *I* put you through? Hayes, when are you going to take responsibility for your own life?"

"When guys like you quit fucking with it."

"Then you better give up your ambitions of being a producer."

"I'm pretty much there."

He poured the drink into a salted margarita glass and handed it to me. "Have a drink and enjoy the party. I'll bring out the film when I get a break."

"It's here?"

"Yeah. The guys showed up with it around five."

"You could have brought it to me. I told you where I was staying."

"I had to help prepare for the party."

"And I'm sure the sadist in you loves watching me sweat one more time."

"These kinds of experiences are good for you. Puts hair on your chest."

"I stay around you any longer, and I'll look like Lon Chaney Jr. during a full moon."

I took the drink and mingled with the ex-sheriffs. They were a lively, friendly bunch. The courtyard was filled with great stories of adventures and misadventures within the department. If they had any idea what had happened on this property the day before, they would hog-tie me and haul me off to the *federales*. I was definitely feeling like that Right Guard guy Clyde was talking about. I tried to make myself invisible, but the paranoid within me was certain the sheriffs were on to me. And it was making me sweat like O.J. on the way to the airport.

The party looked like it would go on until the wee hours of the morning. These old folks had stamina! A lot more stamina than I had. I went to Clyde and told him I was fading. He got Jorge to spell him at the bar. Jorge never looked me in the eye. He didn't know me anymore. I was just another gringo now, not someone who had accompanied him to the body dump the day before.

Clyde went into the guesthouse and brought out three heavy silver cans. The answer print of *Blonde Lightning*. I took one of the cans from him and we walked to my car. I popped my trunk and we loaded the cans in.

"Don't leave these in your car tonight. Bring them into the room with you."

"Okay."

"Tell Vince I'll have someone contact him about ordering prints and delivery items for the various deals. I'm not going to furnish him with an interneg or an access letter to the lab. He'll have to go through my intermediaries."

"He's going to be furious."

"He'll get over it. Besides, I've eaten a lot of his post costs. This makes up for the thirty grand the car accident cost the production. He's coming out way ahead. As usual."

"What about you? What are you going to do?"

"I'm going to blow out of here tomorrow, soon as the vet lets my dog out."

"Where you going to go?"

"South. Mexico is a big country."

"Who's giving up now?"

"I'm not giving anything up. I did what I wanted to do. I finished *Blonde Lightning*. And I finished it in a way they can't fuck with it."

"I think you're underestimating them."

"Maybe, but I've got my own print. And the negative. They can't do anything about that."

"Don't you care how it's released? How it's advertised?"

"I've got no control over that anyway. My job is done. See, Hayes, sometimes making a movie can just be about making a movie. It's its own reward. It doesn't have to be a stepping-stone. It doesn't have to lead to a bigger career."

"No, but it can certainly end careers."

"If that's the case, then it was never meant to be."

"You're probably right." We shook hands and I said, "It's been . . . strange."

"Yeah. I guess I should say I'm sorry or something."

"Don't break with tradition now."

"Good idea."

"By the way, did you ever find that third thing?"

"What?"

"That third thing. The mystery between the cut."

"Oh, that. I was a little delirious when I went on that rant. But, no. I don't think I found it. Maybe next picture."

"Thought you were quitting for good."

"It's just a figure of speech."

"Which part?"

"All of it."

I smiled and shook my head. I think he smiled back, but it was dark out. I got in my car and drove away, not looking back. If I had, I doubt he would have been there.

chapter fifty-four

I considered heading straight home, but I was too tired to make a four-hour drive. I went back to the motel and crashed hard. I slept much later than I wanted, waking around eleven in a bed soaked with sweat. The air conditioner had died in the night, and I had just slept through the sweltering heat.

I showered and dressed and loaded the film cans back into the trunk of the car. I checked out and was preparing to leave when Clyde pulled the Maserati into the dirt parking lot and stopped by my car. I walked over and bent near his window. His dog was in the passenger seat, her missing front leg bandaged at the stub.

"Poor baby," I said and reached across Clyde in an attempt to pet the dog on the head. The dog growled and curled her lips at me angrily. I pulled my hand back just as she snapped at the airspace it had occupied a moment before.

"Emily's not in a very good mood," Clyde said. "I'd let her rest."

"Sorry about that."

"Just thought I'd drop by on my way out of town, make sure you and the movie were safe."

"If you have so little faith in my survival skills, you can feel free to deliver it yourself."

"L.A. is not on my schedule."

"Well, I'm heading there directly."

"Good. Give Vince my regards. And tell him if he touches a foot of that film, I'll kill him."

"He will have no idea how serious a threat that is."

"Vince knows me better than you think."

"So, you're turning your back on everything and everybody? No more movies in Clyde McCoy's future?"

"Listen, I was out of the business for the last few years anyway. Making *Blonde Lightning* was gravy. But I have no interest in making any more movies. It's time to put away childish things."

"What will you do for a living?"

"Hell, it doesn't take much to live down here. I'll tend bar if I have to."

"Maybe *Blonde Lightning* will make us all rich."

"Don't bank on it. Even if it does well, it will be tough to collect from the distributors. They make the Mafia look like choirboys."

"Thanks for telling me that now."

"Hey, you knew the risks going in."

"The fiscal risks. But I didn't know we'd have to kill a bunch of people to get the job done. We could still end up in jail or in a hole somewhere."

"We all end up in a hole sooner or later."

"Nice. What about Emily? Aren't you worried about her?"

"Emily will be fine. No one will come after her."

"And you can leave her just like that? No regrets?"

"Sure there are regrets. But that's the funny thing about life. No matter what you do, the cast is constantly changing."

He winked at me and put the car in gear. He spun dirt in the air as he threaded traffic and ripped onto the *libre* road, heading south at a speed that would have been unsafe even on the toll road.

chapter fifty-five

I crossed the border a little after four and drove straight through, stopping only once for gas and a cup of coffee. It was dusk by the time I got to my apartment. I cruised past the parking lot twice, looking for big rental cars bearing men from the East. The coast looked clear, so I parked and approached my apartment. The place looked undisturbed. I went in and checked to see if Tracy had called, but of course I had ripped the phone and answering machine out of the wall before I left, so no one had been able to leave messages. I couldn't even hear the phone not ring.

I hooked up the phone and called Vince Timlin and told him I was in possession of a finished print of *Blonde Lightning*.

"Can you bring it to my house?" he asked.

"You want me to get you a pizza while I'm at it?"

"All right. I'll come over there."

"Forget it. I went a long way to get this print. I want to see it. Set up some screening room time at Fotokem tomorrow, and I'll bring the print there."

"Fine. I want to see it, too. But you don't have to be such a prick about it."

"Just trying to speak in a language you'd understand." I hung up and stared at the phone. It was almost over.

I brought the film cans up to my apartment, just in case someone decided to steal my crappy car in the middle of the night, and I began to pack up my apartment. Clyde was right about me. I was finished. It was time I left the City of Angels, as well.

chapter fifty-six

Vince booked a screening room for noon the next day. I met him in the lobby of Fotokem, and we brought the print up to the projectionist. Vince was alone. He didn't want anyone else to see this first screening, just in case it was a disaster. He asked about Clyde, and I told him I had no idea where he was, which was the truth. I told him that the negative was in Mexico City and that people would be contacting him so he could order prints and tape masters as his distribution deals warranted. He wasn't happy about any of it, but there wasn't much he could do about it. Clyde had covered his bases pretty well.

We sat and watched *Blonde Lightning*. It wouldn't sweep the Academy Awards, but it was a lot better than either of us expected. Clyde had done a very good job with the footage he had stolen. He had completed a score using a string quartet and a saxophonist in Mexico, and the minimalist sound was somewhat experimental, yet perfect for the dark images he had brought to the film. There were a couple of rough bits of ADR where Clyde had been forced to use Mexican actors to patch up some dialogue problems, but the average viewer probably wouldn't notice. Vince smiled more than once during the screening, always during one of his scenes, of course. It was one of his better performances.

When it was over, Vince said, "Not bad."

"Yeah. I think you've got a winner there, Vince."

"It could use a little trimming."

"I wouldn't advise that, Vince."

"Why not?"

"Well, first off, you don't have any of the raw elements. The only thing you could do is cut into the print itself, and it will be very hard to do that in a seamless fashion. Secondly, you don't have the right to make changes. Clyde has final cut on this thing, and I think you should honor it."

"What's he going to do, sue us?"

"I doubt he'd go to that trouble."

"Then what's my incentive to leave it as is?"

"I think he's dangerous. He was in a pretty bad way when I saw him. You know how people always say things like 'I'm gonna kill you if you fuck with my movie'?"

"Yeah."

"I think with Clyde it's a threat worth respecting."

"Get the fuck out of here."

"I'm serious. This isn't one of those times to mess around. Why don't you just let this one go as is?"

"This is my movie, too. I got the financing. It's my face up there."

"You're good in this. Why would you want to cut anything?"

"I didn't say I wanted to cut any of *my* stuff."

"Oh, I get it. You want to cut other actors' scenes down, so your part will be bigger."

"Don't put it that way. I just thought a few of the supporting character bits wandered."

I looked Vince dead in the eye, trying to make him understand how dangerous this game he was considering playing might turn, without actually revealing anything about Clyde's murder spree.

"Not one foot of film should change, Vince. I'm serious. It's just not worth what you will go through."

"What I will go through? What is that, some kind of threat?"

"Not from me."

Something about my desperately intense expression must have gotten to him, because he suddenly looked startled, and then, if it was possible, a bit afraid. "It's not bad as it is," Vince said. "Not bad at all."

legacy

chapter fifty-seven

I packed my car with what few things I wanted to keep, and I left my apartment, leaving my landlady my busted TV, a stack of quality screenplays, some lousy furniture, and my seven-hundred-dollar security deposit. I didn't want to take the time to cash out on any of it. I just wanted out of L.A. The carpets were shot anyway, and one of the bedrooms had smoke stains on the walls where my ex-roommate used to burn candles while bedding actresses. I figured my landlady and I would come out about even, if I stuck around to do the math.

Before I headed out of town, I cruised by Tracy's house one last time. A big green truck was sitting in the driveway, the words TWITTY LANDSCAPING growing out of a painted forest of bushes on the side of the vehicle. I guess Adam was back to stay. For a while, at least. Tracy Twitty. What kind of a name was that to saddle on anyone?

I hit the 10 and headed east. *Far* east. I kept an eye on Los Angeles as it receded in my rearview mirror. It was like a whirlpool. I feared it would grab me at the last minute and suck me back down into its depths. But I found the faster I drove, the less I felt the gravitational pull of the place. I was going so fast by the time I hit West Covina that a motorcycle cop had to pull me over and give me a speeding ticket. At least I couldn't say the state of California never gave me anything.

After I crossed the California/Arizona border, I slowed down and took a look at the country. I slept for three hours in a rest area in Comfort, Texas. When the morning sun woke me, I saw that I was near the bank of a river. Large appliances and auto parts hung in the branches of the trees along the riverbank like a bad modern art exhibit. I assumed the display was the result of a recent flood. Either that or the Texans hadn't quite grasped the concept of recycling.

I had a few drinks and a good meal in New Orleans and still made it to Boca Raton in record time. My parents, refreshed from their recent fishing expedition, welcomed me with open arms.

"It's about time," my father said. "I told you that business was no good for you."

If only you knew the whole story, Pops. If only you knew.

chapter fifty-eight

I detoxed for a few weeks in Boca, taking in the sun and the sand. And the girls. Oh Lord, did they have girls. This is where the beautiful girls got on the bus that ended up three thousand miles across the country in the land of dreams and schemes. But here they had not gone pro yet. Their dreams were intact. They were beautiful and fresh and happy. No one had crushed their hopes under the heel of reality yet.

But I was just the guy to get that ball rolling for them. Tequila and strangers can do serious damage to bad memories. And I had a lot of people, places, and events I wanted to forget. Charity James and Tracy Twitty were high on the list. They burned deep in my consciousness, but they faded with every drink and each new encounter with a fresh-faced girl.

I was living off my credit cards and they were starting to max out. I needed a new career. Or at least a job. My old man hooked me up with some of his real-estate cronies, and I decided to stay in Florida instead of mining the territories of his youth in Maryland like he had been suggesting over the years. I studied the real-estate laws, and I aced my test. Voilà! I had my license. I fell in with a broker whom my father had befriended when he first moved to Boca, and I sold my first house two weeks later. It was a $200 K fixer-upper in Lantana, the cost of a garage in Los Angeles, but my commission ended up being almost five grand after expenses. I was back in the working world. Moreover, it felt like the first honest money I had made in a long, long time. I could get used to this. And after selling crap to my bosses in Hollywood for so long, selling houses to people who needed them would be a cinch.

After a few months of successful selling, I took a listing for a condo in Delray Beach that I could afford, and I bought it myself. I even pocketed a commission check for my troubles. This was a good racket!

When the smoke had settled and I felt more comfortable in my new life, I put a call in to Vince Timlin. I didn't tell him where I was calling from, just in case there was still any bad business lingering in the air, waiting to descend on me.

Vince was as full of shit as always. "Hey, buddy, how you doing?"

"Fine, Vince. How are you?"

"Great. Got a new company going. We're making twelve films this year, and I own the foreign on all of them. Roger's financing them just so he can have the domestic. It's a sweet deal. You looking for work? We've got plenty."

"It's tempting, but I'm out of the business now. I'm selling real estate."

"Had enough of the good life, eh? Decided to settle down with the audience and call it a day?"

"That's about it."

"So, what can I do you for?"

"I'm calling about the status of *Blonde Lightning.* When's it coming out?"

"We've got a little problem there."

"What kind of problem?"

"The company we sold it to stopped making their payments. Then the asshole who ran it sold the company's assets to one of his in-laws for a dollar—the assets, including the film library, but none of the debt. Then he went BK and closed it all down, burning his creditors."

"That sounds illegal."

"It should be, but not in this country. The laws are set up to protect the corporations, not the artists."

"Can't you go after the guy who has the library?"

"He legally doesn't owe us anything on the up-front money, but if he released the movie, he would still have to pay us our percentage of the profits, if there were any. But there's a problem there, too."

"What's that?"

"He's in trouble with the IRS. They've put a freeze on his accounts, and it looks like he's going to let Bank Leumi take the assets in an attempt to appease them."

"So the IRS will own the movie?"

"Basically. But the IRS doesn't distribute movies. They'll wait for a suitor to make an offer on the library to cash out."

"Can't you get the rights back since they didn't pay the full price? Aren't they in breach of contract?"

"Doesn't matter. They had made payments, and we had a contract. The rights are tied up until someone else comes in and buys the library. We probably won't get paid unless it sees a release somewhere down the line. Maybe not even then."

"This is insane."

"It's business."

"You don't sound too upset."

"That flick got me my current deal. I can't be whining too much about it."

"How's that?"

"I screened my print for Roger, and he was so impressed with what we did on that budget that he offered me this sweet deal."

"What's the *we* get out of that deal? What about the investors? Are we all supposed to eat it while you get rich?"

"You should never put any money into a movie if you can't afford to lose it."

"What about the money that's already been paid? Don't we get any of that?"

"That money went into covering deferments."

"Like your additional salary?"

"That was part of the budget. It's legitimate. The deferments were in first position. The investors get the next money out after the deferments are covered."

"*If* there's next money."

"Yeah, if."

"So I busted my ass for nothing and dumped fifteen grand into a movie that will never see the light of day?"

"That might end up being the case."

"That's really fucked."

"I'm sorry you feel that way."

"You wouldn't even have had that movie to lose if I hadn't tracked Clyde down. Now I wish I hadn't."

"You think I'm happy about this? I'm not."

"You're doing all right, though, aren't you?"

"Hey, so are you. Selling real estate's a lot more stable than producing movies. You made a smart move. Water seeks its own level."

"Nice talking to you, Vince."

"See you around, pal. Or not."

We both hung up. Vince Timlin, the good old sociopath. Getting rich while the rest of us go broke. And smiling all the way.

I called Emily to see if she had heard from Clyde and to tell her the news about *Blonde Lightning*. I was shocked to learn that she had gotten married. And to a lawyer, at that!

"I told Clyde I was going to have a child," she said. "With or without him. I found a guy who could get the job done."

"What about Clyde?"

"What about him? He never calls. I haven't talked to him since that day I called the set. He doesn't care about me. And I sure wasn't going to wait around for him."

"I thought you two were so happy."

"That's a very temporary state of being."

"Are you happy now?"

"No. But I'm working on it."

I told her all about the financial disaster that was *Blonde Lightning*. She took the news without surprise. I left her my phone number with instructions to give it only to Clyde if he were to resurface. She said she thought that was unlikely, and something inside me made me believe that was true.

chapter fifty-nine

One day, after looking at a house up in Lake Worth, I decided to investigate the facts in the strange history of Clyde McCoy. I stumbled across the shopping center he had described when he told me his "struck by lightning" story. Or at least it looked like the place he had described. It contained a Winn-Dixie market and a strip of smaller stores, but there was no movie theater anymore. The thing that gave it away was the tall metal marquee on an island of land between the street and the parking lot. It was the only such marquee that I had seen since my move to Florida. It was thirty feet high, with lighted white panels on either side. The black letters now advertised the latest movies for rent from the video store in the corner of the lot.

I parked and went into the store. It was large for a non-Blockbuster. And there was a downward slope to the floor. If I squinted, I could almost see where the movie screen had been at the bottom of the slope. I approached the front counter and disturbed a kid who was reading *Premiere* magazine behind the cash register. He looked like he was still in high school.

"Excuse me," I said. "Did this used to be a movie theater?"

The kid laughed and said, "Nope. It's been a video store long as I can remember."

I was a little disappointed, thinking I had stumbled upon the Holy Grail of Clyde's past, only to find that I had created the experience in my own mind, probably out of wishful thinking.

Suddenly a gruff voice spoke up from behind a row of shelves to my right. "You can't remember very far back, you runny-nosed punk."

A fat old guy with thick glasses stepped out from behind the shelves. He had a notebook in his hand, and he appeared to be checking off titles.

"Yeah, this used to be a movie theater," he said to me. "Long time ago. The Lake. Back before videotape. That kid was biting ankles back then. I closed The Lake in 1984 and opened this joint. I couldn't compete with the multiplexes. And cable. And video. So I threw in the towel and jumped on the video bandwagon."

"Did you used to have a guy named Clyde McCoy working for you?"

"Hell, yes. He was my assistant manager for a while. Just a kid. Like this punk here. Motherfucker didn't have the good sense to come in out of the rain, but he went out to Hollywood and became a big-shot moviemaker. Can you believe it?"

"What do you mean he didn't have the good sense to come in out of the rain?"

"Oh, hell, everyone knows that story. I sent this dumbfuck out to change the marquee one day, and a storm blew in and he just kept on working. A lightning bolt hit the marquee and knocked him flat on his ass. Letters went everywhere. He was lucky he wasn't killed. Who the fuck stands on a metal tower in a thunderstorm?"

"The movie was *Krakatoa, East of Java,* wasn't it?"

"That's right. So you *have* heard that story, huh?"

"Yeah. But I never believed it."

"Well, believe it. I was here when he came in out of the rain. Funniest damn thing I ever saw. Eyebrows burned to a crisp and his hair curled like he was Goldilocks. Damn, that was funny. I told him he should have just put up the first part of the title and left it at that. You think anyone gives a shit whether they come to see *Krakatoa* or *Krakatoa, East of Java?* Nobody would have known the difference. But that little fucker was such a perfectionist. Almost got him killed. He's a lucky one, though."

"Sounds like it."

The man went back to his paperwork, and I wandered around in the store and browsed a bit, perusing the new titles out on video. Toward the back of the store, down where the movie screen used to be, there was a section devoted to Spanish-language titles. I had a sudden jolt of ESP and began looking through the boxes. I knew I would find it. It had been more than a year now, and I was betting they would have a copy. I realized that was why I was actually here. I hadn't come to find out if Clyde McCoy was a big fat liar. I had come to find our film in the only version known to exist for public consumption. It took a while, but I finally came to a video with a picture of Michelle Kern on the cover, her long blond hair covering her nude body as she stared over her shoulder at the camera. There were inserts of shots supered about on the cover: Vince Timlin firing a gun, Scott Hewitt brandishing a machete, a car blowing up in midair (a shot that did not occur in the film), a number of menacing men lurking in shadows, and, inexplicably, a pit bull growling at all involved. Nevertheless, my heart raced at the realization that the film was out in the world, even if it was only the Spanish-language version. At least people could *see* it. The title, now translated into Spanish, was *Relámpago Rubio.* Underneath the title in small black letters were the words *BLONDE LIGHTNING* in parentheses.

I took the tape to the front counter and spoke to the young man again. "Can I buy this tape from you?"

"No, sir—that's a rental."

"Could you order a copy of it for me to buy?"

"I don't know. I can look it up."

He disappeared into the back room to get his catalogs. The man with the thick glasses came up to the counter again, having heard our conversation. He looked at the tape in my hand. "Why you want that thing? It's a piece of shit. And it's not even in English."

"Well, why don't you sell it to me, then?"

"It's a good rental. I don't have to like 'em to make money off of 'em."

"Did you watch it?"

"No, but José did. He said it sucked."

"Do you know who made it?"

"No."

"Clyde McCoy. Your old employee." I handed him the box.

He turned it over and read the credits. "No shit. I didn't know McCoy spoke Spanish."

"We shot it in English. This is the Mexican release."

"You worked on it, too?"

"Yeah. That's my name right there." I pointed to my credit on the box. My name was misspelled, but it was close enough. "I was the associate producer."

"I'll be damned. How come I haven't seen this movie out in American?"

"The executive producers are having legal problems with their distributor. I don't know when it will come out."

"I'll have to watch this thing, now that I know McCoy made it."

I took the tape out of his hand. "You can watch it as soon as I return it. I'm going to rent it. See you in five days."

The man grunted and went back to his work. I felt like kicking him in his sanctimonious ass. The kid returned with a stack of catalogs, and he finally located the distributor of *Relámpago Rubio.*

"Yeah, I can order it for you. It's seventy-nine ninety-nine."

"Why so much?"

"It's not a sell-through item. It's priced as a rental."

"Fine. I'll take it." I pulled out my credit card. "And I want to rent this copy right now."

"You must really like that movie."

"It's one of a kind."

chapter sixty

A few months later, I was doing paperwork on the sale of a three-bedroom Tudor when the Simpson verdict came down. O.J. had not only stolen two lives, he had hijacked an entire country for more than fifteen months. We were all prisoners in the spectacle of this trial, and now it was coming to an end. A verdict. At last. Now we would know the price of justice in America. Despite the intense coverage of the events, the verdict was still up for grabs in the minds of the public, and our office had been consumed with betting fever for the last two days. The office bets were almost evenly divided between guilty and not guilty. Not that any of us believed Simpson was innocent. Every single person in the office was convinced of his guilt. What many of us were not convinced about was the effectiveness of the prosecution, which had stumbled and bumbled from the very beginning of the process. The integrity of the jury was also a big concern. A year earlier, I was fairly certain Simpson was going to be convicted, but after what I had been through and what I had done, I was no longer sure of anything. The fact that I had come out of it all relatively unscathed had tainted my already-dark worldview. My belief that justice finds its own way had deteriorated to the degree that I bet one hundred dollars that the Juice would be spared further jail time.

When the verdict was read, there was no cheering in the office, even by those of us who had won our bets. We felt inside the way that Dominick Dunne looked—like a fish that had been speared and thrown onto the deck to drown on the air of the land, his mouth hung wide open in stunned silence. Even Robert Kardashian looked shocked, and he was on the defense team! Perhaps the theories that he had been hired by Simpson so he would be ineligible as a witness for the prosecution were more than idle speculation. Kardashian knew the score, but it looked like he was hoping those twelve jurors would do what he couldn't do. Put a killer behind bars. Now it was too late. It's tough when you put loyalty to a friend above your principles. I should know.

The Goldmans wept, the Browns seethed, the Dream Team danced, the Juice looked skyward to rejoice (as if He had also been on his side), and the rest of us just got sick to our stomachs on the certain knowledge that fame and money can override the facts if used properly. And if you can find a jury of fools.

On my drive home, I couldn't help thinking about the hypocrisy inherent in my feelings about O.J.'s acquittal. Who was I to judge him? Who were any of us? The general consensus among the public was that he was a murderer, but twelve people sat on a jury and said he wasn't. He was a free man. And so was I. Maybe I had been looking at the whole thing wrong. Maybe I wasn't as guilty as I thought I was.

The men we killed in Mexico might have just been in the wrong place at the wrong time, but weren't they leg-breakers and murderers by trade? Didn't they know that their jobs could end in their premature demise when they signed up for the long haul with *la cosa nostra*? Wasn't it a professional risk that they embraced every day they showed up for work?

And what of Carmine C.? Hadn't he brought all this about by going crazy and killing Mace Thornburg? No one told him to kill anyone. And then he extorted us. I think there was a very good possibility that Carmine had killed Mace on purpose to pressure us into paying him hush money so that he could pay his debt to Sal the Pro. Were we really in the wrong by taking him out of the game?

And what of Mace Thornburg, after all? Wasn't he the guy who started this whole ball rolling? He threatened us repeatedly, sabotaged our set (maybe), and tried to kill us in Clyde's car (probably). Why should I feel guilty that he was dead, even if his death was a result of actions I had a part in orchestrating? The way I looked at it, there were four dead bad guys out there somewhere, and we were alive—Clyde, Emily, and I. (*If* Clyde was alive. I had not heard from him since that day in Mexico.) Four bad guys dead so that three good guys could live. At least I had to assume we were the good guys, because we were still alive. Didn't the good guys always win in the end? So maybe, by extrapolation, O.J. was actually the good guy, as well. If I was going to live with myself in this brave new world we were entering into, I would just have to get used to sharing it with Mr. Orenthal James Simpson. He had as much right to free air as I did. Maybe more, since his innocence and freedom had already been vetted by a jury of his "peers."

When I got home, I pulled down my $79.95 copy of *Relámpago Rubio* and looked at the cover. There they were—Vince, Michelle, Scott, the stars of *Blonde Lightning*—reframed and matted in the most garish assemblage possible. A truly exploitational cover if I had ever seen one. A cover that promised an even more lurid viewing experience than the one actually on the tape inside.

I turned the box over and stared at the credits. There, in the middle of the credit block, the culmination of fifteen years in the film business, the only thing I had to show for a decade and a half in Los Angeles other than a guilty conscience and a load of debt: my one credit on a movie (even if my name was misspelled).

PRODUCTOR ASOCIADO
MARK HAYS

It would just have to do.

author's note

Due to a series of disastrous corporate takeovers and bank failures, the rights to *Blonde Lightning* remain hopelessly entangled to this day. Even more alarming, a casual search by a bank official revealed that the print of the film, as well as twelve negatives of other films in the package, could not be located. When the lab in Mexico City was contacted so a duplicate print or internegative could be struck, it was discovered that all the elements had been removed by the registered owner of the materials, and no forwarding details had been left behind. The Mexican version of *Blonde Lightning, Relámpago Rubio,* was released on DVD in 2004, promptly going straight to the discount bins of local Spanish-language rental stores around the world. The event was heralded by a groundswell of apathy from film aficionados everywhere.

The killer of Ronald Goldman and Nicole Brown Simpson has yet to be brought to justice. O. J. Simpson continues his search for the murderer, scouring the country's golf courses from coast to coast, often accompanied by Nicole Brown Simpson–look-alike girlfriends: blond, tall, beautiful, and white (perhaps in an attempt to lure the killer out of hiding). His search is painstaking and thorough, but he is determined to succeed through methodical examination of the terrain.

One hole at a time.

acknowledgments

Blonde Lightning completes the saga of Mark Hayes and Clyde McCoy begun in *Earthquake Weather.* Over the fifteen years that I have wrestled with the various incarnations of this story, a lot of people have contributed valuable input—both positive and negative—and these two books are the end result.

On the positive side, I have to thank many of the usual suspects—Sterling and Brandon Lankford; Steve Breimer and Marc Glick—who constantly challenge my very rational prejudice against lawyers (I'm here to tell you, there are at least *two* good ones out there); my agents, Matthew Guma and Richard Pine; the team at Ballantine—Joe Blades, who was the one-in-ten editor who decided to gamble on a guy who hadn't had a book published in seven years (sometimes it takes a while to write these things); Heather Smith and Gilly Hailparn, the publicists who manage to get my books into a lot more heads and hands than I would ever have thought possible; and all the other people who labor without credit to bring writers and readers together. Kim Dower's advice on these issues over the years has also been invaluable. Lisa Cruz, Sandra Petersen, Alan Ormsby, William Petersen, Rick Lasarow, Stephen Eckleberry, John "the Devil" Vogel, Joe Ito Farina, Joan Kern, Anthony Coogan, Joe Lansdale, Scott Phillips, Jeff Parker, Kimberly Ray, David Pecchia, Jane Davis, Winona Franz, Judy Whitley, and the late greats John Alonzo and Bert Remsen, as well as their beloved widows, Jan and Barbara, respectively, provided spiritual nutrition over the long journey.

Special thanks must go to the cast and crew of the ill-fated production of *Blonde Lightning,* or as it is more commonly known by the few who have seen it, *Relámpago Rubio.* The magnificent Karen Black, producer extraordinaire Gary Bettman, harried production designer Yuki Nakamura, tortured script supervisor Jackie Taylor, and beleaguered film editor Bill Shaffer must be singled out for sharing with me what little they could remember of a very trying experience. The real Vince Timlin should also be acknowledged, but our lawyers forbid identifying him—for obvious reasons.

Heidi Sobel and Mike Connelly should be singled out for keeping me alive long enough to complete these books.

On the negative side, there are far too many people to thank for the stories that inspired these two novels. Many of you know who you are. For legal reasons, I won't name you specifically—I also have no wish to further fan your egos. But the simple fact is, if not for the hysterically heinous behavior exhibited by the characters populating this mythical place we collectively call "Hollywood," these stories could not have been written. It is with no malice, bitterness, or irony that I thank the "bad guys" in town for all the lemons they contributed so I could make this lemonade. I couldn't have done it without you!

See you all at the movies!

about the author

TERRILL LEE LANKFORD is the author of *Earthquake Weather, Shooters,* and *Angry Moon.* He has also written, produced, and directed numerous documentaries and feature films. He most recently directed *Blue Neon Night: Michael Connelly's Los Angeles.* Visit his website at www.TerrillLeeLankford.com.

about the type

This book was set in Garamond, a typeface originally designed by the Parisian typecutter Claude Garamond (1480–1561). This version of Garamond was modeled on a 1592 specimen sheet from the Egenolff-Berner foundry, which was produced from types assumed to have been brought to Frankfurt by the punchcutter Jacques Sabon.

Claude Garamond's distinguished romans and italics first appeared in *Opera Ciceronis* in 1543–44. The Garamond types are clear, open, and elegant.